jane

HOLD ON – THE ROAD TO LOVE CAN GET BUMPY!

a novel by Elka Ray

mc **Marshall Cavendish** Editions

© 2011 Elke Ray and Marshall Cavendish International (Asia) Private Limited

Cover art by Opal Works Co. Limited

Published by Marshall Cavendish Editions
An imprint of Marshall Cavendish International
1 New Industrial Road, Singapore 536196

Other Marshall Cavendish Offices:

Marshall Cavendish International. PO Box 65829 London EC1P 1NY, UK •
Marshall Cavendish Corporation. 99 White Plains Road, Tarrytown NY 10591-
9001, USA • Marshall Cavendish International (Thailand) Co Ltd. 253 Asoke,
12th Flr, Sukhumvit 21 Road, Klongtoey Nua, Wattana, Bangkok 10110, Thailand
• Marshall Cavendish (Malaysia) Sdn Bhd, Times Subang, Lot 46, Subang
Hi-Tech Industrial Park, Batu Tiga, 40000 Shah Alam, Selangor Darul Ehsan,
Malaysia.

Marshall Cavendish is a trademark of Times Publishing Limited

National Library Board Singapore Cataloguing in Publication Data
Ray, Elka.
Hanoi Jane :- a novel /- by Elka Ray. – Singapore : Marshall Cavendish Editions,-
2010.
p. cm.
ISBN : 978 981 4328 16 6 (pbk.)
1. Canadian fiction – 20th century.
PR9197.3
813.6 — dc22   OCN669878052

Printed by Fabulous Printers Pte Ltd

For Thien, who makes everything more fun.

Acknowledgements

I'd like to thank my parents, Gisela and Gerry Ray, for providing inspiration and support, as well as an unusual childhood. *Cam on* to the many friends who've encouraged, fed and housed me over the years, including the Trangs, Tini, Nhung, Chad, Hai, Pontus and Melissa. I'm grateful to my early readers, to Stephanie Pee at Marshall Cavendish, and to Steve Christensen at www.lotushanoi.com.vn for designing my beautiful author's website: www.elkaray.com. Finally, thanks to my husband Thien, whose enthusiasm is contagious.

1 Flat Earth

It's my lunch break and I'm standing outside of my office at the Hanoi Scope, staring at a crumpled *To Do* list. Item number three, below *Pay phone bill* and *Buy roach spray*, is *Pick up wedding dress*. I haven't gotten around to the first two but am in the right part of town to fulfill number three. The tailor is only two blocks away. I start walking.

Normally, I'd have driven, but my apple-green 1964 Vespa scooter had failed to start this morning. I'd chosen the bike (against my fiance Wyatt's advice) for its paintjob rather than its mechanical integrity — a decision that, in 36-degree heat, I'm regretting. I yell for a motorbike-taxi but get no takers. The only driver in sight is stretched out on his bike's seat with his bare feet on the handlebars, napping.

At the best of times, Hanoi is a bad place to walk, its streets seething with vehicles and its sidewalks broken, uneven and full of parked motorbikes. Now, in mid-July, the city is like a sauna, albeit one scented with exhaust fumes and bad drains rather than cedar and eucalyptus oil. Resigned, I plod along Trang Tien Street, trying to stick to the thin strips of shade cast by overhanging snarls of electrical wires. Sweat drips into my eyes and trickles down my back. Even my kneecaps are sweating.

I'm about half a block from the tailor's when my phone rings. It's my friend Sigrid, asking whether Wyatt and I want tickets to watch some visiting Bangladeshi dance troupe this Saturday night. Sigrid is always attending cultural events, the more obscure, the better. I tell her that we have other plans, which is a lie. I doubt that my banker fiancé would enjoy Bangladeshi folk dance. I consider calling him, just to be sure that he hasn't already made other, solo plans for Saturday night and forgotten to tell me, but decide not to disturb him.

"Too bad for you. I hear their costumes are fantastic," says Sigrid breezily. "There's a Polish theater troupe the following weekend. I'll let you know if I can get tickets to that one." I remind her that we'll be back in North Carolina for our wedding and she says, "What? You're getting married? Oh wow, how could I have forgotten?"

"Are you mocking me?" I say, because I know that she is. I try not to talk about my wedding non-stop but it's about the only thing that I can think about.

Sigrid laughs. "Only a little," she says. "You're not as bad as some brides I've known. I'm still waiting for you to throw a fit because the icing on the cake is the wrong shade of pink or something."

"There's still time," I say. For a second, I consider asking Sigrid to meet me at the tailor's. Trying on my wedding dress feels like a big deal and it'd be nice to have a friend there. The way I'd always pictured the final fitting, my mom and bridesmaids would be on hand to *ooh* and *aw* and fuss with my tiara. I'd also like a second opinion and Sigrid is honest to a fault. But I hesitate and Sigrid tells me that she's late for a meeting.

"Stop stressing about your wedding," she says, before she hangs up. "It's meant to be fun, not an ordeal, remember?"

Hanoi Jane   9

I stuff my cell phone back into my bag. That's easy for Sigrid to say. She's not about to get married in front of 250 people halfway around the world. Organizing a wedding long-distance has been hell, since I've had no choice but to depend on my mom, Tabitha, which is like asking a peacock to organize a party for a pigeon. My mom can't accept that this isn't her big day and seems determined to rectify that.

Turning onto Church Street, I stop in the shade of St. Joseph's Cathedral and dab my face with a tissue. Even the beggars and postcard vendors are resting, while the cops who usually sit outside of the police station spitting and smoking are probably holed up in some air-conditioned karaoke lounge. I dig another tissue from my bag and mop the back of my neck. At least the tailor shop will have air-conditioning.

The bells of St. Joseph's chime once, a reminder that I'd better get a move on. At 2:30 I'm supposed to interview some French guy who's skateboarding across Asia, then check out a new Indian restaurant at 3:45. This long before the *Hanoi Scope* goes to print, I'd normally have lots of free time, but since I'm about to take six weeks off of work, I have a slew of stories to write. I step into the tailor shop, grateful for a blast of cool air. I figure that I can drop my wedding dress off at home before meeting that crazy French skateboarder.

Seeing me, the tailor smiles. "It's ready," she says, then ushers me into the sole changing cubicle. I peel off my shirt and use it to swipe the sweat from my back, then turn to survey my plastic-wrapped wedding dress.

The tailor, a tiny, cheery woman named Huong, is a

genius. Bias-cut from silk overlaid with cream lace, the dress makes me look taller, slimmer and much more elegant than I really am. The hand-beaded bodice has just the right amount of sparkle. I am so grateful that I'm speechless.

"You lose weight," says Huong approvingly, when I bounce out of the cubicle. I want to kiss her.

Back out on the street, now clutching a pink plastic garment bag, I feel dizzy with happiness. Trying on the dress has made my wedding day seem even closer. In less than a month I'll be married! If it weren't so hot I'd do a little dance on the sidewalk. I want to call all of my girlfriends and gush about how well my dress fits. Instead, I scan the street for motorbike-taxis. It's too hot to hang around outdoors. I need a long, cold shower.

The only *xe om* driver around is an old guy in dark glasses and a pith helmet. After setting a price that's too high he spits loudly into the gutter, my attempts at bargaining met with further expectorations. Since I'm short on time and no regular taxis are around, I clamber aboard his Chinese scooter. Following a final discharge of phlegm, we start moving.

Through the Old Quarter, where there's little room to maneuver, my *xe om* drives sedately. But as soon as we hit the dyke road he accelerates, the bike weaving wildly between slower traffic. I hug my flapping garment bag and wish that I'd called a proper taxi. How tragic would it be to die just weeks before my wedding?

"Slower," I yell, one of five Vietnamese words that I've learned, the others being *Khong* and *Toi la nguoi My*, which translate as 'No' and 'I am American'. Unfortunately

for me, Vietnamese is a tonal language. A single syllable can have six different meanings depending on the inflection. Since I can't differentiate the various tones, let alone reproduce them, only other similarly tone-deaf foreigners can understand me. "*Cham cham!*" I yell again, then, attempting another tone: "*Cha-am cha-am!*"

The driver turns to gape at me. "Eh?" he says, his mouth like a black-and-white photo of London during the Blitz. "*Noi gi?*" His lack of comprehension needs no translating.

Hit by the sour scent of alcohol fumes, I lean back. "Look where you're going!" I yell in English, gesturing straight ahead of us. I glance up at the sky. It has started to drizzle.

The driver takes one hand off the bike's handlebars and waves it around in a gesture of incomprehension. Turning off of the dyke road, we come perilously close to hitting a three-wheeled cart full of flowerpots. I resolve to keep quiet. I'm gripping the bike's luggage rack so tightly that my fingers hurt. The motorbike hits a bump. I shut my eyes and hang on grimly.

Five harrowing minutes later the *xe om* pulls to a stop in front of the row-house that I share with Wyatt. When I scramble off, my knees are shaking. After paying the *xe om* driver I sift through my bag for my keys, the drizzle now turned to rain. My bag's so full of stuff — work notebooks, spare shirt, laptop, cell phone, sunglasses, three tubes of lip gloss, a water bottle, a bag of gummy bears, a fork for takeaway lunches, wadded up tissues — that I'm soaked by the time I find them.

Like most houses in Hanoi, ours is tall and skinny, the layout on each of the four floors identical with a big front room, a bathroom, a central stairwell, and a small back room. Wyatt rented this house before I arrived in Hanoi, since I stayed on in Raleigh for an extra month to finalize our wedding details. We're getting married in the same chapel where my parents wed. Just thinking about it makes me shiver. Ever since I was a little girl I've imagined myself walking down that aisle and now it's finally happening.

A retractable metal gate covers our front door, which is wide enough to drive a car through. Before reaching through the bars to unlock the two padlocks, I gaze up at the house. When I first saw it I'd been dismayed, since it looks like a rent-by-the-hour love hotel and I'd imagined us living in some quaint, French-style villa. Wyatt chose this place because it's close to his office.

After unlocking the last padlock I step inside, the ground floor serving as both coatroom and garage. My green Vespa is parked where I left it this morning in a puddle of motor oil. I wonder what's wrong with it this time. Maybe Wyatt was right and I should have bought a new Honda Dream after all, even if they are ugly and boring. As soon as this thought enters my mind I feel disloyal, as if my dodgy, old Vespa is a mind-reader. I give the bike a guilty pat. I'll get it fixed this weekend.

Next to the stairs, a half-dozen boxes are filled with so-called essentials that I'd had shipped from New York, where I spent the last seven years studying and working. I look away, the boxes yet another source of guilt. I've been here for four months and have yet to get round to unpacking them. It'll have to wait until after the wedding.

Hanoi Jane   13

I kick off my wet flats and shake the raindrops off of my garment bag, imagining the dress within. I picture Wyatt's face when he sees me in it for the first time, then check my watch. There's still time for me to have a quick shower and try the dress on again. I want to see it with my shoes and tiara.

Our bedroom is on the fourth floor, so I'm panting by the time that I get there. A glance in the hall mirror reveals that my mascara has run. My hair's a mess too, the longer bits lank and the bangs frizzy. I make a face into the mirror, wishing, as usual, that my face weren't so round. While six months of dieting have allowed me to look great in my wedding dress, no cheekbones have surfaced. I suck in my cheeks and sigh. It's hard not to compare myself to my little sister, Lauren, who has the bone structure of a Slavic ballerina.

When I step into the bedroom I stop. The curtains are drawn, which is weird, and the air-conditioner is on full-blast. Has Wyatt come home sick today? I start to call his name but think better of it. Maybe he's sleeping.

Without realizing what I'm doing, I sniff. There's a strange flowery smell in here. In my damp clothes the room is freezing. Tiptoeing towards our bed I see that the duvet is piled into a heap. Some toes are peeking out. "Honey?" I say softly. "Are you okay, babe?" The toes wiggle.

In the gloom, it takes a moment to register. I lean closer. My mouth goes dry. The toes feature shiny red toenails.

The bottom of the duvet rustles and Wyatt's head pops out, just inches from those red-painted digits. His dark hair is sticking straight up and there's a smear of red lipstick on his chin. Seeing me, his eyebrows shoot to the top of his face and his mouth forms a little *o*, giving him the look of a cartoon hedgehog. "Oh," he says. The toes stop wiggling.

I hug the garment bag to my chest and take a small step backwards. "Wyatt?" I say. "What are you…"

The top end of the duvet is tossed back to reveal a woman, her pretty face framed by long, black hair. Registering my presence, her dark eyes glint with triumph. I take another step back and she smiles, as though she finds my shock amusing.

"Oh God," says Wyatt. He burrows under the duvet and reappears at the top end, his head now beside the woman's. "Jane, damn it, I didn't mean for you to find out like this. God, this is…" He shakes his head, then glances at the woman beside him. "This is so awkward."

"Awkward?" I say, the scene still unreal to me. How is it possible that Wyatt, who less than a year ago had asked me to marry him and move to Hanoi, is now lying in our bed, naked, with this this…? I glance back at the woman — early twenties, attractive, Asian but doesn't look local. "Aw-awkward?" I stammer. "Our wedding is three and a half weeks away." I'm too stunned to be angry.

Wyatt pulls the duvet closer to his chin. He says that he's sorry.

"Sorry?" I parrot, my mind blank.

Wyatt scratches his ear. He looks uncharacteristically nervous. "I didn't plan to feel this way about Lindy… I just…" He glances beseechingly at his bedmate and shrugs. "It just…happened."

At this the woman's smirk curves into a sly smile. I continue to stare at Wyatt. What is he trying to tell me? That he is in love with this woman? I feel sick to my stomach.

"You two need time to talk," says the woman, her French accent as manicured as her toenails. She gives me a condescending smile, her expression revealing neither pity nor embarrassment. "Can you get me a robe? I saw Wyatt's hanging in the bathroom."

I open my mouth to respond but no sound comes out. Is this really happening to me? I wonder if I'm going to throw up. I count to 10 and try to breathe slowly.

The woman, Lindy, looks exasperated. With an exaggerated sigh, she turns to Wyatt. "*Cheri*," she says. "Could you get me that robe *please*? I can't get out of bed like this with her," she nods my way, "just standing there."

I wait for Wyatt to say that he's not her *cheri*, but he's too busy looking under the bed for his boxer shorts. "Hold on a sec," he says when he's found them. He turns away from me to slip into them.

I expect him to come over to me, to try to hug me, to start to explain, but instead he just stands there. When he starts to walk towards the bathroom, he moves like a man who's been at sea for days. "Wyatt?" I say, my voice so small that even I don't recognize it. "Aren't you going to say something?"

He shrugs. "What can I say?"

I nod. He's right. What can he say? Our wedding is less than a month away and he and this woman were just fu- fu- fu... I can't even bring myself to think it. I take a deep breath. "Our wedding," I say. "What about our wedding?"

Even as I say it, I know how pathetic I sound. I just caught my fiancé cheating on me and yet I'm still thinking of marrying him. Am I crazy or just totally desperate?

I figure that I'm a little of both given that, even with this other woman lying naked in our bed, my main concern is the wedding. But how could it not be, when I've spent my whole life planning it?

Long before I liked boys, I was obsessed with all things bridal. At age four I refused to go anywhere unless I had a long swathe of mosquito netting pinned to my head, like a veil. While other kids collected rocks or stickers I collected those hideous plastic pom-poms that people in the 1970s and 1980s used to decorate their wedding cars. I had hundreds of the things, which I'd wash and blow-dry before arranging into fluffy pastel rows on my bookcase.

I've been with Wyatt for six years: five of them spent waiting for him to propose and the last one organizing our wedding. But the wedding planning didn't start with Wyatt. I've envisioned every guy I ever dated, including the ones I didn't especially like, as potential husbands. There was Willy Dobson, who stuck his tongue in my mouth at Camp Pocahontas when I was 15. There was Brent Gobrowsky, the guy who took me to prom after the guy I wanted to take me to prom (who I also envisioned marrying) asked my little sister instead. There was my college boyfriend Doug, who later dropped out of school and reportedly became a Zen monk. I even imagined my one and only one-night stand, a Norwegian dive-instructor named Brokk, saying 'I do' in his sexy Scandinavian accent.

Given all those years of anticipation, the idea that this wedding might not happen seems impossible. It's like being told that the earth is flat after all, and that I'm about to fall off of it.

"We can't," says Wyatt. "I mean, I can't." His eyes slide back towards Lindy.

I too look at Lindy and immediately regret it, her smug smile bringing hot, angry tears to my eyes. Rather than cry in front of her, I turn and careen down the staircase.

At the bottom of the stairs I stop. I am trying not to hyperventilate. Clinging to the banister, I shut my eyes and wait, sure that Wyatt will follow me. He'll want to explain. I imagine what he'll say: he was drunk; she seduced him; it only happened this one time and he is so, so sorry.

Just when I think that I can't wait another second I hear him, descending the steps so slowly and quietly that I wonder if he's on tiptoes. I look up to see him shuffling across the first floor landing as if he's stepping across a hangman's scaffold. He looks so wretched that if I hadn't just caught him cheating on me, I'd feel sorry for him.

Seeing me, Wyatt stops walking. "Jane?" He swallows hard. "I… I feel really bad about this but I can't, we can't…" He studies his hands. "We can't get married."

I want to tell him that he's wrong, all the invitations have been sent, all the napkins have been ordered, all the food has been catered, but no sound comes out.

"I know this is awfully sudden but I need time to figure things out, to figure out what I want. We need to take a break." The words speed out of him, crash against each other and pile up in a mangled heap, like a train wreck.

I hear the sound of screeching brakes and a wild, crazy clanging. With all of that noise going on inside of my head it's hard to think. "A break?" I whisper. "But our wedding..."

"I — I can't," says Wyatt. "We have to cancel—"

Still pressing the garment bag to my chest, I feel the world tilt. Is it really possible? I grip the banister.

Seeing my face, Wyatt stops talking. "Postpone," he says. "We need to postpone the wedding. We can't get married right now, not like this. I need to figure this out." He shakes himself, then stands a bit straighter.

I have a vision of Wyatt in some meeting negotiating with difficult clients, trying to convince them that what he wants is in their best interest. "We need time to work through this," he says, looking down as if to survey some imaginary notes. "You'd better call your parents about the arrangements." He clears his throat. "I'll deal with my family."

I'm not sure what pushes me over the edge but all of a sudden I'm sobbing. It's as if all the tears and snot that I've been holding in come out all at once, so that one moment I'm relatively self-possessed and the next I'm blotchy, slimy and blubbering.

Wyatt stays put, leaning over the balustrade of the first-floor landing. We're like the antithesis of Romeo and Juliet, me on the ground, sobbing, and Wyatt peering down at me. "Don't cry," he says. He looks alarmed and revolted, like I'm a slug that he just stepped on.

I throw my wedding dress to the floor, grab my bag and stuff my feet into my still-wet ballet flats. Making a conscious effort not to look back I stumble out the door, too blinded by tears to see where I'm going. I can hear Wyatt calling after me but he sounds half-hearted.

Once outside, I turn left and start walking, the street mercifully deserted. It's raining harder than ever, the clouds so dense that it's as if dusk has set in. Someone is cooking *bun cha*, the street smelling of grilled meat and fish sauce. I pass a pagoda, its tiered roofs dripping and its empty courtyard full of mud puddles. In the fading light the street looks unfamiliar, the pagoda's curved roofs a reminder that I'm far, far from home. Behind the pagoda's wall a gong sounds, its long quavering note giving voice to my desolation.

Bowing my head against the deluge I feel sick and bewildered. What should I do? Should I go to a hotel? I wish that I were home in Raleigh or back in New York. At least there I could run to an old friend, someone who really knows me.

Taking imperfect shelter beneath the pagoda's spreading banyan, I stop and pull out my cell phone. Still fighting back tears, I scroll through the list of names until I get to Sigrid's. Although we've only been friends for a few months, Sigrid will know what to do. She is, after all, an expert in Disaster Management.

2 Sympathy & Suspicion

I'm about to call Sigrid when a *xe om* appears, the driver waving to get my attention. I hesitate for a split-second before nodding at the man, who's engulfed in a pink plastic rain poncho. I recite Sigrid's address and he sets a price, the two of us communicating through repetition and sign language. Twenty-thousand *dong*, or just over a dollar. A total rip off. Out of habit, I start to bargain, then remember that saving 30 cents isn't a big priority right now. I'm in desperate need of some hot tea and a dry place to cry my eyes out.

The bike lurches forward before I'm properly settled, then teeters precariously. When we pick up speed the rain stings my eyes. I hope that the driver can see more than I can, although death doesn't seem as unappealing as it did a half-hour ago.

Clutching the seat with one hand and my cell phone with the other, I call Sigrid. After three rings she picks up, her smooth tone making it clear that she'd been expecting a work call. "GEMS, Sigrid Olsen speaking." The office she runs, Global Emergency Management Solutions, specializes in disaster preparedness and response, consulting on everything from office evacuation plans to oil spill cleanups.

"Sigrid!" I yell. "Where are you?"

There's a pause, followed by a tentative, "Jane? Is that you? Why is it so noisy?"

"I'm on a *xe om*," I yell. "I need to—"

Sigrid cuts me off. "You know that's a bad idea. Someone could drive by and snatch your phone and pull you off the bike. Call me when you get to where you're going."

"No!" I scream. "No don't hang up! Please!" The desperation in my voice must register, since there's a pause before Sigrid asks what the matter is. I swallow hard, solicitude drawing a fresh sob from my throat. "I — I just found Wyatt in bed with… with… My bed…They were in my bed…Our bed. A F-French woman. With Wyatt. In my bed. N-n-naked."

"What?" says Sigrid. "Oh no. Can you hold on a moment?" She must be covering the phone with one hand and speaking to someone else, since her voice is suddenly muffled. When she returns she sounds calm and authoritative. "Go to my place. I'll be there in 15 minutes. Wait for me round back, out of the rain. I need to lock up the office."

"I'm… on my way," I say but Sigrid has already hung up on me.

The *xe om* driver twists around to get another look at me, no doubt wondering why this panda-eyed Western woman is sobbing hysterically on the back of his motorbike. I return the phone to my bag and retrieve a wad of damp tissues, my efforts to scour the mascara from my cheeks having little effect. It's still raining and I'd applied three coats of Ultra Black to my pale lashes this morning. It will take a lot more than a Kleenex to clean up this mess. I dig out my sunglasses.

As soon as the bike stops I pay up and vault off. Sigrid's apartment lies smack in the middle of the Old

Quarter, near a bunch of popular shops and cafes. It's prime property for Hanoi's expats, and the only thing that could make me feel worse than I already do would be to run into someone I know.

Feeling like a fugitive, I scurry towards the low doorway that leads to Sigrid's building. A dark, covered alley runs beneath a shop house to a small courtyard. Smelling of mold and cat pee, this narrow tunnel is barely wide enough for a single bicycle, the floor tiles so warped that I lurch drunkenly. I'm not sure how Sigrid manages to pass this way unscathed after a big night out in high heels.

At the far end of the tunnel a rusty sliding gate usually bars access to the courtyard, but somebody has propped it open with a tricycle. Security isn't an issue, however, as two old ladies pop up over windowsills to examine and dismiss me. A Chihuahua peeks out of a doorway and yaps until one of the old women kicks it.

Once in the courtyard I make my way through a maze of plastic baby toys, dog crap and potted plants, the sounds of a half-dozen voices drifting out to me, along with those of a TV quiz show and Strawberry Fields sung in Vietnamese. I climb a dim, bare-cement staircase to the fourth floor, then sink onto Sigrid's braided doormat.

Located on the top floor, Sigrid's place overlooks a haphazard collection of red-tiled roofs on one side and a street lined with souvenir shops on the other. Although it's tiny and noisy, I've always admired Sigrid's apartment, which she's decorated with a few choice antiques and paintings by local artists.

I'm sitting with my eyes shut when I hear footsteps below, Sigrid's dark, tousled head coming into view.

Hanoi Jane 23

Despite the hot, wet weather, Sigrid looks chic and professional, her petite frame clad in a cream-colored shirtdress. Although she's just 5"1, I never think of Sigrid as small. Like usual, she's wearing outrageously high heels, but it's not just the shoes that make her seem taller than she is. Sigrid has a big personality. Her high heels clatter up the staircase.

When she reaches the landing she stops and studies me, then shakes her head pityingly. I'm sitting with my back to her front door, some wadded-up tissues scattered around my feet and another pressed to my nose, which is dripping.

"You've had an awful shock," says Sigrid. "Let's go inside. I'll make tea."

With a Chinese-American mother and a British father, Sigrid grew up shuttling back and forth between New York, Hong Kong and London. While she looks Asian and sounds American, she is very British in her eating habits. Tea is her solution to everything. I bet that Earl Grey is listed in all of her Emergency Response Plans.

I manage a wan nod and she holds up a shopping bag. "I bought ice cream. One tub of extra dark chocolate and another of raspberry."

My eyes well up with gratitude. Sigrid is a good friend. She has bought my favorite ice cream flavors. "Thanks," I say, although even ice cream would stick in my throat right now. Sigrid extends a hand to help me up, then unlocks the door. I follow her inside obediently. Her kitchen smells of fresh-cut limes and oregano.

After washing my face, blowing my nose, sitting on the toilet to sob, and having to blow my nose all over again,

I return to the kitchen to find Sigrid pouring boiling water into a cobalt-blue teapot. She has changed out of her work dress into sweat-shorts and a grey tank top. I watch as she sets two mismatched mugs on the kitchen table and retrieves a Pyrex dish from the fridge. "Carrot cake?" she says. "I made it two nights ago." She sets two plates on the table.

Faced with tea, cake and sympathy, I'm overcome by fresh tears. I pull out a wooden chair and sit down, then shake my head angrily. "God, I wish I could stop crying," I say. "This is so pointless."

Sigrid pours the tea, then hands me a mug. "Would you rather not talk about it?"

I stare into my mug, then squeeze my eyes shut. "No, it's just that I can barely believe it. I mean, this is Wyatt we're talking about. We're about to get married. And the way he looked at that girl, it was like he was crazy about her…" I don't usually take sugar, since I've been trying to stay skinny for the wedding, but after Sigrid's done with the spoon I add two heaping spoonfuls to my tea. I take a sip. It is hot, sweet and delicious.

Sigrid hands me a serving of cake. "Who is she?"

I shake my head. "I've never seen her before. Younger than me, maybe in her early twenties. Long, black hair. Pretty but mean looking." I take another sip of tea, trying to calm myself. "She looks Asian but has a horribly sexy French accent. French Viet Kieu, I guess."

"She must have been mortified."

"No," I say. "She didn't seem embarrassed at all. It was like she was pleased with herself, like she found the whole scene amusing."

Sigrid, who'd been in the process of slicing another thick square of carrot cake, looks outraged. "Really? But that's crazy. Did she say anything?"

"She... she asked me to get her a robe. It was more of an order, actually..." I shake my head, the mortification that I'd felt at that moment coming back to me. "I turned and ran away. It was so awful."

"Hmph," says Sigrid. "What was her name?"

"Lindy," I say. "That's what Wyatt called her. Lindy."

Sigrid hands me a roll of paper towels, the house's supply of tissues already exhausted. "So what do you want to do now?"

I shrug and admit that I don't know. "I guess I have to call my sister, get her to deal with the flower people and the band and the caterer." I lick some icing off of my fork, then set it down. I have no appetite. "I'll have to contact all of the guests, postpone the wedding..." I rub my eyes. Just thinking about it all makes my head ache.

One of Sigrid's eyebrows goes up as her mug comes down. "Postpone?" she says. "Don't you mean cancel?"

"Um, yeah," I say. I study my mug, unable to meet Sigrid's eyes. Surely Wyatt will come to his senses and fix everything. We've been together for *six* years. We picked out a china pattern together, Royal Doulton's Precious Platinum...

Sigrid purses her lips. "You still want to marry him?"

I feel myself blush. Having gone to journalism school and spent three years working at *Chic!* in New York, I've interviewed loads of people. But Sigrid is a natural interrogator, her ability to detect bullshit earning her almost as many enemies as friends. I'm sure that both are a bit scared of her. I look away. "I love him," I say, appalled by how pathetic I sound. I just caught the man cheating on me. I ought to be plotting how to castrate him. Instead, I can't imagine my life without Wyatt.

Sigrid sighs. "I understand that," she says. "But do you really think you can forgive him?" She chews thoughtfully. "Could you trust him again?"

I shrug, but I'm not thinking about trust. I'm thinking about my wedding dress, and how well it fits. I'm thinking about stepping into the chapel on my daddy's arm, and about the white roses and the jazz quartet and my carefully chosen party favors.

"Jane?"

I look up guiltily. "He made a mistake," I say. "Whoever this girl is, he can't love her like he loves me. We're part of each other's families. We both want two girls and a boy." I swallow hard. "We both love crime novels."

Sigrid, who reads military history for fun, frowns. She starts to speak, then stops herself, although it's clear what she's thinking.

"You think I'm in denial," I say sullenly. "That it's a lost cause, that I should forget about him."

"I don't know," she says. "I can't tell you how to feel. You're in shock. It's a major betrayal." She tops up my mug. "So yes, I think you should cancel, postpone—whatever—the wedding and give yourself some time to get your head around this."

I study my friend's face. Technically, Sigrid's not beautiful, since her nose is too prominent, her forehead too high and her jaw too square. But somehow her odd features work well together. I bet that even people who

Hanoi Jane 27

don't like her are attracted to her. "You don't think I should call him?" I say.

"Not now," says Sigrid firmly. "I can go by and get your clothes. You can stay here for a while."

"What about Fergus?" I say, fresh tears prickling my eyes at the thought of the scrawny orange cat that I'd found in an alley two weeks after moving here. I feel like a stray myself at this moment.

"Leave the cat with Wyatt for a while." Sigrid is a dog person.

I take a deep breath and nod, then ask if she'll do me a favor.

"What's that?"

"Will you help me to find out everything you can about this Lindy woman? We could, I don't know, check her out on the Internet…"

Sigrid's eyes narrow into chocolate shards. "What for?" Only her closest friends know that she's a hardcore computer geek, having been given her first Mac at the age of seven by her Uncle Don, an FBI computer crimes expert back in Los Angeles.

"I just need to know," I say, my voice thin and sniveling. "Can you understand that? I need to know who she is, what he sees in her, and why this is happening to me."

Sigrid pushes back her chair and stands up, then walks around the table. She pulls my stiff shoulders towards her. I allow myself to bend to fit Sigrid's body, which is compact and muscular, like a cheerleader's. Not that Sigrid's the cheerleader type; she'd been on three teams back in high school: Fencing, Computers and Orienteering.

Sigrid leans back to examine me. "Are you going to be okay?" I give a feeble nod and she rubs my hair, which is still damp and frizzy. "Try not to torture yourself," she says. "One day none of this will seem as important as it does now."

I nod again, although I don't believe her, then blow my nose. "So you'll help me find out about Lindy?"

Sigrid sighs. "Yeah," she says grudgingly. "But we'll need her last name." She licks the cream cheese icing off of her cake and grins wickedly. "I'll help you destroy Wyatt's hard drive too, if it makes you feel any better. There's a new virus going around, a really nasty one that forwards gay porn to all of your email contacts before frying your entire system."

I manage a slim smile. "That might help," I say. "At least a little bit."

• • •

A city of six million, Hanoi still feels like a small town, few of the buildings in the city center standing higher than a few stories. In the Old Quarter, the houses are even lower, while the streets are so narrow that only one car at a time—or about three honking motorbikes facing in each direction—can negotiate them.

For Hanoi's expat community the city feels smaller still, with most foreigners frequenting the same shops, bars and restaurants that offer a taste of home, or at least staff who speak English. With this in mind, I start to fish around, being subtle, of course, for info on Lindy. Someone I know must know her. So far, only my friend

Michelle thinks that the name rings a bell. A French-Vietnamese woman named Lindy or Mindy works out at her gym and hogs the treadmill during peak periods. Michelle thinks that she works for some charity.

I look around the office and stifle a yawn. Despite having downed two glasses of red wine and half a valium last night I slept badly. Three different people have stopped by my desk this morning to tell me how awful I look. Tact, apparently, is not a virtue in Vietnam.

At just before 11:00 a.m. on a Thursday, the office is so quiet that I can hear the clock ticking. This far from deadline, that's not unusual. Two days before *Hanoi Scope* goes to print the room will be packed, everyone clamoring to use the computers and yelling into their cell phones.

While I don't miss *Chic!*'s constant stories about hairspray and 'Spring's Hottest Lipstick Trends', working at the *Hanoi Scope* is a big step down, the magazine a glorified flyer full of advertorials and government propaganda. Aimed at expats and foreign tourists, the *Scope* has only one native English-speaker on the payroll. As such, I serve as managing editor, reporter, copywriter, proofreader and Journalism 101 coach.

Most of the *Scope*'s staff were trained back in the days when reporting the facts was the last thing that a conscientious Vietnamese journalist would do. Unfortunately, the *Scope* is produced by a state-owned company, which means that laziness, craziness and illiteracy aren't grounds for dismissal. Short of murdering the deaf octogenarian editor-in-chief or desecrating Ho Chi Minh's mausoleum I doubt that there's anything that the senior staff could do to get fired.

Luckily, there are a few talented exceptions, like my assistant, Tuyet, who's now standing beside my desk, studying me. "What's wrong with your eyes?" says Tuyet, whose name means 'Snow', ironically something that Tuyet has never seen.

I sniff. "I have a cold."

Tuyet nods. "Ah. It's the weather. You must be careful when the weather changes." Twenty-four-years-old, Tuyet is gorgeous but doesn't seem to realize it, her large, almond-shaped eyes hidden behind unflattering green glasses and her admirably straight black hair pulled back into a low ponytail. Contacts and a haircut would transform Tuyet into a fox, but since I've left *Chic!*, I'm not going to waste time handing out beauty tips.

"I need your help," I say. "I'm trying to find someone. A French Viet Kieu woman named Lindy. She might work for some non-profit organization. Any idea how to find her?"

Tuyet nibbles on the end of a ballpoint pen, revealing perfectly even little teeth. I bet that, unlike me, she never wore braces. "There's a book listing all the NGOs in Vietnam. If she's permanent staff her name might be in there," says Tuyet. "How do you spell her name?"

I cock my head and consider. "Hmmm, not sure. Probably L-I-N-D-Y. But it could end in an I, or maybe an I-E."

"And her last name?"

"Uh, sorry, no idea," I say.

If Tuyet is curious as to why I want to find this woman she doesn't get the chance to ask, because at that moment my phone rings. Tuyet gives me a thumbs-up and walks off. I grab the phone, convinced that it's Wyatt calling to beg for forgiveness, but it's just Sigrid checking up on me. "I'm fine," I say, but it's hard to keep a tremble out of my voice. I'd been so sure that it was Wyatt. Why hasn't he called me yet?

"Have you spoken to Wyatt?"

I take a deep breath. "No. He hasn't called."

"Asshole," says Sigrid. "Oh, about that woman. I did some checking online. Her name is Lindy Tran. She runs an NGO called Highlands Outreach. That's HO for short," she snickers and I manage a tired smile. "Anyways, hmmm, where was I? It provides small business loans and other forms of assistance to impoverished ethnic minority women." She sounds like she's reading.

I shut my eyes. Great. Not only is Lindy Tran hot, but she's also devoted her life to helping poor people.

"Jane?" says Sigrid. "You still there?"

"Yup."

"That's not all I found."

All of a sudden, I lack the energy to care. Just talking about Lindy, Lindi or Lindie has sapped the life out of me. I keep seeing Wyatt's face when he'd looked at her, like everything else in the world was invisible. I can hear Sigrid on the line, waiting. "So what did you find?" I say.

"It seems she's living with another guy," says Sigrid. "An American lawyer named Jason McCallum. They live out by West Lake in one of those giant fancy villas with a turret." She snorts. "My friend Emma went to a party out at their place a couple weeks ago and said it seemed really serious between them, I mean between Lindy and this lawyer guy."

I ponder this information, wondering what the implications are for me. Maybe Lindy has no interest in a relationship with Wyatt. Is it just a fling? I'm finding it hard to breathe again.

"You still there?"

I rub my eyes, which are itchy and puffy. "Uh, yes. Anything else?"

"Yeah, something really weird. I called my friend Tracey who works for Save the Children UK. I figured she might know this Lindy Tran seeing as they're both in the NGO crowd. Well it turns out that she does, but not through work. They were both members of the Hanoi Players community theatre group. Remember how they performed *Little Shop of Horrors* last Christmas? Oh, right, that was before you got here. Well anyways, Tracey said that Lindy was a total snot, complained that her costume didn't fit right, wanted it shortened to make it sexier, etcetera etcetera…"

I grit my teeth, wishing that Sigrid would get to the point, if there is one. I'd thought that I wanted to know all about Lindy but now I'm not so sure. Every time Sigrid says her name my throat constricts and my headache intensifies.

"So anyway," says Sigrid. "Tracey said that Lindy was dating the guy who did the show's lighting, some Canadian named Graham, a graphic designer, apparently totally hot. Of course that was last December so I just figured they broke up but then Tracey said no, she'd seen them together only last night, making out in the River Bar."

I try to take this all in. "Sooo," I say. "Lindy is dating three guys at once."

Hanoi Jane   33

"And living with at least one of them," says Sigrid.

"Wow, that's insane," I say. "Or maybe they all know and are, like, fine with it. Maybe they've all agreed that they can see other people. You couldn't keep that kind of thing secret in Hanoi."

"Well from what Emma told me about Jason it seems that he and Lindy are practically engaged. And Tracey said that Graham is really sweet, definitely not the kind of guy who'd be okay with his girlfriend sleeping with someone else's fiancé."

"Maybe she's just wrong," I say. Until yesterday, I'd have sworn there was no way that my fiancé could be sleeping with anyone besides me.

"Or maybe he doesn't know."

"Maybe," I say skeptically. "But if she thinks she can pull that off in a town like Hanoi then Lindy Tran is a lunatic. I mean come on. Everyone knows everything about everybody."

"Yup, she's got balls all right," says Sigrid, then, "Whoops. Gotta go. I got a long distance call."

I set the phone back into its cradle and massage my temples. Maybe I'll go home early today. I feel exhausted and in danger of crying again.

"Uh, Miss Jane?" says a soft voice.

I raise my head to see Tuyet. "Oh hey, Tuyet." I sit up straighter. "What's going on?"

Tuyet holds up a computer printout. "I think I found the information you needed. She skims through the small print, then starts to read out loud. "Lindy Tran is director of Highlands Outreach. Says here that it's a non-profit organization created to provide assistance to disadvantaged ethnic minority women in Vietnam's North-Eastern Highlands in the areas of small business loans and training, healthcare and education." She passes me the printout.

I manage a smile. "Great work. Thank you Tuyet."

"Uh, there is something else," says Tuyet. "It might not be important but, if you read down here…" She points several paragraphs down the page. "It says that last year Highlands Outreach ran a basic healthcare training program in Mai Chau for Red Dao women. Hand-washing, nutrition, food-safety, basic prenatal and postnatal care." She reads from the paper, then looks up, her pretty face troubled. "Well, see, a friend of my sister's is an anthropology PhD. Her name is Van and she's been in Mai Chau for the past two years working with Red Dao women. So I figured that she'd know Lindy Tran and Highlands Outreach, since Mai Chau is very small. But when I called her, Van said that she'd never heard of them." She stops talking and nibbles on her ballpoint. "Isn't that strange?"

"Uh, yeah," I say, my head throbbing harder now. "That is strange."

"Right, well, anyways, all the contact info is on there," says Tuyet. "You need me to do anything else?"

"No," I say. "This is great. Thanks again, Tuyet."

"No problem." She pauses, taps her pen against a perfect tooth, then says, "Miss Jane? You do not look fine today. Maybe you should go home and rest until this bad weather improves."

"Right," I say, already stuffing papers and notebooks into my tote bag. "I think I'll do that." Tuyet keeps standing

there, as though she's waiting for me to say something else. Since I really do like her, I feel an urge to tell her everything. But I resist and turn off my computer.

With a final admonishment to take care, Tuyet is off. Watching her retreat towards her own desk, I feel a surge of self-pity spiked with envy. Five years my junior, Tuyet seems so smart, poised and proper. I can't imagine *her* being cheated on. As I stalk out of the office I take stock of my failings: I'm 29 years old, working in a dead-end job, recently and humiliatingly dumped, homeless, and disheveled…

The list is so dismal that I feel incapacitated. Even small steps towards self-improvement seem beyond me. My head is so full of all the things that I should do—wash my hair; eat a decent meal; call my parents to cancel the wedding bookings; decide whether or not I'm going to stay in Hanoi—that I can't do anything. I take a taxi back to Sigrid's house and curl up in a ball on her couch, feeling like I did as a kid when I got sick: dull, sticky and listless.

I turn off all of the lights and shut my eyes, wishing that I had mumps or measles instead of this terrible sense of loss and failure. I fall asleep wishing that my dad would appear with a glass of flat ginger ale and an offer to read me a story.

3 On Hold

Woken by my buzzing cell phone, I sit up in a panic. Sigrid's living room seems strange in the dark. I feel under the couch but can't find my phone, my alarm growing as I fumble under the cushions. The phone must have slipped down there; I can feel it vibrating below me.

Judging by the lack of light it's still late at night. Sigrid's bedroom door is shut. Who, besides Wyatt, could be calling at this hour? I picture him wracked with remorse, unable to sleep, begging me for forgiveness. My fingers close around the phone and I shove it towards my mouth. "Hello?"

"Jane? Honey, is that you?"

I sink back down against the couch, tempted to hang up. I could always claim network failure. That sometimes happens here.

"Honey?" My mom's voice comes again. "Lauren told me that Wyatt's brother called, that he asked her to rearrange the chapel and the country club..." There's a pause, as if my mom is waiting for me to refute this claim.

I curse myself for having answered the phone without checking the caller I.D. display. Right now, my mom, Tabitha, is the last person I feel like talking to.

"Are you and Wyatt having some sort of problems?" she says. "Has one of you gotten cold feet? That's not unusual, you know..."

"Uh, Mom, it's the middle of the night," I say. "You just woke me up. Could we talk about this some other time?"

"Like when?" snaps my mother. "In case you've forgotten your wedding day is three weeks from now. And all of a sudden you want to postpone it. The venue's been booked for the past year, and you *know* how many strings Daddy had to pull to get the club on a Sunday."

I grit my teeth, my mom's voice growing increasingly hysterical.

"So do you want to tell me why Lauren was told to cancel the caterer after I spent weeks, no, make that months, going over the menu with him? Your Uncle Bob's allergic to shellfish and your bridesmaid Molly doesn't eat meat and Cousin Dale's new Korean wife is lactose intolerant and, really Jane, you had better tell me what's going on over there."

"I…" I take a deep breath. "I'm sorry, Mom. It's so…" I swipe at some newly-formed tears. "It's so humiliating." I can hear my mom sucking on something, no doubt a sugar free mint. Tabitha consumes a couple of tins of sugar free Altoids a day in a bid to stay slim, no doubt reasoning that, if her mouth is full of mints, she'll be less likely to put real food into it.

"I knew it!" shrieks my mother. "He's gay, isn't he?"

"No!" I say. "Wyatt's not gay. I just caught him ch—cheating on me. With another w—woman."

"Hmmm," says Tabitha. "Another woman? Are you sure about that? I saw a show on the Discovery channel about those Thai lady boys. Men dressed up like pretty girls and you'd never know it in a million years—they looked so good. Do they have them in Vietnam too? I always thought Wyatt might be long in his loafers…"

"That's light in the loafers," I say, "and you've got it all wrong, Mom. Wyatt is not gay!"

"So is it over between you?"

I bite my lip. "N—no! I mean, I don't think so. We haven't talked since I…since I found out about… her."

"Well what are you waiting for?" says my mom. "Your Grandma June is flying in from Florida next week. And your Uncle Dwayne's getting a tailored tux, for God's sake, since they don't sell them that big off the rack. Aunt Lorraine had to book him two seats on the bus because she hates to fly." She stops to bite on a mint. "So what am I supposed to do about all of this? What should I tell everybody?"

"He was cheating on me, Mom!" I wail. "In my bed. With another woman."

There's a pause, so that I wonder if the phone has gone dead after all, but then I hear her mint tin rattling, followed by one of my mother's long, theatrical sighs. "I always thought something like this would happen," says my mom, an I-told-you-so ring to her voice.

"What are you talking about?" I say. "And why didn't you say something?"

"Ah, well," says Tabitha. "It's not like you listen to me anyway. What I mean is that I always wondered if he was really in love with you. Smart, successful guy like Wyatt. And handsome too, if a little on the short side." She sniffs. "I just wondered, that's all."

"So you think I'm not good enough for Wyatt?" I say, my voice thickening with self-pity. "Not, what? Successful enough? Pretty enough?"

"There you go again," she says. "Always taking things the wrong way. I never said that. What I meant was that Wyatt seems so in love with himself I'm not sure there'd be much left over for anyone else."

Mollified, I blow my nose, then feel an urge to defend Wyatt. But before I can get a word in, my mother is off again. "But you know, honey, if you had gone into broadcast journalism like I suggested you could have been on TV by now. And well, let's face it, ever since you left that fashion magazine you've been looking a little..." The mint tin gives a jaunty shake. "Feral."

"Feral? I squeak. "So what, now it's my fault that Wyatt cheated on me?"

"Men are simple enough," says my mom lightly. "They're easily distracted. You have to pay attention, keep them occupied. It was one of those Vietnamese girls wasn't it? Personally I don't know what men see in those Asian girls but I guess they find them exotic, so skinny and, well, most of them are desperate, aren't they? I mean they'll do just about *anything* for a Green card, won't they? Really, Jane, didn't you understand what it'd be like over there? I told you that going to Vietnam was a lousy idea..."

"You don't get it," I wail. "I didn't do anything wrong. Wyatt betrayed me. Three weeks before our wedding." The tears are coming hard and fast now, my breathing increasingly irregular. "And she's French!" I hiccup. "I can't believe he did this to me."

"Well, you better believe it, missy," says my mom. "The question now is what are you going to do about it? Do you still want this louse or should I tell Uncle Dwayne he won't be needing that tux after all?"

"I … I don't know," I sob. "I … I love Wyatt."

Tabitha starts on another of her theatrical sighs, then seems to think better of it. When she speaks again, her tone is softer. "I know you think you do," she says, "but really, honey, I'm not sure if you actually love Wyatt or just the idea of him."

"Wh—what's that supposed to mean?"

"Well, getting married is romantic, but living with someone for your whole life takes some doing. You have to have a lot in common, something really special together."

"And you don't think that Wyatt and I have that?"

"I think now's the time to find out."

"So, so what would you do?" I say.

"Ha! I'd skin the jerk alive," she says. "But I'm not you. Just try to figure out what you want before your dad's mother arrives next week. If this wedding isn't going to happen, I'd rather she stayed in Florida. Oh and honey, remember that no matter what happens you can always come home."

I feel my alarm spike to a new high. I'd rather face jail-time than return to live with my folks. Even Lauren, who's the perfect daughter, felt compelled to move to a new town, albeit one only a few hours' drive away.

"Some of my friends here have very nice-looking sons," continues my mom. "Luanne Jenkins's eldest is an orthodontist. And he's so *masculine*."

I turn the phone away and blow my nose, then take a deep breath. "Wyatt's not gay, Mom."

"Right," she says. "Whatever you say, honey. Just make up your mind ASAP. The calla lilies are being special-ordered all the way from Mexico. And I can't hold off on printing up the menu cards forever…" Then with an air kiss and a rattle of mints Tabitha hangs up, leaving me unable to breathe through my nose and fresh out of tissues. I shuffle towards the bathroom.

After splashing cold water on my face and blowing my nose I feel slightly better. Studying myself in the bathroom mirror I realize that my mom's right about one thing: I need to talk to Wyatt as soon as possible and see if our relationship can be salvaged.

• • •

At two minutes past two in the afternoon I'm hiding in a bathroom in the Metropole Hotel, checking my makeup for the dozenth time and psyching myself up to walk into the Garden Bar. Following Sigrid's advice I arranged to meet Wyatt in a public place, since it'd be way too easy to get overemotional back at our house.

I check my watch, then return to my reflection in the full-length mirror. I dressed casually but carefully: dark jeans and a sleeveless blue silk tank that brings out the color of my eyes. Considering that I've had two nights of bad sleep and cried buckets I don't look too bad, the dark circles beneath my eyes and the redness around my nose more or less masked by foundation, while some pink blush has lent my cheeks more color than they normally have. I wonder if I've overdone the blush but dismiss the idea, still smarting from my mother's claim that since leaving *Chic!* I've gone "feral".

I enter the bar to find Wyatt waiting for me, just as I'd expected, punctuality being an obsession of his. He looks handsome but strained, his mouth tightening when he spots me and his eyes sliding off to one side, unable to meet my gaze. I sink into the booth across from him without speaking, glad that I'd gone for that extra foundation and blush. Not that Wyatt is actually looking at me.

"Hey," says Wyatt, his eyes fixed on the bar's art-deco-style floor tiles. "How's it going?"

I shrug. Seeing Wyatt is harder than I'd expected it to be, a vision of his face next to Lindy's red-painted toenails causing my throat to burn. I try to look hurt but brave. "Okay. You?"

Wyatt shrugs, then asks what I wanted to see him about. All of a sudden I'm too angry to respond. What does he think I want to see him about? I bite back my rancor, struggling to keep my voice neutral. "We need to discuss what to do about us, about our…" I swallow hard. "Our wedding."

Wyatt tugs at the knot of his striped tie, a gift from my sister Lauren a couple of Christmases ago. I wonder why he chose to wear that one today. Does it mean anything? I tell myself to stop overanalyzing everything, then dab at my eyes with a tissue.

At the sight of my tears Wyatt's nostrils flare. Raised in a family where handshakes substitute for hugs, shows of emotion make Wyatt nervous. "Please," he says, then seems to remember that he's the guilty party and manages a sympathetic sigh. He pats my hand, my heart lurching at his touch. "I never meant to hurt you," he says gruffly, "It's just that, well, meeting Lindy has changed everything."

Sometimes, if I have a sore in my mouth, I can't stop myself from running my tongue over it. Hearing Wyatt say Lindy's name triggers a similarly masochistic response. "How did you meet her?" I say. "And how long has it been... " I swallow hard. "Happening?"

Wyatt sighs. "What's the point of getting into this?" Our table has a view of the hotel's pool, where an attendant, dressed all in white, is using a net attached to a long stick to scoop leaves out of the pool. Instead of looking at me, Wyatt is staring out the window. I want to smack him.

Classical music is being piped into the lounge. In a bid to stay calm, I focus on the tune, trying—and failing—to identify the composer. "I just want to know," I say. I sit up straighter. "You owe me the truth, Wyatt."

Two French businessmen walk past our table, both of them laughing about something. Clearly anxious lest I cause a scene, Wyatt waits until the two guys have stepped outside before answering. "Okay, I met her playing golf," he says. Every few weeks, Wyatt and his colleagues play golf—an activity that, on the scale of human futility, I rank right up there with training chickens to dance and building ships inside of bottles. Wyatt claims that it's essential for doing business in Asia.

"How long ago?" I say. I try to recall Wyatt's last golf date.

Wyatt's Adam's apple shimmies and I know that he's debating whether or not to fudge the numbers. He frowns. "I've been seeing her for about, um...two months," he says.

Two months. That's 60 days, or 1,440 hours, of being lied to. And during all that time I'd been blissfully ignorant.

He had slept with her and then slept with me. Just the thought of it makes me want to bathe in disinfectant.

"Jane?" His hand is back on my arm. My first instinct is to shrink from his touch. Then I meet his eyes and my anger takes a back seat. Hope is at the wheel again. "I do care about you," he says. "And I really am sorry."

I nod, glad that Sigrid and my mom can't see me now, since no matter what Wyatt's done, I'd still marry him. I want things back as they were, the way they were going to be. The white wedding, the honeymoon in Bali, the condo back in New York once Wyatt's contract in Hanoi ends... I try to pull myself together. "This is crazy," I say. "We've been together for six years. We went to Aruba with your parents last Christmas and to Hawaii the year before with mine. There are 250 people coming to our wedding... we want the same things in life." I try for a stoic smile. "And you want to throw it all away for this woman you just met?"

Wyatt studies his hands, which are small and neat, like the rest of him, good grooming one of the secrets to his allure. Even now, Wyatt appears dapper and confident, as though he's dealing with a troublesome client rather than his wronged fiancée. He steeples his hands beneath his chin. I hold my breath. "Please Jane," he says. "I need time."

I feel nauseas. "Time for what?"

"To figure this out." He reaches for a silver bowl of mixed nuts, extracts a couple of cashews and examines them daintily. "It's not that I don't love you or appreciate what we have together, but being with Lindy makes me feel so..." He's searching for the word when the waitress appears. An unsmiling middle-aged woman in a cream-colored traditional Vietnamese tunic, she stands, note-pad at the ready, like she's about to issue a traffic ticket. "A lemon soda for me," says Wyatt, who's not one to be intimidated by surly wait staff. "With ice. Sugar on the side. Extra lemon wedges." The woman turns to go, ignoring me. Not trusting myself to say more, I croak out that I want the same.

The waitress frowns. Wyatt's missing adjective hangs there, tormenting me. "She makes you feel so what?" I say when we're alone again, the waitress having sauntered off without acknowledging my order. I can see her standing by the bar staring into space, an aggrieved look on her face. No doubt it's her nap time and she's annoyed that she has to deal with customers. Back in the good old State-subsidized days she could have resolutely ignored us.

Wyatt waves a hand as if to say that it doesn't matter and leans back against the booth's brocade-covered backrest. "We can't get married," he says. "I'm sorry that it happened this way but I don't know what I want. We need to take a break."

I twist my napkin. "A break? As in breakup, or as in some time apart?" My engagement ring catches the light— 1.6 carats, princess cut, platinum setting, everything I'd ever wanted. I try not to look at it.

"A break," says Wyatt. "Time to figure out what we want."

I know what I want, I think, but another voice, seldom heard and screeching with delinquent rage, is screaming obscenities in the back of my head. I grit my teeth. "Then you should take this," I say. I try to twist off my engagement ring.

"Aw no, you keep it," says Wyatt, a blush—is that embarrassment? Regret?—traveling down his chiseled jaw. The ring, tangible evidence of his broken promise, clearly makes Wyatt uncomfortable. My heart cartwheels with hope. All the DeBeers ads I've ever seen flit through my head. Surely our love, like diamonds, will last forever?

I can hear the nasty adolescent voice in the back of my head scoffing, telling me to stop believing cheesy advertising. I feel an urge to tug off the ring and chuck it at him, aiming for his eyes. But Hope, naturally, triumphs, my ring-twisting efforts ceasing as fresh tears flood my eyes. "Wh—what about your parents," I say. "Have you spoken to them?" So far, neither his mom, or dad or sisters have contacted me. Given how uncommunicative his family is, I hadn't expected much, but they could at least have called to check up on me. I can't help but interpret their silence as proof that they hadn't wanted Wyatt to marry me after all.

Wyatt picks out another cashew, some unwanted peanuts spilling from the bowl. He explains that he's emailed everyone.

I stare out towards the swimming pool, a few well-off tourists sprawled on lounge chairs, their handbags costing more than the waiters and pool boys earn in a year. I imagine news of our broken engagement spreading through our network of friends and acquaintances, my Inbox filling with concerned enquiries, everyone fishing for gossip. "What did you tell them?"

Wyatt looks confused, as though the answer should be obvious. "Well, that the wedding is off and that—" At that moment his cell phone rings. He flashes me a familiar, apologetic smile before answering it, then stands up and heads for the courtyard, because, as I well know, mobile reception is bad in here. He returns a few minutes after our soda waters have arrived, then announces that he's got to get going, but, by the way, what should he do about the cat? Will I be taking it home?

"Wh—what?" I say, my mind in slow motion right now. "What do you mean?"

"Well I figured you'd be going back to New York," says Wyatt. "I mean if we're taking a break. Since coming to Vietnam was my idea, I just thought that you'd go back." He takes a quick sip of soda and reaches for his briefcase.

For a moment, I sit stunned. A break, to my mind, holds the possibility of reconciliation. But how can we work things out if we're in different continents? Or does Wyatt plan to finish his contract in Hanoi, have some fun, then return to the States and resume his old life, sure that I'll be there waiting for him?

"No. I'm going to stay," I say, surprised by the certainty in my voice. I had, of course, been considering leaving Hanoi. The thought of being the object of gossip and pity is appalling. The city's expat community is so small that by now news of Wyatt's dalliance must be common knowledge. I could go back to New York. I've got lots of friends and contacts there; one of the women's magazines would probably hire me.

Wyatt, I realize, is still studying me, waiting for me to elaborate. I've finally gotten his attention. "I figured

I'd look for an apartment," I say, reaching for my tote bag. "You can keep Fergus until I find something." For a moment I feel brave and defiant, a wronged woman carving out a life for herself in a strange city, head held high, but then I realize that I'm just sticking around to try to win Wyatt back. I clench my fists. Fury, I know, should be buoying me, but instead I feel crushed. Is this heartbreak? Why doesn't the certainty that Wyatt doesn't deserve me stop me from wanting him?

I think back to the moment when I fell in love with Wyatt, six long years ago. We'd been dating for a few weeks when he'd taken me trail riding, an activity that I'm crazy about. We'd ridden for maybe 10 minutes when I'd glanced back and seen Wyatt's face, which was green-gray with motion sickness and terror. At that instant I'd realized three things: his claims to the contrary, it was Wyatt's first time on a horse; he would never, ever ride again; and he had tried to overcome his fear of horses in an effort to make me happy.

This memory is interrupted by a beep from Wyatt's cell phone, alerting him to the receipt of a text message. As he types in his response, I wonder whether I'd misinterpreted the import of that long-ago trail ride. He had, after all, been lying—too concerned with trying to look cool than to admit to a fear of horses.

Wyatt has signaled for the bill when I decide to broach my final topic, wondering how best to approach it without destroying my last shreds of dignity. "There's one other thing," I say. "About this girl, Lindy." I pronounce her name with careful distaste, the way one might a rare malady. Wyatt's grey eyes narrow. He stays

silent and I plunge ahead, opting for a tone of wide-eyed innocence. "I just wondered if you knew about her other boyfriends," I say. "The American lawyer she's living with and that Canadian guy she was kissing at the River Bar on Monday night, that's the night that I..." I glance down at my engagement ring, then look back at Wyatt. "The night I found out about you and her." Wyatt's eyes, I see, have grown greyer and narrower, as have his lips. I'd never noticed their lack of pigment before.

"That's ridiculous," he says. "You're jealous. Bad-mouthing Lindy isn't going to help. I have feelings for her. You just have to accept that."

I struggle to control my own feelings, fresh tears threatening. "It just seems so tacky," I say. Appearing tacky, I know, is one of Wyatt's greatest fears. "Sleeping with someone who's living with another guy and then making out in a bar with someone else..." I wave my hand, 1.6 carats flashing.

Wyatt's eyes snap back towards me. "What's tacky is you spreading stupid rumors. I know Lindy. None of this is her fault. She felt terrible about getting involved with me when I was..." he pauses, has the grace to look sheepish. "When I was still with you. So don't try to drag her into this, telling me crazy gossip or just making it up."

"I'm not making it up!" I say, outrage making my voice squeak. "Don't you see how awful this is? You breaking off our engagement for someone who's running around with a bunch of different guys..."

Wyatt glares at me. "Lindy broke up with that lawyer ages ago. And as for being in the River Bar, that's impossible. She took the night train to Lao Cai on

Monday. I dropped her off at the train station. She works up there, helping people." The last two words are spoken with extra emphasis. Being a banker, Wyatt has little experience with NGO workers. No doubt Lindy strikes him as some kind of adventurer-saint, braving nasty night trains to bring hope to Vietnam's deep, dark countryside.

I feel my certainty slipping. Lindy could very well have ended it with that lawyer weeks ago. As for the sighting in the River Bar, in that dark, smoky room a lot of longhaired Asian girls would look just Lindy Tran, especially with their faces mashed up against some white guy's.

Wyatt glances at the booth across the aisle from us, now occupied by two Japanese businessmen, both smoking heavily. I get the impression that Wyatt would love a cigarette. He'd smoked in college but quit years ago, back when smoking stopped being cool and became a sign of poor willpower. I watch Wyatt's eyes travel from the men's mouths to their pack of 555s, his lips twitching into a pout.

He grabs his briefcase and stands up. I do likewise. "Look Jane," he says. "I'm sorry I lied and that I didn't tell you sooner. I handled this all wrong. But if you want to hate someone hate me. Leave Lindy out of it."

4 The Other Woman

"Getting dumped isn't the end of the world," says Sigrid, a shrimp cracker heaped with lotus stem salad in one hand and a glass of cheap burgundy in the other.

"He didn't dump me," I hiss. "We're taking a break." Half a bottle of wine has diluted what little sensitivity Sigrid has. I remind myself that Sigrid is actually trying to help. Consoling people just isn't one of her strong suits.

"Um, right," says Sigrid, the entire shrimp cracker vanishing in a single bite. "All I meant is that it might be for the best. Better to realize that he's a wanker now than to end up getting divorced later. I've been in two bridal parties where the couples have already split up."

"Remind me to never ask you to be my bridesmaid," I snap.

Sigrid snorts. "As if. I saw the dresses you picked out for those poor girls. The only way that shade of pink will ever come close to my body is if I have indigestion."

"The color in the photos was different from real life," I say. I think sadly of my now on-hold bridesmaids, my cousin Leah and my college roommates Molly and Sybil. Those carefully-chosen pink dresses are now hanging unworn in their closets.

Perhaps sensing the threat of tears Sigrid leads me closer to the buffet table and hands me a plastic plate. For the past four days I've barely eaten, this spread of deep fried spring rolls, chicken wings, salads and crackers doing little to tempt me. I glance around the art gallery, grateful for the thin crowd. The few familiar faces down at the far end should be easy to outrun if need be.

We'd arrived at the launch party late, it having taken Sigrid some time to haul me off of her couch. The sooner I got out and about the better, Sigrid had insisted. It'd stop everyone from speculating that I'd had a nervous breakdown or attempted to kill myself. But now, surrounded by a mix of young, artsy Vietnamese and assorted expats who've come for the free wine, I wish that I were back at Sigrid's place. I don't feel up to socializing.

While Sigrid loads up on canapés I pretend to study the art, this show by some young Hanoian artist who reportedly draws inspiration from Vietnam's countryside. Looking at the romanticized images of grinning kids on water buffaloes and red-cheeked ethnic minority women, my thoughts turn, inevitably, to Lindy Tran. Is she still off in the countryside doing good or is she back in Hanoi doing Wyatt?

I'm still pondering Lindy's whereabouts when Sigrid reappears in the company of a petite brunette dressed in cargo pants and a black tank top. A chunky beaded necklace swings past her belt buckle. I know that I've seen her before but can't place her. Sigrid introduces her as Katy Demoines. Noticing Katy's grease-stained fingers, I suddenly recall having spied her roaring around town on a Russian Minsk motorbike, the preferred mode of transport for Hanoi's younger, edgier and poorer expats. "Katy works for the NGO Resource Center," says Sigrid brightly. "I asked her to look into Highlands

Outreach, you know, to follow up on that information you gave me."

I nod warily. I'd handed my assistant Tuyet's findings over to Sigrid, who'd obviously been intrigued enough to call Katy. But now, faced with Katy's scrutiny, I feel myself blushing. If the rumor gets out that I'm trying to dig up dirt on my romantic rival I'll die of embarrassment. I nod and sip my wine, wishing that I'd stayed in my nest of damp Kleenexes on Sigrid's couch after all.

From the way the conversation progresses it soon becomes clear that Katy has no idea about any connection between me and Lindy Tran, Sigrid having fed her some story about my having a wealthy aunt who's keen to donate to some woman-friendly cause. Katy, who evidently prides herself on being a key figure in the city's charitable scene, rattles on and on about her work, how the NGO Resource Center operates and, finally, what she knows about Highlands Outreach. I only half listen. I wonder if I should go back to New York after all.

"So I looked up that training you mentioned," says Katy, her lowered voice a cue for me to pay attention again. "It's really weird." She bites into a spring roll and scans the room, no doubt searching for attractive men. At this reminder that I've joined the legions of single foreign women who come to Asia in search of adventure only to spend their stays bemoaning the lack of good men, my heart plummets. I look around. While I can spot at least five women who'd qualify as attractive, the guys are a different story. There's a tanned guy in the far corner who'd be alright if he lost his beer gut, and an older, silver-haired fellow near the front door who'd look downright distinguished if he weren't groping the spandex-spackled butt of a Vietnamese girl half his age… What, besides my sad inability to accept that it's over between me and Wyatt, is actually keeping me in Vietnam?

I take another gulp of wine and force myself to look back at Katy.

"What was weird?" says Sigrid, who despite all of the cheap wine she's consumed, seems the most focused of our trio.

Katy brushes a curl out of her eyes. "Um, oh right," she says, her eyes sweeping the front door. She's obviously hoping to spot some guy who hasn't shown up. I fight back a weepy urge to commiserate. I'd better lay off the red wine or risk gushing about my shattered love life to total strangers.

Perhaps having had the same thought, Katy sets her half-drunk glass of wine onto a windowsill. "So in those papers you gave me it said that Highlands Outreach had employed ENDA to organize their small business training in Mai Chau. ENDA specializes in setting up workshops and trainings like that." The gallery's front door swings open and Katy looks up hopefully, her face falling at the sight of three young Vietnamese women. After retrieving her abandoned wine glass, she keeps going. "So anyways, when you faxed me it just so happened that Marc Porter was in my office. He works for ENDA. So I asked him about that Highlands Outreach training and he didn't remember off the top of his head but he said he'd find out who'd done it. Anyways, he called me back later to say that actually ENDA hadn't done it after all, which is like totally weird."

"If ENDA didn't do it, who did?" I rub my temples. I wish that I'd drunk less wine or eaten more. My stomach rumbles.

"Well, it could be that one of ENDA's regular consultants did it on a freelance basis, but Highlands Outreach just listed it as ENDA. Or it might be a mistake."

"So how would we find out?"

A waiter appears to top up our glasses, Katy at first declining, then reconsidering. "Well Marc was going to ask around, see if any of their consultants had done it. But it'd be easier just to ask Lindy." She peeks back towards the front door, then stares moodily into her wine glass.

"I called her office a couple of times and there was no answer," says Sigrid, her cheeks prettily flushed. In the months that I've known her, Sigrid has never mentioned any boyfriends past or present. She doesn't seem to mind being single. I wonder how she manages it.

"Did you call Lindy's mobile?" says Katy.

"Yeah. Voicemail."

Katy shrugs. "Well, it's a small operation. Maybe all the staff's off in the countryside. Try dropping her an email."

I recall Wyatt's story about Lindy taking the night train to Lao Cai. I take a deep breath, determined to keep my voice neutral. "Do you know Lindy Tran?"

"I've met her," says Katy. "She came into the center to drop off some brochures."

I wait, not wanting to seem like I'm fishing. Once again Katy's attention is drawn to the front door, which opens to reveal a tall, good-looking blond guy accompanied by an Asian woman, her unusually curvy figure showcased in skinny blue jeans and a tight red top. I feel my stomach lurch with recognition: It's Lindy Tran.

"Hey, there she is," says Katy.

I'm already moving towards the restroom. "Uh, excuse me," I mutter. "I'm not feeling so well."

I speed-walk to the toilet only to find it occupied, which forces me to hide, head down, behind a potted palm. That brief sight of Lindy Tran *has* left me feeling ill. I clutch the palm's trunk, overcome by stomach-churning misery. Peering out through the palm fronds I see that Lindy and the cute blond have now joined Sigrid and Katy, Lindy talking and the other three listening. Katy looks curious while Sigrid's expression is unreadable. I eye the route to the front door, wondering if I could slip out unnoticed. Would it be better to dash out now or to wait until Lindy has moved further into the room? The cute blond guy, I see, has retreated towards the bar. Lindy is still talking animatedly. I shut my eyes and breathe deeply.

"'Scuse me. Are you waiting?"

I turn to see the blond guy gesturing towards the restroom. He'd walked up behind me.

"Ah, yes," I say, my cheeks turning scarlet. I must look insane, hiding behind this potted plant.

He raises an eyebrow, then reaches tentatively for my elbow. "Are you okay? You look a little… faint or something. Do you want to sit down?"

I do feel dizzy but shake my head forcefully. "No, I'll be fine," I say. "I just think I ate something bad… I mean I did." I make a face.

He looks sympathetic. "Poor you. Happens a lot here, doesn't it? Any idea what it was?"

"Seafood," I say, saying the first thing that pops into my head. "Crab soup, out on the street. I knew it'd get me sooner or later."

The blond guy nods. He's even cuter up close, with sparkly green eyes and a wide mouth that reveals an adorable gap between his front teeth. "*Bun rieu*," he says. "There's a woman on this little street by Cho Hom who makes the best crab noodle soup in town."

"That's where I usually get it," I say. "From the soup lady on the alley with all of the fabric stores." Just around the corner from my office, this crab noodle soup stand is one of my favorite spots for a quick lunch. "But I went somewhere else today," I add, not wanting to slander my blameless soup lady.

He holds out a hand. "I'm Graham Hall, by the way." He studies me intently, causing me to blush harder. "Do you work at *Hanoi Scope*? I think I've seen you there." His hand feels cool and solid.

"Yes," I say, the sight of that delicious, gap-toothed grin momentarily evicting all thoughts of Wyatt, Lindy Tran and Highlands Outreach. I'm sure that I've never seen Graham Hall before. He's far too handsome to forget. Realizing that he's waiting for some further response I release his hand and manage to stammer out my name. "Jane Moxley. But I don't think we've met before."

"I went by the *Scope* to pick up some images from one of the photographers," says Graham. "I run a graphic design company, Onyx Design."

I'm about to ask about what kind of design work he does when the power cuts out, the crowd roaring with surprised laughter. It takes a minute for the staff to light candles. I turn to look for Sigrid and realize that Lindy Tran is no longer with her. She could be on her way over here. "I'd better go," I tell Graham.

"What about the washroom?" he says. Whoever is in there is taking an awfully long time.

"I'll wait till I get home," I say. "It was nice meeting you."

"Yeah, you too." His gapped teeth shine white in the candlelight. "Take it easy. I hope your stomach gets better."

Having already forgotten my food poisoning story, it takes me a moment to respond. But Graham's attention is elsewhere, Lindy Tran's unmistakable, breathy French accent calling his name from the shadows. The hairs on the back of my neck stand up. I turn and dart towards the exit.

I've just stepped outside when I hear Sigrid call out to me. "Jane! It's me! Wait up!"

The power is out on the entire block, the sky dark and moonless. It's a hot night, the air smelling of wood smoke and wetness, it having rained earlier in the evening. I fan myself with a gallery brochure as Sigrid strides over to me.

"You were right," she says triumphantly. "That girl is full of shit."

Before I can ask what she means she's walked off to where her bike is parked. Waiting for Sigrid to retrieve her motorbike, I feel tired and homesick. In a nearby house, an unseen woman is singing a Vietnamese folk song, her voice impossibly high and plaintive. I rub my eyes. I don't want to think about Lindy Tran, with her perfect body, sexy accent and mean smile. What am I trying to prove by staying here anyways?

"Ready?" says Sigrid. Her bike, a Honda '67, is the kind of small, old-style motorbike once popular with *xe om* drivers, most of whom have long since upgraded to newer models. Fully original, Sigrid's bike is in decent shape, with a black vinyl seat and chrome engine casing. She hands the guard her ticket and a 5,000-*dong* bill, then maneuvers her bike down a low ramp. After giving me a helmet, she secures her own. "As I was saying," she says, "I asked Lindy about that training that ENDA did and she acted really weird and said that she couldn't remember."

I adjust the strap of my helmet and shrug. "It was more than a year ago."

"But it was a big project. A weeklong training course attended by 30 women, way up in the mountains. If you'd organized something like that, wouldn't you remember who was working for you?" Even in the darkness, I can see Sigrid's eyes shining. Having started out as a reluctant sleuth, she's now obviously keen to keep digging. She swings a leg over her bike. I climb up behind her. "I don't trust that girl one bit," she says. "I can't put my finger on it but really, Jane, I think you're actually onto something."

As we drive toward Sigrid's place, I wonder if I've set my friend off on a wild goose chase. "There's probably some simple explanation," I say glumly. "Somebody must remember who ran that training course."

"Not if it never happened," says Sigrid firmly.

At close to 10:00, the streets are fairly empty, the bad weather having obviously deterred most people from going out tonight. As we drive past Hoan Kiem Lake a gust of cool wind whips off the water. Illuminated by a single spotlight the tiny tiered temple in the center of the lake looks ghostly. Staring at this frail-looking temple, I ponder Sigrid's suggestion. Surely, Lindy Tran wouldn't be that brazen. Inventing an entire training project would be like asking to get caught. "It's too easy to check," I say. "Nobody's that crazy."

We turn left onto Hang Gai Street, the souvenir and silk shops now shuttered for the night. A few beggars can be seen sleeping on door stoops. "Yeah, but who'd be crazy enough to secretly date three guys at once in Hanoi? Or do you really think Lindy and that cute Graham guy are just friends?"

Remembering Graham's sweet smile, my spirits plummet afresh. Not only has Lindy Tran stolen *my* fiancé, but she's also managed to snag this other guy too. I wonder if Graham is unaware of Lindy's other men, and if so, what can be done about it? What is Lindy telling these guys?

My thoughts are interrupted when Sigrid jumps the bike onto the curb. My butt leaves the seat only to reconnect with a thud. Sigrid's bike has no suspension. I yelp. She pulls up at the covered alley in front of her house. "Oops, sorry about that," she says. "It's bumpier on the back, isn't it?" She clicks off the engine. The sudden quiet causes one of the prone beggars to stir.

Sigrid wheels her bike through the tunnel, darkness seeming to intensify the familiar odors of mold and cat pee. I follow, still rubbing my posterior. Waiting for Sigrid to unlock the inner gate, I wonder what Wyatt is doing right now. Does he still think that Lindy Tran is in the countryside? Should I tell him that I just saw her with Graham Hall at that art opening?

Glancing up, I see Sigrid eyeing me suspiciously. "What are you thinking about?" she says. "No, let me guess. You were wondering if you should call Wyatt." She locks the gate behind me.

I start to shake my head, then concede. "Yes," I admit. "If he knew that she was out with this other guy…"

"You already told him and he didn't want to hear it." She wheels her bike into a corner and sets it onto its kickstand. A dog starts to yap. The courtyard is dark except for a single, cobweb-shrouded light hanging in the bare-concrete stairwell.

"She lied to him," I say, as we start to climb. "She said she was going to Lao Cai for work."

"So you're willing to believe that she's lying to Wyatt but not that she's scamming cash from this supposed NGO she set up?"

"No… but…" I shrug. "It just seems a little extreme. What you're suggesting is that the entire NGO is fake. You think she's just raising money and taking it all?"

"I agree it sounds outrageous," says Sigrid. "But so does dating three guys in a small, gossip-ridden town like this one. And like I said, I just got a strange vibe from her."

We're now on the second floor landing, the staircase daubed daily by a woman armed with a mop and a bucket of grey water. Since soap plays no role in this ritual, the dirt is merely transformed to mud. The tiles are slippery and treacherous. "What kind of vibe?" I say.

"Like it came up that I went to Stanford and she just *had* to tell me that she graduated from L'Ecole Nationale d'Administration, which is like probably *the* most prestigious school in Europe and only accepts about a hundred students a year."

Breathing heavily from the climb, I shrug. "Lots of people talk about what school they went to, especially if it was a good one."

"I mentioned that I speak Cantonese, Italian and Spanish and it turns out that she speaks Swahili, Urdu, Tagalog and the language of the Dao ethnic minority group. See, as well as working full time for that non-profit, she's also doing a PhD in Linguistics at Cambridge."

I groan, struck afresh by the sick feeling that I'd gotten upon seeing Lindy Tran step into the art gallery, looking confident and sexy on the arm of yet another handsome guy. "Great," I say. "So as well as being a do-gooder with a great body she's also brilliant."

Sigrid snorts. "How many 24-year-olds do you know who are doing PhDs?"

"Not many but I'm sure they exist."

"Uh huh, well get this. Next Graham asked what I do here and I explained a little, we talked about how I went to Sumatra to help out with relief efforts after the 2006 tsunami, and guess what?" She stops talking to unlock her front door and switch on a light.

I follow her indoors. "What?"

"It turns out that Lindy was actually *in* Sri Lanka when the tsunami hit and only managed to survive by clinging onto a palm tree for six hours while cradling a four-month-old baby whose mom had drowned." Sigrid rolls her eyes. "I mean, I don't think so."

I pull off my shoes. "It could be true. Things like that do happen you know."

"Oh please," says Sigrid. "Like I said, the girl is full of shit."

Although it's only 10:30, I feel too tired to judge whether or not Sigrid's skepticism is justified. I sink down onto a kitchen chair. "What would be the point of lying about something like that?"

Sigrid, now filling the kettle, turns to stare at me in surprise. "Oh come on, it's obvious isn't it? She's got this compulsive need to outdo other women, to make herself seem smarter, sexier, more successful..." She waves a hand for emphasis. "More heroic." After setting the kettle on the stove she opens the fridge door and peers inside. "There's still a little of that carrot cake left. You want some?"

I nod, considering Sigrid's theory. Might Wyatt have fallen for a compulsive liar? And if Sigrid can see through Lindy in just one meeting, why can't Wyatt, Graham, and that lawyer Lindy's supposed to be living with?

"Believe me," says Sigrid, her nose wrinkling. "There's something very fishy about that girl." She peels the saran wrap off the cake pan and retrieves two plates from the cupboard. The old-fashioned kettle starts to whistle.

Scraping the icing off of my cake I wonder what I should do next. Focusing all of this energy on Lindy Tran can't possibly be healthy. Instead of wasting time worrying about Wyatt and Lindy I should be worrying about my career. As it now stands I'll end up broke as well as alone. I consider asking Sigrid, who just turned 32, whether she worries that she's doomed to a life of spinsterhood, but it seems rude. I take another bite of cake, barely tasting it.

Feeling glum, I picture myself at ages 35, 40, 45, chain-smoking and bitching to my gay friends about the dearth of good straight men in the world, then going home to bed with my cats. By the time I'm 50 I'll have an animal shelter's worth of them, my house reeking of stale cigarette smoke and cat piss… Mercifully, this dismal vision is interrupted by the sound of Wyatt's voice emanating from Sigrid's answering machine. My heart ricochets. "Hi, it's me. Jane, I've been trying to reach you but your mobile is off. Could you call me? Thanks."

I shut my eyes, unwilling to see Sigrid's disapproving expression. I take a deep breath, then another, Wyatt's words still ringing in my head. Was I imagining the vulnerability in his voice, the hint of sadness? My tiredness, I realize, has suddenly vanished, washed away by some new emotion that I struggle to identify.

Sigrid sets two mugs of peppermint tea onto the table. "You're going to call him, aren't you?"

Of course I'm going to call him. I try to fight back a smile. "Maybe something's happened," I say. What I'm feeling, I realize, is hope.

5 Torn

I shut my eyes, willing myself to calm down. I can hear Sigrid in the shower singing her favorite karaoke song, *Hot Stuff,* and the water pump, which probably dates back to colonial times, chugging and stuttering in an effort to draw water to the fourth floor. My fingers are shaking as I dial.

Wyatt's phone rings twice. While expected, his hello still takes me by surprise. His first greeting is followed by another, slightly impatient this time. "Ah, hi," I say. "You asked me to call?"

"Jane. Right. How's it going?"

There's a weariness to his voice that hadn't been there the last time we spoke. I hold my breath, increasingly sure that he's seen the light. I wonder how he'll explain himself: he got cold feet; he panicked and went crazy; he needed this time apart to realize that I'm The One and Only.

"I'm fine," I say cautiously. I don't want to sound too eager, too keen to forgive him, but nor do I want to sound bitter, not now when he's about to grovel. Sigrid has started crooning *Love is a Battlefield.* I try my best to ignore her.

Wyatt starts to speak, his voice suitably solemn, when another phone rings. "I've got to get that," he says. "Can you hang on a minute?"

He's gone before I have time to acquiesce, the line humming as I'm put on hold, a bath-robed Sigrid now stepping out of the bathroom and padding towards her bedroom. Seeing me on the phone she mouths the words "good night", her eyes, beneath a towel turban, both curious and concerned. I wave. She pulls her door shut.

I check the screen of my mobile; the line's still connected. I wonder who Wyatt is speaking to. It's pretty late for a work call.

A moment later he's back. "Sorry about that," he says. "Long distance call. Look Jane, something's come up." I examine the ring he gave me, which I haven't had the heart to remove, and wait for Wyatt to continue. "My grandmother's had a stroke," he says. "My father's mother."

"Your Granny Beryl?" I picture a small, unsmiling old woman with nail-thin lips and hair the same cut and color as Wyatt's. Upon first meeting her, I'd assumed that she was wearing a wig, but Wyatt had sworn otherwise.

"Right," says Wyatt, his surprised tone making it clear that he'd forgotten that I've met both of his grandmothers at numerous family gatherings, along with the rest of his dour, ancient relations.

"I'm so sorry. Is it serious?"

"Yes," says Wyatt. "Which is why I'm calling. The doctors don't think she'll last long so I have to go back to Raleigh."

He stops to clear his throat and I wonder if he's crying. I wait, sure that he'll ask me to go with him, to be his shoulder to cry on. I picture the two of us sitting hand-in-hand beside Granny Beryl's bedside, our wedding delayed

Hanoi Jane 67

for an appropriate—but not too long—period following the funeral.

"I should be there for around a week," continues Wyatt. "So you'd better take care of the cat."

I blink. "You what?"

"The cat," says Wyatt. "You'd better feed it."

"Why don't you ask Lindy," I say, unable to keep the bitterness from my voice. I screw my eyes shut, already chastising myself for having hoped that he'd changed his mind. I am such an idiot.

"I would but she travels a lot," says Wyatt. "And frankly, Jane, you *are* the one who wanted that cat in the first place."

While this is true, Wyatt's tone of voice makes this fact seem somehow shameful, as though my yearning for a cat was a sign of my inevitable spinsterhood, proof that my future would be short of men and full of increasingly mangy felines. I feel a few hot, angry tears escape my squeezed-shut lids. "Fine," I say. "I'll come by and feed Fergus."

"You still have the keys, right?"

Before I can answer I hear another voice, unmistakably Lindy Tran's, a sexy purr and what sounds like a nuzzle. For the second time in two minutes I freeze in shock. I guess Wyatt knows that Lindy's back from the countryside after all. But did she really leave her gallery date with Graham and go straight over to Wyatt's? Where does the girl possibly find the energy, not to mention the nerve?

I stab off my phone and bury my face in my hands, the diamond of my engagement ring poking into my cheek and scratching me. Rubbing at the scratch I know that more tears are inevitable. I burrow my face into a sofa pillow. When am I going to get it? Wyatt doesn't want me. He wants too-good-to-be-true Lindy.

• • •

When Sigrid calls to say that she's outside I scoop up my tote bag and head for the exit. While the office was about two-thirds full this morning, most reporters have long since gone out for lunch and a midday nap.

Tuyet, however, is still staring at her computer. I stop by to offer to pick something up for her. "No thanks, I already ate some boxed rice," she says, motioning to the Styrofoam box now wedged into the garbage beneath her desk. "Oh, by the way Jane, I could not contact that Lindy lady you asked me to call. I'll try again after lunch."

"Ah, right," I say. I smile guiltily. I'm not entirely sure that it's ethical to use Tuyet to sniff out dirt on Lindy Tran. It's not purely personal, I tell myself. After all, there could be a *story* there…

Tuyet looks at me curiously. "Anything else, Miss Jane?"

"No, thanks Tuyet. See you later."

Stepping outside, I note that the sun has come out, a brisk breeze sweeping a school of tiny yellow leaves up the narrow street, while some larger, redder leaves flutter downwards. Under bright blue skies the old houses look picturesque, their mottled and chipped paint artistic instead of depressing. The passerby look cheerier too, their plastic rain ponchos shed to reveal summery clothing. One old man is actually whistling.

Seeing me, Sigrid waves. She's wearing a black dress and a red scooter helmet, the red making her hair look extra black and shiny. "Sorry I'm late," she says. "It's been a crazy morning. My computer crashed and the phone wouldn't stop ringing. But at least the bike's running well."

Sure enough, Sigrid's old Honda is puttering happily, the dry weather as welcome to Hanoi's vintage motorbikes as it is to its residents. Sigrid waits for me to mount, then asks what I want for lunch. "Or should we go feed your cat first?"

When I'd told Sigrid about my conversation with Wyatt she'd volunteered to feed Fergus, no doubt reasoning that I'd find going back to the house traumatic. We'd finally agreed to have lunch and stop by together. "Let's go there first," I say. I'd rather get it over with.

"Right-o," says Sigrid. "Hang on tight."

At the sight of Wyatt's house—so recently ours—my throat tightens. It looks exactly the same, four stories of brown-tinted windows in cheap aluminum frames and that ridiculous domed skylight, like a bun on a squat, ugly babushka. The upstairs curtains are all drawn, while the washing line on the upper terrace hangs empty.

Not trusting myself to speak, I pull back the accordion gate in silence, my fingers faltering as I unlock the inner door. The house's familiar smells hit me like a series of slaps: motorbike oil, kitty litter, lemon floor cleaner, mold (no doubt growing in the unpacked boxes brought all the way from New York), and a hint of Allure Homme, Wyatt's favorite aftershave.

After the bright sunshine outside, the interior is dim. My gaze is drawn to the pink garment bag that contains my wedding dress, still lying where I'd tossed it. I force myself to look away. Sigrid clears her throat. "So where's your precious cat?"

Fergus' bowl, I see, is still half full. Wyatt must have set out extra food before he left yesterday. The maid, Chi Phuong, will be in tomorrow. "He's probably passed out upstairs," I say, determined to actually see the cat since I made the effort to come over here. I miss the little guy. And he must be lonely locked indoors by himself all day.

Sigrid peers doubtfully up the staircase. "You going to go check on him?"

I nod and head for the stairs, Sigrid following dutifully. Sure enough, the cat's in the bedroom. Walking towards the bed I'm unable to fight back a vision of that last, dreadful time I entered this room. Sound asleep on the bed, Fergus' orange-spotted belly rises and falls. His white whiskers quiver.

"Not much of a guard cat, is he?" says Sigrid, her eyes scanning the darkened bedroom. Wyatt had obviously packed in a hurry. Some unwanted clothes are strewn across chairs and the closet doors lie open.

I also peer around, my eyes catching on each familiar item—the embroidered white duvet cover that I'd picked out, the mirror that was a gift from my sister. What's missing from the room, I see, are the photos of me and Wyatt, the bedside tables now holding nothing but a few books and magazines, *The Economist*, *Forbes* and *A Guide to Economic Indicators* on Wyatt's side, a half-read novel on what was mine. Even though I can barely remember the plot, I stuff it into my tote bag.

I bend to stroke the cat and Fergus stirs. His green eyes stare up at me, neither startled nor enthusiastic. "How are you little guy?" I murmur. "You miss me?" The cat yawns and rolls over, its eyes already closing.

"Charming creature," sniffs Sigrid. "I'm sure he misses you like crazy but can't say so." She moves towards the door. "Let's go. I'm starving." Her stomach growls in confirmation.

After giving Fergus a final unreciprocated cuddle, I rise to join Sigrid. I'm turning to go when I spot an unfamiliar bag poking out from under the bed. Bright pink and covered with rows of silver sequins, it's obviously not Wyatt's, which must mean that it's...

Following my gaze, Sigrid walks over to the bag and grabs it. "Now whose might this be?" she says. "It looks like something that little hussy would carry." She shakes the bag and it rattles.

I can't help but smile, more at Sigrid's use of the word "hussy" than at her antics with the handbag.

"What do you reckon?" says Sigrid. "I bet it's jam-packed with condoms."

"And cash," I say. "Wads and wads of hundred dollar bills."

"And crotchless panties."

Before I can add anything Sigrid has unzipped the bag. Peering inside she looks disappointed. "Just a bunch of papers," she says. "Although... hmmm, bank statements. This could be interesting after all." She spreads the papers out on the bed. I eye the door nervously, as though Lindy Tran might barge in at any moment and demand to know why we're snooping.

"Do you really think that we should be riffling through her bag?" I say. "It seems kind of…"

"Dishonest?" says Sigrid.

"Well, yeah. And sneaky."

"Dishonest and sneaky as in cheating on people or as in robbing poor ethnic minority women?"

"We don't actually *know* that she's robbed anyone," I say. *Except me*, I think sadly. *She stole my fiancé.*

"What we do know," says Sigrid triumphantly, "is that an awful lot of cash has been transferred into her personal account in the US over the past year. Here, look at this." She thrusts a bank statement into my hands. "Last May, $7,204 from the law firm of Nguyen & McCallum." She bites her lip. "Now where do I know that name from?"

I look doubtful. "Nguyen?"

"No. Half the country's named Nguyen," snorts Sigrid. "McCallum." She snaps her fingers. "Got it! Jason McCallum. The lawyer Lindy's reportedly living with. Now why would his firm be transferring money into her personal account in May and…" She flips through a few more pages. "Again in July and September and November? And they're not the only ones making transfers. In the past year, she's gotten an average of five, no, closer to six thousand dollars a month."

"Maybe that's her salary."

"Working for a small NGO? Oh come on. I don't think so."

"She could be doing other consulting work," I say doubtfully.

"Possibly, but it seems like a lot of money." She squints, then holds up some pages of what looks like recycled paper. "Now what's this? Any idea what alphabet this is?"

Bending closer, I see that the rough brown sheets are covered in some strange, swirly script. "I dunno. Sanskrit?" I say. "It doesn't look like Thai. What languages did she claim to speak?"

"I can't remember," says Sigrid. "But these might be important too." She inserts all of the papers carefully into her purse and shoves Lindy's pink bag back under the bed. "I'll get these photocopied. We can replace them tomorrow."

"What if Lindy comes by before then?" I say. I hate to think that Wyatt has given her a set of keys but it is possible.

Sigrid pats the cat absent-mindedly. "Then you copy them and drop them off tonight after work. And you should go speak to that Jason guy. Maybe he's in on it." She extracts the papers from her bag and hands them to me.

I take them reluctantly. "How am I supposed to do that?" I say. "I can hardly tell the guy that I've been snooping through his girlfriend's bank records, can I?"

"You're the reporter," says Sigrid, already heading for the door. "I'm sure you'll figure something out."

Before following her, I cast a final look at Fergus. The cat stretches and flops over to reveal some colored paper that was wedged beneath him. It is, I realize, one of our wedding invitations, now ripped in half. Both sides are badly crumpled. The tiny photo of me and Wyatt has been defaced, my neck slashed with red ink and my eyes scribbled out, the effect ghoulish.

Hands shaking, I pick up the two pieces and fit them together. Did Lindy Tran leave this here for me to find, knowing that I'd stop by to check on Fergus? It seems too cruel and spiteful. But surely Wyatt wouldn't do such a thing…

"Are you coming?" yells Sigrid. Her voice echoes up the stairwell. "I'm starving!"

I shove the torn invite into my pocket and descend the stairs. The more I learn about Lindy Tran the nastier she seems. There must be some way to make Wyatt see this.

• • •

According to her voicemail message, Lindy Tran is out of town, on a "mission" to the Northeast Highlands. Listening to the recording I wonder why aid workers use words like "mission", casting themselves as saints or secret agents. Stepping into the lobby of Nguyen & McCallum I hope that Lindy's claimed absence is real: I'd hate to run into her here, or anywhere else for that matter.

"Yes?" says a frowning receptionist. Partnered with her aggressively plucked and arched eyebrows, this single word makes it clear that she thinks I have no business here. (She's right too.) Located in a newly finished high-rise, the lobby smells of fresh paint and carpet glue.

"I'm looking for Jason," I say. I figure that calling him by his first name will give her the impression that I'm a friend of his, someone with a plausible reason to just drop in and say hi.

The receptionist isn't buying it. "Do you have an appointment?"

"Ah, no." I lower my voice. "This is personal."

If the receptionist is curious she doesn't show it, her perfectly-painted lips curving into a discontented moue. "He has a client with him."

"I'll wait," I say. I grab a couple of well-thumbed magazines. All of the chairs are empty. I head for the one closest to the fish tank.

The woman sniffs. "Mr. McCallum is booked the rest of the day."

"It'll only take a minute."

"I don't—"

I cut her off. "When you get the chance, you might want to tell Jason that Jane Moxley from the *Hanoi Scope* has popped in. We're doing a story on legal services in Vietnam and were hoping to include Nguyen & McCallum." The promise of free publicity, I figure, should bear fruit. Sure enough, not five minutes later I'm ushered into the large corner office occupied by Jason McCallum.

He appears to be in his late thirties, somewhat older than I'd expected, and better looking too, with light brown hair, astute brown eyes and what appears to be—beneath his blue oxford shirt and grey pants—an extremely well-toned body. When I enter he rises from his chair and extends a hand, his handshake vigorous without being crushing. His desk is the size of a small car. "Miss Ha said you're with the *Scope*," he says, revealing a set of admirably white teeth. "How can I help you?"

I figure that Lindy Tran must have a thing for teeth. Graham, Wyatt and this guy all possess grins worthy of a toothpaste ad.

"I was hoping to do a profile on foreign lawyers working in Vietnam," I say, flying by the seat of my pants. "The challenges of working here, the changing legal system, what sort of cases you're seeing…" I trail off, hoping that Jason will take it from there. I wish that I'd thought out a plausible story ahead of time. What was I thinking?

"Sounds interesting but I'm afraid it'll have to wait for another day," says Jason, casting an eye at his watch. "I'm booked solid until closing…" He gives me a charmingly apologetic smile. I wonder if he's flirting with me. Behind him, I can see sky and rooftops.

"Just pick a date," I say chirpily. "Whenever works for you."

Jason grabs his Blackberry. "How's next Monday afternoon?"

Next Monday? I nod and smile, knowing that, if this were for a real story, next Monday would undoubtedly be too late. "Great," I say. "Oh and Jason, if I could just ask you one quick thing. It's actually about another story I'm working on right now, about local charitable organizations and transparency, regulations to ensure that the money's being properly spent, that sort of thing." Before he can get a word in I rush on, explaining that I've been looking into a few organizations including Highlands Outreach and that someone had mentioned that he was a key supporter.

Jason rubs his chin. "Highlands Outreach?" he says. "No, I'm not involved with it. But my girlfriend Lindy is the director, so maybe your source got confused…" He looks at his watch again, more pointedly this time.

By now, it's got to be after five. I wonder how late Jason usually works.

"So you're not a donor? I was told that you were making regular donations to their US branch?" I hold my breath, aware that I'm on shaky ground here. Jason looks wary. For a moment I think that he'll get mad, but instead he just shakes his head.

"Oh, wait," he says. "I *have* been helping Lindy to transfer some cash back to the US. There's been some problem with her visa paperwork..." He waves a hand. "You know how it is in Vietnam, always some catch-22. Anyways, she doesn't have all the forms she needs to send dollars overseas so I've been doing that for her every once in a while."

I'm about to ask more when there's a knock on the door, the receptionist poking her head in. "Mr. Morrison is waiting," she says, each word somehow directed at me. Jason stands up. "I'm really behind schedule," he says. "Can you send me an email about Monday?"

After thanking him, I dash out the door. While I'd have liked to have gotten to the bottom of this now, the interruption may be just as well. If Jason hadn't been so distracted he'd probably have wanted to know how I knew about those bank transfers. Hopefully he won't give my visit too much thought.

Riding the elevator back to the ground floor, I reflect on what I just learned. Jason seems nice enough, but where is Lindy getting all of that money?

When I step outside, it's 5:20. Dusk isn't far off, the afternoon overcast and muggy. I head down the street to Au Lac, order a lemon juice and some shrimp curry and pull out my laptop. I'm meant to be working on a story about Hanoi's art scene but can't get into it. I flip through the notes that I made during various interviews with young artists in an attempt to get inspired. Maybe it's just my mood, but their statements all seem banal and their art commercialized. I set down my notebook.

Across the street I can see people working out in the Metropole's gym, one wall of which is a plate-glass window. I used to go there with Wyatt and can't help but look for him, but of course he is back in the States with his sick grandmother.

My curry half uneaten, I collect my things and signal for the bill. By the time I start walking back to Sigrid's it is fully dark out. I cross the street and cut through tiny Toad Park with its ornate, non-functioning fountain, then walk through another larger park to the lake. Near the blocky, Soviet-style war monument I cross the street so as to avoid the giant banyan that always gives me the creeps, since I imagine all sorts of malevolent spirits hiding in its dark, tangled roots. An ice cream vendor pedals past, his bell clanging.

Watching couples and families stroll around the lake, I wish that I were going home to Wyatt, to a cozy take-out dinner for two and an evening of snuggling in front of a video. Instead, I'll spend the night on my friend's couch. Am I crazy to stay in Vietnam? Is it time to cut my losses and go home?

Pulling a stick of gum from my pocket I find the torn wedding invitation. In the light of a streetlamp I bend to examine it, Wyatt's smile handsome but fake, my eyes replaced by scary red dots. Looking at this scrap of

paper I feel indignant. I'd bet anything that Lindy Tran left it on Wyatt's bed to torment me. Does she know that I've been asking questions about her? Was this a way to threaten me?

I stuff the ripped invite back into my pocket and unwrap the gum, aware that if I go back to New York, Lindy will get away with everything. "I am not giving up that easily," I say aloud. "I'm going to get her."

An old woman chaperoning a toddler eyes me warily, no doubt wondering who this crazy white girl thinks she's talking to. I smile at her and the old woman scoops up her charge and crosses the street, just to be on the safe side.

As I walk around Hoan Kiem Lake I think of the golden turtle that's supposed to live in its depths. According to legend, this magical beast presented the fifteenth century king Le Loi with a sword that enabled him to ward off Chinese invaders. Every couple of years someone manages to snap a blurry photo of this purportedly supernatural turtle, which then appears on the cover of various newspapers. Like a comet or a red moon, these sightings are interpreted in various ways, with some people convinced that the turtle is lucky and others viewing it as a warning.

Staring at the dark water, I feel my resolve harden. Vietnam offers lots of opportunities. Not only will I expose Lindy Tran, I'll also find some more meaningful work, something that I'm really passionate about. No more *Chic!* specials about how to shave inches off of your thighs. No more *Hanoi Scope* advertorials about bar openings. I wonder what else I could do. What are my strengths? Lately, I haven't felt like I have any.

It happens so fast that I'll never be sure whether I imagined it or not, but for one gasping second I see the turtle, its tapered snout pointing straight at me. A gust of wind blows the scent of milk flowers into my nostrils. And then the turtle is gone again, the lake's surface unbroken.

I turn around to see if anyone else saw the turtle but the sidewalk lies empty. I wish that I could tell Wyatt about it but he'd probably just say that I'd imagined it— no turtle could survive in water that polluted.

6 Trouble

My Vespa freshly fixed, I drive down Youth Road. It's a
Saturday night and the street is packed with young couples
on motorbikes. Most of the guys drive with an arm casually
draped across their girlfriend's thigh. Many of the girls
ride sidesaddle, one high-heeled foot dangling.

Looking at all of these loved-up couples I can't
help but think of Wyatt, due back from North Carolina
tomorrow evening. His Grandma Beryl—tough old bird
that she is—has made a miraculous recovery. Wyatt sent
out a group email in which I'd been included.

Turning onto Truc Bach Road I weave through the
throng of motorbikes idling around the ice cream shops.
It's a hot, still night and the ice cream cafes are packed.
As I pass, the café touts try to intercept me by throwing
themselves in front of my moving bike. I wonder how
often these guys get hit on an average night. Injuries
seem inevitable. When I've finally run the gauntlet, I
breathe a sigh of relief. This stretch of road ahead is dark
and quiet.

The Indian restaurant where I'm meeting Sigrid
is lit with yellow lights. Walking in, I spot Sigrid in the
prized corner booth, a tall, fair-haired guy beside her.
Rob Emmett is new to Hanoi, Sigrid having met him at
some work function and invited him to join us for dinner.
When she'd mentioned his single status I'd assumed that

she was interested in him, but I now get the feeling that she's trying to set *me* up with the guy.

While I appreciate her attempt to cheer me up, I'm annoyed too. I don't want help meeting some new guy. I want help getting my fiancé back.

"We already ordered," says Sigrid as I slide into the booth beside her. Whether from the heat or a glass of wine, her cheeks are rosy.

"Hope you're hungry," adds Rob, already pouring me a glass. "We may have gone overboard with the ordering." He extends a large, warm hand for me to shake. My own hand is clammy.

An Australian engineer, Rob seems pleasant enough, with a wide, open grin and gingery sideburns. He's been in Hanoi for three weeks. I give it another fortnight at the most before he's shacked up with some savvy Vietnamese babe. It's his first time in Asia.

While we're munching on pappadams we discuss Hanoi, our respective jobs, and the sultry weather. The restaurant starts to fill up with locals and foreigners, most of the Westerners' faces familiar to me. When the first of the entrees arrive Sigrid turns the conversation to Lindy Tran. "I tried to call her this morning but got that same voicemail message," she says. "Did you find anything out?"

I nod. "My assistant Tuyet got an email from her today, saying that she's in Mai Chau for the next four days setting up a sewing workshop." I reach for my wine and take a gulp. "Teaching ethnic minority women to embroider pillowcases and handbags and stuff for the export market."

Hanoi Jane 83

"Oh, I know Lindy Tran," says Rob. "Her boyfriend Jason and I played rugby together last weekend. Touch." He smiles apologetically, as if embarrassed by the implied lack of toughness. "I've got a bad knee." He rubs the offending knee. "An old snowboarding injury."

I'm about to fish for more details when Rob adds that he just ran into Lindy. "She was coming out of that little bottle shop next to the American Club carrying two bottles of Moët," he says. "She said that she'd just gotten back to Hanoi."

Sigrid tears off a hunk of garlic naan and chews thoughtfully. "Two bottles of champagne. What was the occasion?"

Rob smiles. "Mmmm, I asked her that. Turns out it's her and Jason's second anniversary." He offers me some more *baingan masala* but I decline, my appetite having vanished upon mention of Lindy.

Sigrid accepts the bowl and scoops out a generous amount, then reaches for more naan. "So you know Jason?"

"Yeah, seems like a good bloke. He and Lindy have a place out on Tay Ho, just a few doors up from mine. Lindy travels a lot. She's always off in the countryside with that NGO of hers."

Sigrid chews her butter naan thoughtfully. "Except at the moment."

"I guess she came back specially, it being their anniversary and all," says Rob. "She seems like a sweet girl. And impressive too, being such a fine athlete."

Sigrid gives me a pointed look. "Oh is she?" she asks innocently.

"Yes, she's an accomplished mountaineer," says Rob. "I haven't been at it long myself, done a few mid-level climbs in New Zealand, Mount Apo in Indonesia, Mount Buffalo back in Aus. But we got to talking about it and it turns out that Lindy's done some serious peaks in the Nepalese Himalaya, Peru, Mt. Kilimanjaro." He shakes his head in admiration. "She's a lot tougher than she looks, that's for sure."

I'll bet she is, I think. I recall Sigrid's suspicions about Lindy Tran being a compulsive liar. I try to tally up Lindy's reported accomplishments: honors PhD student, fluent in God knows how many languages, tsunami survivor, expert mountaineer… What can't the girl do?

When our dinner plates have been cleared, Sigrid proposes that we go to the Apocalypse. "We could dance off some of that chicken curry," she says, patting her belly. "You up for it?"

"Lead the way!" says Rob, obviously keen to check out this Hanoi institution. Picturing Apo's cramped, smoke-drenched interior, I stifle a groan.

"Oh come on," says Sigrid. "There's nowhere else to go."

I can hear people at tables nearby having similar conversations. "I may as well come for one drink," I say grudgingly.

"One drink, hey?" smirks Rob. "I've heard that before."

• • •

Sure enough, one drink leads to another, which leads to a few more. By the time Apo is ready to close I'm

swinging between drunken euphoria—*I love Abba!*—
and alcoholic despair—*why doesn't Wyatt want me?*
Rob has disappeared with some lycra-wrapped Vinababe
and Sigrid, dancing in a circle of shimmying gay men, is
singing *Billie Jean* at the top of her lungs.

The lights flick on and off, a warning that the club will
soon be bathed in a fluorescent glow. I make a dash for
the door. Seeing the Apocalypse illuminated is like being
forced to study yourself hungover at dawn in one of those
powerful magnifying makeup mirrors. A terrible sight
indeed, and not one that I, in my fragile, post-Wyatt state,
have the stomach for.

While I don't normally smoke, I'm both depressed
and drunk enough for the idea to seem pleasant. After
bumming a Marlboro Light off a guy I barely know, I
sink down on the club's front steps to wait, the cigarette
providing some minor distraction. I inhale, cough,
and inhale more forcefully, trying to make sense of
the information that Rob had provided about Lindy at
dinner. Lindy and Jason are definitely living together.
Champagne. Their second anniversary. Wyatt is being
lied to. There must be *some* way to convince him.

I decide I need proof—irrefutable evidence—that
Lindy is romantically involved with Jason McCallum,
something that Wyatt can't dismiss as a product of my
jealous imagination. I need photos, pictures of Lindy and
Jason going at it, the kind of black and white photos that
private investigators stuff into manila envelopes, the kind
that people use to blackmail each other.

I wonder whether I could hire a private eye, then
dismiss the idea. I'm a reporter; surely I can do this alone.

Recalling the rows of couples making out by the curb on Youth Road, I wish that Lindy and Jason were into PDA. But how hard can it be to get a picture of two people who live together doing something intimate? I just need to get close to them...

I've nearly finished my cigarette when Sigrid materializes from the club, shiny and breathless, a posse of gay men in tight black clothes trailing after her. "I can't believe it's already closing time," she wails. She sinks down beside me and pouts. "I could have danced all night." She taps her sky-high snakeskin sandals for emphasis.

The Apocalypse' front steps are now full of people, everyone asking each other where they're going next, and if anywhere's still open. I watch as two drunken Australian guys drag their even-drunker mate towards the parking lot. A loud altercation starts up between two groups of hookers and the club's bouncers intervene. The warring hookers instantly join forces to screech abuse at the bouncers.

Stubbing out my cigarette, I consider whether or not to fill Sigrid in on my plan to snap compromising pictures of Lindy and Jason. While Sigrid is definitely keen to collect evidence that Lindy is defrauding her charity, she seems less concerned about her cheating ways. This, I realize, is because Sigrid doesn't understand that Wyatt is a victim too, a man misled in a moment of weakness by a professional con-woman... I shake my head. Clearly, it's up to *me* to pull the wool from Wyatt's eyes.

"There's a house party near Lenin Park," says Sigrid. "You want to check it out?" She gestures towards one of the gay guys. "It's at a friend of Andre's..." Andre walks

over to say hi to me. An old college friend of Sigrid's, he moved to Hanoi three years ago and now owns a successful PR company. On air-kissing terms with every pop star, actor, model and wannabe in Vietnam, he always knows where the best parties are. His boyfriend, Phi, a former model turned hairdresser, walks over to us. "Let's get going," he says. "Are you coming, Jane?"

I shake my head. "Naw, you guys go ahead. I'm going to call it a night." I stand up and dust off my jeans. Sigrid does likewise.

"Okay, well you've got keys to my place," she says. "You driving?" Phi and Andre go off to retrieve their motorbikes.

I hesitate. If Vietnam does have laws against drunk driving I've never heard of anyone being stopped, not that that makes it all right… I cast a guilty glance towards the parking lot, telling myself that at this time of night the streets will be deserted. "Yeah. Don't worry, I'll go slowly."

Since Sigrid is set to climb onto the back of Andre's bike, and Andre looks none too steady, she's in no position to argue.

"Mwah! Mwah!" says Phi, blowing an exaggerated air-kiss.

"Drive safely," says Andre.

They roar away from me.

The streets, sure enough, lie desolate. I drive slowly, enjoying myself. At night, Hanoi is ethereally lovely, the worst of the dirt and disrepair hidden by darkness. The big trees form strangely shaped silhouettes against the few street lights. I amuse myself by imagining tiny fairies and devils hiding in the foliage.

On the road that cuts through the military citadel I pass no other vehicles, the streetlights few and far between, the silence total. In the dim light the old brick wall looks even older than it is, the giant wooden gates reminding me of the entrance to a castle. On a whim I stop the bike and dismount to snap a photograph of the old gates, doing my best to keep the camera steady. The result, framed in the digital camera's tiny screen, is disappointing. The gates' carved double happiness symbol is barely distinguishable in the gloom.

The cool air has sobered me up a bit, so that by the time I turn onto Tay Ho, the street where Lindy and Jason live, I'm questioning the wisdom of this escapade. While my zoom lens is decent, is my compact camera really up to this task?

The first problem, however, is finding Jason's place. Rob Emmett's house lies at number 44 and he'd said that Jason's was a few doors up. I slow my bike and peer through various gates, looking for a house with a turret. Sure enough, there it is at number 48, the house set beside a kidney-shaped swimming pool.

I pull the bike up onto the curb and cut the engine, the sudden silence startling me. I can hear nothing but some frogs croaking in the nearby *rau muong* ponds and the squeaks of bats overhead. The night air smells of still water and rotting vegetation.

Jason's gold-painted gate is locked, although the stone wall that surrounds the house is only chest-high. I figure that I'll have no problem clearing the wall, although tight jeans and high-heels don't make the climb any easier. My flailing alerts the neighbor's toy poodle, which starts to

yap frantically. This sets off a chorus of mutts all over the neighborhood.

By the time I've scaled the wall my favorite jeans have a rip in one knee, which is bleeding. Flustered but undaunted I trot across the sodden lawn, noting that an upstairs light is still on and that the curtains are open. As I watch, the silhouette of a fit man appears. A curvy, long-haired woman saunters over and puts her arms around him. My heart beats faster. Both figures appear to be naked.

Creeping closer, I extract my camera from my bag and aim it up at the window, the flash taking me by surprise. Did anyone else see that? I dive into some shrubbery.

Crouched in the shadows of a bougainvillea bush, I wait, half expecting someone to come running. But even the neighborhood dogs seem to have given up, their barking replaced by the soft croak of frogs. I squint up at the lit window, considering. If I can get onto the porch roof I might be able to get a good shot. There's a trellis that I could scale. Fuelled by alcohol, heartbreak and adrenaline, I decide that it's possible.

I kick off my high heels. While I wish that I'd worn looser pants, I'm too close to give up now, especially when Wyatt will be back in town tomorrow. I imagine his face when he sees the incriminating photos. "What was I thinking?" he'll say. "It was the pressure of my new job and our wedding...trying to figure out the seating plan for all my relatives who hate each other... Lindy Tran's not my type at all. She's too skinny... and busty."

This fantasy evaporates when my foot slips off of the trellis. I grab at a vine to steady myself, a sharp pain in my hand eliciting a yelp. Closer inspection of the vine reveals that it's a climbing rose. I grit my teeth against the pain and keep going.

I'm struggling to haul myself onto the porch roof when there's a loud yell. I freeze, then turn just in time to be blinded by a blazing white light. While I can't see a thing I can hear agitated male voices, all in Vietnamese, and the sounds of footsteps crunching on gravel. One man, to my utter horror, starts bellowing into a megaphone.

Legs trailing off of the ledge, I kick frantically. Strong hands grasp my ankles. I try to cling to the roof but am pulled down, my fall broken by the three men who are holding my feet. All of them are wearing khaki-green police uniforms. I feel sick with terror.

A fourth policeman, still clutching his megaphone, shines a high-powered flashlight into my eyes. He barks something in Vietnamese, which, naturally, I fail to catch. I wonder if they're about to shoot me. "Stop!" I yell, then, in desperation, "Help! I'm American!"

If these words are understood they have no effect whatsoever. Blinded and dazed, I'm frog-marched towards the driveway.

At that point, the house's front door flies open to reveal Jason McCallum dressed in checkered boxer shorts and armed with a golf club. Lindy, wrapped in a gold satin robe, stands in the doorway behind him, her hair sexily tousled.

"What the fu…" says Jason, his words dying at the sight of me, firmly clasped between a pair of policemen. Jason lowers his golf club. "Jane? From *Hanoi Scope*? What are you doing here?"

The cop with the megaphone, who seems to be in charge, starts speaking rapidly to Lindy, who, it's soon obvious, can't understand him. Despite my dire situation, I feel grimly pleased that Lindy-the-stellar-linguist doesn't seem to speak Vietnamese, despite her Vietnamese heritage. You'd think that she'd have opted to learn her mother-tongue before studying Urdu and whatever else she claims to have mastered. Jason, on the other hand, seems fairly proficient, since he's now saying something to the head cop, who nods and withdraws a notebook.

If Lindy recognizes me she doesn't let on. "You know this person?" she asks Jason. The four policemen all eye her appreciatively. Lindy unfurls the belt of her robe and reties it, pretending to be unaware of their attention.

"We met today," says Jason, his confusion obvious. He turns my way. "What's going on here? Our guard saw you climbing our wall…"

I shake my head miserably. "This is all a terrible misunderstanding," I say. "I can explain everything. Please let go of me." The guys who are holding me, both of whom look to be in their teens, tighten their grip. To make matters even worse, I have started to hiccup. Stress, not to mention booze, sometimes has that effect on me.

"I'd say she was snooping," says Lindy imperiously, anger making her French accent stronger than usual. "Trespassing on private property. Breaking and entering." She looks pointedly at Jason. "I told you not to talk to reporters. They're always trouble."

"Did she *hic* tell you that she's sleeping with my *hic* fiancé?" I blubber. "His name's Wyatt *hic* Dumfries. He's assistant manager at *hic* Citi-*hic*. Go and ask him yourself if you don't be-*hic*—"

With a toss of her head, Lindy cuts me off. "You're insane," she says. She turns to Jason and puts her hands on her hips. "Just look at her. She's drunk and obviously unstable. Can you tell the cops that she's been hassling me?"

The head cop seems to be following some of this, for he now says, in passable English. "So you meet this lady before?"

Lindy rolls her eyes. "Briefly."

"Where you meet?"

Lindy doesn't bat an eye. "Through her former boyfriend. I'm the director of a small NGO and he was advising me on some banking regulations, taxes, etcetera."

"They were in my *hic* bed together!" I squeal, tears springing to my eyes at the injustice of it all.

"Enough," says the policeman, who doesn't seem inclined to question any of us any further. After writing down Lindy's and Jason's names and telephone numbers, he nods in my direction. "We take her to station," he says. He barks some orders to his men, who propel me towards the street. A sheepish-looking guard materializes out of the shadows to open the gate for us. I guess he was sleeping on the job when I'd scaled the wall earlier.

"Ow!" I say as the cops push me towards a waiting army jeep. "Let me go. I want to *hic* call my *hic* embassy. Where are you taking *hic*?"

Before I'm bundled into the canvas-roofed vehicle I turn to see Lindy and Jason standing in the doorway,

Lindy snuggled up against Jason's bare chest. He's got his arms around her and his nose burrowed in her hair. I hang my head. It would have made the perfect photograph.

• • •

The room is empty but for two wooden chairs and a battered Formica-topped table. A single light bulb hangs overhead, wrapped in cobwebs. My watch and mobile phone having been confiscated, I have no idea what time it is. I've been here long enough for a hangover to have kicked in but not long enough to feel truly sober. I am desperately thirsty and in need of a toilet. The scratches on my hands sting, my scraped knee throbs, and my mouth tastes like something died in there. The longer I wait, the worse I feel. Why, oh why, am I such an idiot?

I'm considering putting my head on the table to weep when the room's single door opens. A tall, slim Vietnamese man in an immaculate grey suit enters. His confident demeanor makes him seem much older than me, but he's got a young face. I guess that he's in his early to mid-thirties.

"Jane Moxley?" he says, reading my name from a manila folder. He regards me impassively.

I sit up straighter. "Yes, right. I'm Jane."

"I am Mr. Thai," he says, "with the Department of Foreigner Control under the Ministry of Public Security…" He pauses, as if to allow the weight of these words to sink in.

I bite my lower lip apprehensively.

Mr. Thai takes a seat, his pant legs drawing up to reveal perfectly coordinated grey socks, tucked into shoes so shiny that I can see my face in them, warped and scared-looking. He opens his folder, extracts a sheet of paper and starts to read: my date of birth, passport number, date of entry into Vietnam, place of employment, permanent address. For current address he reads the address of the house that I'd shared with Wyatt. I decide not to correct him. My living arrangements with Sigrid are temporary. Why drag her into this?

Only when he's gotten to the bottom of the page does Mr. Thai glance up at me, his dark eyes shrewd. "So, Miss Jane. What were you doing at number 48 Tay Ho Street?"

Faced with his intelligent gaze, I make a split-second decision to confess the full story. Eyes watering, I start at the beginning, back when I discovered Wyatt and Lindy in bed together. From there, I explain my suspicions about Lindy's misuse of charitable donations, ending with my ill-fated decision to go over to Jason's place and collect evidence.

Mr. Thai raises an eyebrow. "Evidence?"

My blush deepening, I'm forced to admit that I'd been hoping to snap some photos of Jason and Lindy being intimate. Mr. Thai's gaze never falters. He extracts an expensive-looking pen from his breast pocket and scribbles some notes, then closes the pen's lid with a snap. "And with these photographs you were hoping to do what?"

"To prove to Wyatt that Lindy is lying," I say. "She's . . ." I lower my eyes. "She's having relations with three different

men. And Wyatt and I are … were about to get married …"
I bite my lip hard, aware of how pathetic I sound.

"Having relations with multiple partners is not illegal,"
says Mr. Thai. "But breaking and entering is."

I hang my head. "Yes, I know that," I gulp. "And I'm
very sorry. I got carried away trying to prove that she's …"
I shake my head in frustration. "That she's dishonest.
That training her NGO supposedly held up in Mai Chau,
for instance …"

Mr. Thai raises a well-manicured hand. "You studied
journalism, is that not so?"

I agree that it is. Mr. Thai goes on to a long list of
questions relating to my work, stories that I've done
and stories that I'm working on, publications that I've
freelanced for, my role at the *Scope*. I'm wondering
where he's going with these questions when he whips
a photograph out of his folder. "Did you take this?"
he says.

I peer at the image, my overwrought, hung-over brain
struggling to work out where I've seen it before. Then I
remember: I took this photo earlier tonight in the military
citadel. As I'd expected, the result is poor, the flash having
washed out the foreground and left the carved wooden
gates in darkness.

"How do you explain this?" says Mr. Thai. He looks
victorious.

I shrug in confusion. "It's the gate of the citadel," I say.
"It didn't turn out very well."

If his manner had seemed tough before it now gets a
lot tougher. Who asked me to photograph this site? Who
am I working for? What was I hoping to capture here?

I shake my head. "Nobody," I say. "I just thought it was pretty, the way the shadows of the streetlight emphasize the wood carvings…" I stop, realization dawning on me. "You think I'm a spy!" I gasp. "Is that why you're asking me these things?"

Mr. Thai's nostrils flare. "You are in a very risky position," he says quietly. "You have broken several of the Socialist Republic of Vietnam's laws: trespassing on private property, taking clandestine photographs of forbidden military sites in the dead of night."

"I didn't know it was a forbidden site!" I say. "And I wasn't trying to hide anything! Climbing into Jason's yard was a mistake, I admit, but there's nothing more to it than what I've already told you." Fighting back tears, I wish that I'd never, ever, set foot in Vietnam.

Mr. Thai springs to his feet and strides to the door, where he barks something into the corridor. A moment later a younger man appears bearing a glass of water and a box of tissues, both of which are deposited on the table before me. I nod gratefully and reach for a tissue.

"We could keep you incarcerated," says Mr. Thai. "Or we could expel you."

I hold my breath. Given the choice of being thrown into a Hanoi jail or being deported I'd obviously prefer to go home, and yet, all of a sudden, the thought that my time in Vietnam is over makes my eyes burn.

"Or we could release you with a strong warning and a reminder that we will be watching you closely," says Mr. Thai.

I look up hopefully.

"So please, no more detective work." He rises to his

feet, his stony expression broken by a flicker of mirth so quick that I wonder if I imagined it. He checks his wristwatch and makes a notation in the folder.

"I..." I dab at my eyes. "Thank you," I say. "I'm really sorry for the trouble I caused."

Mr. Thai nods ever so slightly and retrieves his folder. He's almost out the door when I call out to him. "Excuse me, Mr. Thai, but could you follow up about Lindy Tran? There's something not right about her. Like I told you about all the cash she's transferring to the United States and then there's the mystery of how her charity's money is being spent..."

Mr. Thai frowns, his eyes narrowing dangerously. "I warned you, Miss Jane. Stop while you're ahead." His lips curve into a grim smile. "And remember, it's *you* who we are watching."

7 Bad Calls

I dream that I'm in a dank, gloomy jail cell, my leg—which is in dire need of shaving—secured to the wall by a rusty chain and leg iron. I run a hand up my stubbly calf and a noise causes me to look up. Wyatt and Lindy are gazing in through the bars, smirking at me.

"Ugh. What a mess," sniffs Lindy, who's dressed as a porn-movie prison guard, her black thigh-high boots featuring chrome heels as thin as chopsticks. She flicks a riding crop in my direction. "She looks feral, doesn't she?"

Wyatt is carrying a briefcase, from which he now pulls a manila folder. He flips through some papers and wrinkles his nose, his grey eyes disapproving. "It says here that you're a spy," he says. "Do you have any idea what the penalty for espionage is here?"

Lindy cocks her index finger and thumb at my head. "Pow," she giggles. "Guess you should have minded your own business."

She pats Wyatt's butt and he blushes. "Not here, *cheri*."

I try to move closer to the bars only to be stopped by the chain, the iron ring digging deeper into my ankle. "I'm not a spy!" I wail. "Please, Wyatt, you have to tell Mr. Thai that it's all a mistake…"

Lindy whacks at the bars with her riding crop. "Just look at yourself." She rolls her eyes. "Do you really want to live anyway?"

The next moment, I find myself gazing into a mirror, shocked to see that I'm wearing my intended wedding dress, which is now far too small for me. It's as if my whole body has been pumped full of helium, my thighs and belly threatening to burst through the cream silk, my breasts bulging. I cry out in shock and the dress starts to tear. I try in vain to hold the thin fabric together.

"She actually believed that you'd marry her?" shrieks Lindy. Wyatt doubles over with laughter. I squeeze my eyes shut as the dress' seams give way. There's a loud explosion.

When I open my eyes, the cell is littered with beads and shreds of silk. I am standing, huge and hairy, in my underwear, my bra barely covering my nipples.

"I got it on video!" crows Lindy. She waves a camcorder and titters.

"We'll put it on Youtube!" says Wyatt.

Lindy laughs harder.

I'm begging Wyatt for mercy when the phone rings. I turn around in confusion. My cell lies bare. The phone's ringing grows louder...

I sit up and the jail cell gives way to Sigrid's living room. The curtains are drawn but some light filters through. My cell phone is in the pocket of the jeans that I wore last night, which lie crumpled on the floor where I'd stepped out of them.

I reach for the phone, relieved to see that my arm is normal size. A quick peek beneath the sheet confirms that I was having a bad dream. I clear my throat. My mouth tastes dreadful.

"Hello," I say, my voice thick with sleep and the remnants of too many margaritas. I retrieve my watch from the floor: 9:45 a.m. My head pounds. I wonder what time I got to sleep last night. It had been close to 4:00 when I'd finally been allowed to leave the police station.

For a moment, the line just hums. I sink back down onto the sofa cushions only to sit back up again at the sound of my mom's voice. "Jane? Are you there Jane? I don't know what's wrong with the phones over there. It's been what, more than three decades since the war ended? Why can't those people get it together and build a decent communications network? I mean, really Jane, what is the attraction of living somewhere so…" Her mint tin rattles. "So backward?"

On a better day I might actually respond to this, but I'm still too traumatized by my dream and recent brush with the law to attempt it. Instead, I manage a faint, "How's it going, Mom?" to which Tabitha takes affront.

"How do you think it's going?" she snaps. "All those wedding guests I had to contact. The caterer and the band and God only knows what else. All that good money wasted." She sniffs. "I should have made you come home and deal with it all yourself. Your Aunt Kitty's tickets were non-refundable so she and Uncle Donald spent a week with us. All that pair wanted to do was play bridge, day in day out. They drove me half crazy, always whipping out those damn playing cards." She pauses to draw breath. "Well? Are you still there?" barks my mother. "What's the matter with you Jane? You've barely said a word to me!"

"I'm sorry, Mom. I really appreciate it." I take a deep breath. My head is throbbing and my entire body aches. "How's Dad? Has he been playing golf lately?"

My mother sighs. "Skippy's worried about you."

Hanoi Jane 101

"Nothing to worry about," I rasp. "Of course it was a shock with Wyatt and all but things are back on track."

"What do you mean?" Tabitha sounds suspicious. "You're getting back together again?"

I squeeze my eyes shut. I feel too wrecked to be speaking to my mom, my every statement fraught with the potential to be misunderstood and exaggerated. "No," I say. "Not yet but we're ..." I search for words that won't add up to an outright lie. "We're talking."

"Hmmm, well, I don't know that there's much to talk about. But that's your business. Although from what I heard Wyatt didn't seem too cut up when he was back in town last week visiting that old battleaxe of a grandma."

"I... what are you talking about?" I say, trying to keep my voice level. The year before last my folks had had Easter dinner at Wyatt's parents' place, an invitation that had not been re-extended last year. Since my dad had gotten drunk on sherry (the only alcoholic beverage on offer) and repeatedly referred to Wyatt's stout Grandma Beryl as "Cracker Barrel", this wasn't surprising.

"Your sister Lauren ran into Wyatt in some bar or other. Apparently he mentioned that he was seeing someone new over there, which I thought was rather unnecessary given the trouble that Lauren had to go through canceling the florist." My mom shakes her mint tin for emphasis. "I mean, not a word of apology for the trouble he's caused us."

The trouble he's caused you? I think, self-pity threatening to swamp me. What about me? But I don't say anything.

My mom's mints rattle harder. "Jane? Are you still there?"

"Yes," I say, my voice very small. "I…" I try to fight the impulse to ask more but give up. The thought of Wyatt telling my perfect sister that he's already moved on is too much to bear. "What…what else did she say?"

"What else did who say?" says my mom, there being only one real subject in her stories, namely herself.

I grit my teeth. "Lauren," I say. "What else did Lauren say about Wyatt?"

"Oh, Lauren. Mmmm. She said he looked good and that his grandma was fine. False alarm, fit as a fiddle. I could have told them as much. It's not easy killing off someone that grim. She'll outlive all of us."

"So Wyatt didn't say anything else about…" I pause, aware that questioning my mom is not only pointless but possibly dangerous.

"He mentioned he was dating someone," she says, her voice vague. "An Asian girl. Lauren was a little shocked since she thought that your wedding was just on hold and that there was some chance that you'd reconcile. Is that what you told her, Janey, or did Lauren misunderstand? You know how Lauren can be sometimes…"

I bury my face in my hands. "What…what did she say to him?"

"Who?" says Tabitha, then, "Oh, you mean Lauren? Well I don't know. You'll have to ask her. But really Jane, Skippy and I are worried about you. Why you insist on staying over there is beyond us. Since it's clear that you and Wyatt are finished don't you think it's time to come—"

"I like it here," I say, then wonder if it's true.

This causes my mom to pause, but she recovers quickly. "But…but why?"

Hanoi Jane 103

I eye Sigrid's door, which is pulled shut. No doubt Sigrid is still asleep. I envy her. "There are lots of interesting people here," I say, thinking of last night's run-in with Mr. Thai of the Department of Foreigner Control. "Everything's so different. There's so much to learn. It's a different culture."

"Mmmm," says Tabitha, clearly unconvinced. "Well, you can tell us all about it when we're there."

I swallow hard. "When you're what?"

"We're coming to visit," she says brightly. "Skippy wanted to see for himself how you're getting on over there and, well, you know how I hate long-haul flights but I could see that in this situation…"

"No!" I gasp. "No, Mom, that's really not necessary."

"Oh I think it is. We're flying Cathay Pacific via Hong Kong, arriving on the 22nd." Tabitha's voice is firm. "I'll email you the dates so that you can arrange a hotel."

I count on my fingers: that's 19 days from now. I shut and open my eyes, hoping against hope that this is another bad dream. "But you'll hate it here," I say weakly. "There are no big shopping malls. And what about Dad? He'll miss his golf buddies. And it's so hot and humid here right now. Plus the traffic… it's crazy! Oh Mom, honestly, Vietnam is not your kind of place at all."

Tabitha sighs, "Really Jane, if it's so dreadful, what are you doing there? And can't you even pretend to be happy about seeing us? I mean, honestly, we're coming all that way just to see you and you're acting like it's the end of the world. What's the matter with you?"

I shake my head in frustration. Skip and Tabitha regard Hawaii as unacceptably foreign. "No, no, it's not that

Mom. Of course I'll be happy to see you but it's just that, well, remember how much you hated Mexico? Wouldn't you be better off going to Florida?"

"Skip and I were unlucky with that stomach bug in Mexico," sniffs Tabitha. "And the resort looked nothing like it did on the Internet. But you'll be able to take us to all the good places. Skippy's been watching all sorts of movies to prepare for this trip. He's really excited about it. Now email me if you need me to bring anything. Do they sell Clearasil there? I noticed your complexion was suffering in those last photos you sent us. Maybe some concealer?"

I grit my teeth, willing myself to stay calm. "No Mom, it's fine thanks. I'll email if I think of anything."

"Right-e-oh," says my mom cheerily, then, "Oh! Hold on! Your dad wants a word with you."

There's some rattling and rustling as Tabitha hands the phone to my dad, who booms out a hearty hallo, followed by, "Janey! So your mom let the cat out of the bag, I hear. We were gonna surprise you and just show up, but you know Tabitha." He chuckles. "Never could keep a secret."

"Well, I'm surprised anyways," I say, which is the truth.

"Yeah, we figured you'd had a rough month and could use some cheering up," says Skip. "What with being ditched so close to your wedding date and all that."

"I'm fine, really."

"Right, well you know, you're not the first person it's happened to. My aunt Lucia, that's your great aunt, ya know she got stood up at the altar. The guy just never showed up, if you can imagine the humiliation of it, her waiting at the church and everything...."

I have an unwelcome vision of my Great Aunt Lucia, gaunt and doleful like a female version of Christ on the cross, complete with facial hair. I search for some response and fail. Skippy plows ahead cheerily. "So it could have been worse," he says. "We managed to get half the deposit back on the country club. And as for that tux that your uncle Dwayne had special-ordered, well, I'm sure he'll be wearing it in no time. Things seem pretty serious between Lauren and that neurosurgeon of hers. Great guy too. Did you know he's an Ironman? Wants to take her to St. Tropez on vacation and I'm guessing that he plans to propose."

At this mention of my perfect sister and her perfect relationship with her equally perfect boyfriend, I find myself gripping my cell phone so hard that the screen starts to flicker. Two inches taller, three dress sizes smaller and multiple shades of blonde fairer than I am, Lauren could have modeled back in high-school, had something as crass as modeling appealed to her. Instead, she'd been fixated on interior design and now, at age 26, owns a successful interior décor company. She's made for this job, looking like the women who populate ads in *Perfect Homes*—the kind of cool, willowy blondes who have immaculate walk-in closets and fridges stocked with Evian and organic raspberries.

As my dad continues to fill me in on Lauren and Luke's vacation plans, I try to breathe deeply. It's not right that I resent my little sister just because her life is perfect.

"Janey?" says Skip. "You still there? You're awfully quiet today, hon. You sure you're okay?"

"I'm fine, really," I say.

"That's my girl!" says Skip. "Oh and by the way. I just went out and bought a mosquito net but do you think we should be taking anti-malaria pills too, honey?"

"Uh, no," I say. "Not unless you're planning to spend time way out in the countryside, jungle trekking or something."

"Well, I've been doing some research on Vietnam," says Skip proudly. "You know, catching up on a bunch of movies, *Apocalypse Now* and that one with Chuck Norris, plus *Rambo I, II* and *III*, and well, it seems to me that we'd be better off taking those anti-malaria pills."

"Um, Vietnam is nothing like it is in those movies," I say. "Hanoi's a city of six million people…" I trail off, wondering if my dad's actually listening to me.

"Sure. Whatever you say, hon," says Skippy. "Can't wait to see you! Your mom's been out shopping for resort wear."

I hug a pillow. I can picture them both perfectly, my dad in a Hawaiian-print shirt and my mom in something equally bright, flimsy and inappropriate. I promise to email important info, aware that it's unlikely that either of my parents will actually read it.

"It's going to be great honey!" says Skip. "I can't wait to see you!"

"Same," I say, with as much enthusiasm as I can muster.

"And remember hon, if your great aunt Lucia could get over being stood up at the altar, well, you can too. Oh of course Lucia never remarried but she's fine with that, really. And that doll collection of hers is something else. She's got thousands of them, all shapes and sizes. She buys them off the Home Shopping Network, a real passion of hers. And she makes her own little clothes for them. So you just hang in there kiddo."

"Right," I say. "Love you Dad."

"Love you too Janey."

As soon as I've hung up, I burst into tears, the lack of sleep, hangover and stress of last night suddenly too much to take, especially combined with the knowledge that Wyatt actually told my sister that he's dating someone...

I imagine Lauren's surprise at the news of my broken engagement. She wouldn't be mean about it—Lauren's never mean—but merely baffled at how I could have made such a mess of my life. Romantic upheavals, like catsup stains, have no place in Lauren's world of St. Tropez getaways and white carpeting.

Crying, I know, will only make my eyes puffier than they already are. I haul myself up off the sofa and limp towards the bathroom, my knee having stiffened in the night. The scrape looks red and angry.

Letting the hot water run over me, I shut my eyes. How, at 29 years old, have I allowed my life to get so badly off track that my parents feel compelled to fly halfway around the world to check up on me? And even more worryingly, why does a small part of me want to collapse into a heap and let my mom and dad solve everything?

I remember how it was when I was little, back when Skip had seemed infallible. I wish that I could crawl into my daddy's arms and find that nothing is as bad as it seems—Wyatt, Lindy, my cancelled wedding, the Department of Foreigner Control, all of them with no power to hurt me.

I dry off carefully and study myself in the mirror. It is not a pretty picture. While my whole face is doughy, two small, unbaked croissants seem to have been stuck beneath my eyes in the night, my eyes so small and red that it's a wonder that I can see out of them. The only thing on my face that's not puffy is my mouth; my lips appear thin, chapped and bloodless.

Normally, at this point I would look away, but this morning I lean in closer. As my mom had pointed out, my skin is a mess. The woman staring back at me resembles an aging, bleary-eyed teenager.

Studying this ragged creature, the reality of my parents' phone call sinks in: *They are coming to Hanoi.* I can't possibly allow them to see me like this—wan, covered in spots, scratches and bruises, in trouble with the authorities, and camped out on my best friend's couch. I'm 29, for God's sakes, not 14. I'd better pull myself together fast. No more tears. No more whining to Sigrid. No more stupid run-ins with Lindy Tran. And no more margaritas.

"Chin up," I say to the tired-looking woman gazing back at me. "What you need is some coffee, foundation and a new place to live." *And Wyatt*, I think, then chastise myself.

• • •

My little sister is engaged. I heard the news from three sources: my mom, who called —as usual—in the dead of night; my friend Amy, who's also good friends with Lauren; and Lauren herself, via email, since I've been avoiding her phone calls. Ever since news of my breakup reached my parents Lauren has been trying to reach me. I know it's awful but I just can't face talking to her.

Of course, this is stupid and wrong. Lauren won't judge me. She loves me and misses me and deserves so much better. Or that's what I tell myself whist dialing her number, since the other reason that I might be calling now is to find out what Wyatt had told her about Lindy, and I'd rather not be that pathetic.

Lauren's phone rings twice before she answers it, her pleasure at hearing from me so evident that I feel bad for not having called sooner. "I've been trying to reach you for ages," she says. "Why didn't you call me back? I've been so worried about you."

Since I have no excuses, I'm forced to tell the truth, which is that I've been too embarrassed to talk to her.

"Embarrassed about what?" says Lauren, her voice genuinely mystified.

"Embarrassed that my life is such a wreck," I say. "You've done so much to help with my wedding and then with less than a month to go it's cancelled and all that work and money's wasted. And everybody knows. It's all so…" I take a deep breath. "Humiliating."

"It's hardly your fault," says Lauren. "Mom told me that Wyatt cheated on you. I couldn't believe it. I mean, God Jane, I've felt so helpless with you being so far away and all. It must have been hell for you. Mom and Dad are worried too. We're all worried."

"Well stop worrying," I say. "I'm fine, really." I take a deep breath. "And congratulations, by the way. That's great about you and Luke, truly."

"Yeah, thanks," says Lauren. "It is great. But I feel pretty bad about announcing our engagement now, right after this thing with you and Wyatt. I actually wanted to keep it quiet for a while but Luke gave me this amazing ring and I just had to wear it, you know? Anyways, of course Mom spotted it right away and then I had to tell her."

I grit my teeth. Details of this ring have already traveled across the ocean: 2.2 carats of natural pink diamond surrounded by smaller white stones. It'd be hard to keep something like that hidden.

"Don't be silly," I say. "I'm happy for you." This is true, except that that happiness has a bad aftertaste of self-pity. But of course I don't mention that.

"Well, thanks," says Lauren. "How are you, anyways? When are you coming home? Mom said that you were planning to stay in Hanoi for a while?"

"Yes," I say. I ask if there's any way that she can convince Mom and Dad not to visit me, since this is the second reason why I'm calling her.

"But why?" says Lauren, again sounding genuinely perplexed. "I figured you'd be so happy to see them."

I'm glad that Lauren can't see my face. Is she serious? "Our parents aren't exactly world travelers," I say. "Remember their trip to Mazatlan?"

"Mmmm, they said the accommodation was rough," says Lauren.

"It was a four star resort," I say. "It's not like they were camping in the slums. Hanoi's a whole lot rougher than that. It's hot and chaotic and, geez Lauren, I don't think they'll like it at all." Dumb words like 'geez' and 'gosh' that I'd never normally use have a way of slipping out when I talk to Lauren, just as, when we're together, I'm guaranteed to spill something all over myself.

"They've already bought their tickets," says Lauren. "And Dad's really excited about it. He bought one of those photojournalist vests with lots of pockets and zippers."

I stifle a groan, able to picture my dad perfectly. He'll pair that vest with shorts and a fanny-pack. On his feet will be white sports socks and Tevas.

As Lauren goes on and on about my parents' preparations for their trip, I wonder how to change the topic to her recent encounter with Wyatt. I figure that sooner or later she'll ask what's happening between us, but there's always the risk that she'll be too sensitive of my feelings to get into it.

When I ask about her trip to St. Tropez I can tell that Lauren is torn. On the one hand, she doesn't want to subject me, her newly dumped sister, to details of her picture-perfect love life. On the other, she's dying to talk about her romantic holiday. As a result, the details come out in drips and drabs, like a leaky faucet. I'd rather she just gush and get it over with.

When I can't stand it any more, I blurt out that Mom had mentioned that she'd run into Wyatt back in Raleigh. "What did he say?" I say, the desperation in my voice all too evident. I bite my lip. There's a real risk that Lauren will report this conversation to my mom. I wish that I'd kept my mouth shut.

There's a pause as my sister figures out how to respond and when she does, she sounds worried. "Yeah, I ran into him in Zen, it's this new club with a Japanese vibe. He was there with some friends so we didn't really talk much. I didn't know what was happening between you guys and there were all these other people around so I couldn't really ask."

I swallow hard. "Did he mention me?"

She sighs. "He said that he was, um, seeing someone new," says Lauren, who can't lie. "I was kind of surprised since I thought that you guys were trying to work things out." There's a pause. "So is it like, over between you?"

"I don't know," I say. There's now a weird echo on the line, which only intensifies the desperation in my voice. I shake my head. "I, I guess it is," I say. I wait and so does Lauren. Swallowing down the last of my pride, I ask what Wyatt had said about this other woman. I know that this conversation will intensify Lauren's concern but feel compelled to ask anyways.

"He said that she runs a charity over there," says Lauren. "I'm sorry. I didn't know what to say. It was all so sudden, you know. Afterwards I was really mad at him. I wish that I'd told him what an idiot he was being. Like he doesn't deserve you, you know?"

"Yeah," I say.

In my mind's eye I can picture Lauren, clad in cream cashmere with pearl earrings, and that ring hanging off of her slender hand like a Christmas bauble. She'll be sitting at her desk, which, unlike mine, is spotless, a pot of white orchids set beside her chrome laptop. Since she's worried, she might be twirling the phone chord, or perhaps twisting one of her earrings. "Do you really think you could forgive him?" she says. "He's been such a jerk."

"I don't know," I say, but I think that I could.

"Well, I think you deserve so much better."

"Thanks," I say. Since tears are threatening, I change the subject to her wedding plans.

"Mom's taking care of most of it," she says. "But that reminds me. I know you probably don't want to even think about weddings right now but would you mind being my maid-of-honor?"

"Sure," I say. She's right—I don't want to think about weddings, especially hers, but I can't very well say so. I realize that I'd asked my college roommate Molly to be my maid of honor, not Lauren, and wonder if she'd been hurt by that.

"Are you sure you're up for it?" says Lauren.

"Of course," I say. "I really am happy for you, Lo. And I'm honored to be your maid of, um, honor. It'll be great." The strain of lying is making my teeth hurt.

"Oh good, I hoped you'd feel that way," says Lauren, sounding relieved. "I miss you so much, Jane. When are you coming home? I know that we haven't lived in the same city for years but New York never felt like it was that far away. Like I could always come for a long weekend but now it just seems like ages since we've seen each other. And so much has happened."

"Like what?" I say. As long as Lauren is talking I won't have to. As she fills me in on the new place that she and Luke are planning to buy, I reflect on why it is that I'm such a bad person that I can't be genuinely happy for my only sister. Why, when Lauren has always adored and possibly idolized me, have I always resented her? Even as a child, she possessed none of the annoying traits that my friends' younger siblings exhibited. She never broke my toys, and never borrowed and ruined my clothes without asking. All she'd wanted, all those years, was to be close to me. And all those years I'd pushed her away, repelled by her sheer sweetness and perfection. It's lucky that Luke is perfect too or else they'd never survive. For regular fuck-ups like me, living with somebody that perfect is exhausting.

"Jane? Are you still there?" says Lauren and I realize that I haven't been listening.

"Yeah, the line's getting bad," I say. "You were fading in and out."

"Oh," says Lauren. "Hello? Hey Jane?"

"It's okay now," I say. "I can hear you."

"Oh good," she says.

"I'd better go," I say. "Give my love to Luke. And our parents too, if you talk to them soon."

"Oh that reminds me," says Lauren. "Mom's on a new diet again."

"Oh God," I say. "What is it this time?" Nothing but ostrich meat, I bet. Or organic chickpeas and goat's milk consumed between 1:00 and 5:00 p.m. facing southwards.

"Canteloupes," says Lauren. "That's all she's eating. Can you get them over there?"

"Nope," I say, my spirits rising. "You'd better tell her. Vietnam has all kinds of melons but I don't recall ever seeing a cantaloupe. I guess they don't grow here. If she comes, she'll have to break her diet." There is a slight hope that my mom will abandon her trip over this.

"I don't think she'll cancel her trip," says Lauren, who's obviously figured out what I'm thinking. "She'll probably just switch to watermelons or guavas or something."

"Great," I say. When my mom's starving herself she's even harder to deal with than usual.

"Take care of yourself," says Lauren. "I miss you."

"Same here," I say. And I do. "Good luck with that new place."

"Can I send you some photos of wedding and bridesmaid dresses?" she says. "I could really use your advice."

Why Lauren, who's always immaculate, would want my advice on matters of style is a mystery. But I say sure, I'd be happy to say what I think of them.

"Thanks," she says. "And our new place. I want your opinion on that too. It needs a lot of renovation and you always have such good ideas."

"Um, sure," I say.

Before signing off she says that she loves me. Long after I've hung up, I just sit there, thinking. Will I ever manage to stop comparing myself to my little sister? Will I ever just accept her and myself as we are? I do, after all, love her.

The big irony, I realize, is that all of her life Lauren has looked to me for approval. I don't need to see her wedding gown or her new house—I know without a doubt that they will be perfect. I wonder if, somehow, Lauren has failed to realize just how great she is. I want to call her back and tell her that everything she touches turns to gold, and how impressive and brutally annoying that is.

Instead, I go into Sigrid's kitchen and help myself to some graham crackers. I wish that there were some way to get out of being Lauren's maid of honor, then feel guilty for even thinking about it. I tell myself not to worry. She's planning a spring wedding, which means that I still have ages to turn my life around before I have to face everybody back in Raleigh. Nine months is long enough to meet the love of my life, get a great new job, or even, God forbid, have a baby. The graham crackers are stale but I eat them anyways. I try to visualize this new, improved me, so happy and successful that no one will remember my failed nuptials.

I find a pen and some paper and start to make a list, but I've only gotten to point four when the ink runs out. After tossing out the pen I go to check my email. Sure enough, Lauren has sent me the photos already. I hesitate. Do I really want to see her potential wedding dress and new home tonight? Maybe I should just read a book or go to bed early. But of course I will open them and feel jealous and disgusted with myself.

8 Homemaking

Getting my own place is my first priority, but finding the kind of apartment that a responsible, 29-year-old adult should inhabit in Hanoi isn't easy on my meager budget. In the company of various realtors, all of whom refer to themselves as "David" when they are clearly Minhs or Longs, I've spent the last two days visiting places which, I was assured, were quiet, bright and conveniently located. One place had no natural light whatsoever and another was located over a metal-work shop. And those weren't even the worst ones. One apartment was at the end of an alley so dark, narrow and convoluted that I'd been scared to let "David" out of my sight in case I never found my way out again.

After five dumps in two hours my spirits are at a new low. My parents are due to arrive in 17 days and I remain homeless. "I have one other place," says David, whose real name, I gleaned from an envelope in his office, is actually Chau.

"Is it quiet?"

Chau nods.

I sigh, fully aware that Chau's definition of "quiet" includes places located next to and above preschools, karaoke lounges and abattoirs. Questions about natural light and location all elicit the desired responses, not that that means anything. Grudgingly, I say that I'll see it. I am, after all, desperate.

Chau ferries me by motorbike to a quiet, leafy street some minutes from the city center. A narrow path cuts between two old French houses, the vacant apartment located on the third floor, off a small courtyard. Climbing the stairs, which are none too clean, I try to keep an open mind. The location is good and it seems quiet enough, the most prominent noise being that of someone on the second floor strumming on a guitar. "The door's open," says Chau, when we reach the third floor. I bend to remove my shoes but Chau tells me not to bother. "The floor's dirty," he says. "Nobody has lived here for some months." I step into a small, dimly lit hallway.

Ignoring Chau's sales pitch, I wander into the living room, a large, high-ceilinged room that would be bright if its three windows weren't filthy. Dusty sheets cover the furniture, the floor so dirty that I leave footprints as I cross the room. With some effort I manage to pry back the folding windows to reveal a view of old villas and milk flower trees. While basic, the kitchen is sufficient for my culinary expertise (making toast, coffee and cereal) and the bathroom well-ventilated. By the time I've reached the bedroom I can barely conceal my excitement. Beneath a thick layer of dirt, this room features a tiled fireplace, a wrought-iron bed and a balcony. It's the kind of old, charming place that I'd dreamt of before moving to Hanoi. And it's cheap. I turn to find Chau standing behind me.

I wonder if it's possible to get the place cleaned and repainted before my parents show up. Chau studies my face, then shrugs apologetically. "This building is very old," he says. "I have one other place that you will…"

I cut him off. "I'll take it," I say, unable to hide my excitement for another moment.

• • •

It's a Saturday morning and Tuyet, Sigrid and I are in the Old Quarter, the two of them having agreed to help me shop for my new apartment. So far, we've bought towels, a coffee maker and a shower curtain. Next up is a crockery stall that Tuyet knows, located in Hang Da Market. Tuyet leads the way on her shiny silver Piaggio. Sigrid and I follow on Sigrid's old Honda.

Ever since I cancelled my trip home and admitted that my wedding's off, Tuyet has been extra helpful. News of my failed engagement spread around my office like a bad flu, my colleagues reacting as though I'd been diagnosed with some terminal illness. Some of my unmarried female co-workers have taken to avoiding me altogether, as though spinsterhood were contagious.

When I say this to Tuyet, she smiles. She and Sigrid have just parked their bikes and retrieved their bike tickets. Sigrid stuffs hers into the hip pocket of her cargo shorts. Tuyet places hers in her purse. "If you're not married by 25 here, everyone thinks you're an old maid," says Tuyet, whose English, while excellent, seems to have been partially gleaned from a nineteenth century phrasebook. Despite the 95-degree heat she's wearing a wide-brimmed hat, jeans, a jacket and long gloves in an effort to avoid getting a suntan. She removes her floppy sunhat and tucks it into her purse too. "My finding a suitable husband is about the only thing my mom talks about."

We squeeze between parked bikes to get out of the parking lot. Sigrid rolls her eyes. "And you're what, 12?" she says.

Her long black hair pulled back in an Alice band, Tuyet does look about 12 today. She turns to Sigrid and frowns. "I'm 24," she says haughtily. This is the first time that Sigrid and Tuyet have met and they don't seem to be hitting it off. I worry that Sigrid will say something offensive.

The three of us walk through the section of the market that's devoted to selling caged birds. Located outside the main market building, which has two stories, this section consists of a handful of low shacks. Bamboo and wire cages cover the walls and hang from wires overhead. Most of the cages contain birds, all of which seem to be chirping and squawking. The smell of bird shit is overpowering.

Sigrid steps around a cage full of pigeons. Tuyet does likewise. "Twenty-four is way too young to even think about getting married," says Sigrid dismissively. "I don't think anyone should marry before 30."

"I didn't say I was thinking about it," says Tuyet, somewhat defensively. "Just that my mom does." She stops to peer at a cage holding a pair of lovebirds. "I don't even have a boyfriend yet."

I examine the birds too. Their pretty plumage is missing in places. One of them tries to peck at the other. "Great," I say. "Not even the lovebirds can get along." Neither Sigrid nor Tuyet seems to hear me, since they're both walking again, heading for the main entrance to the market. The guy who's selling the lovebirds shoves a calculator under my nose. I shake my head and saunter off to catch up to Sigrid and Tuyet.

As soon as she's safely in the shade, Tuyet plucks off her long gloves. "I plan to marry at 28," she says matter-of-factly. I imagine a spreadsheet titled: "Tuyet's Life Plans". Grad School. *Tick*. Good job. *Tick*. Promotion. *Tick*. Proposal. *Tick*. And so on.

She removes her hat. "Are you married yet?" she asks Sigrid.

After the bright light outdoors, the market building is dim. Sigrid pushes her sunglasses up onto her head. For a second I think that there's a weird, wistful look on her face. But it's probably just a trick of the light. She clears her throat. "Nope," she says. "I'm single."

I listen in on this exchange with some curiosity. I've never heard Sigrid or Tuyet discuss guys before. While I'm hoping that some personal details will emerge, none do. The next thing I know, Sigrid and Tuyet are comparing wedding customs in the East and West. Their earlier standoffishness seems to have vanished and they're behaving like old pals. I wish that they'd either divulge details of their love lives or get off the topic of weddings altogether. The day that Wyatt and I were due to wed is nine days away.

While this recollection engenders a moment of gloom, I force myself to focus on my new apartment. It's going to be great, I tell myself. At this very minute a wall in my bedroom is being painted a gorgeous shade of periwinkle. I'm excited to see it.

"Where's your list?" says Sigrid.

I realize that she's speaking to me and extract the creased list from my pocket. "Plates, bowls, mugs, chopsticks," I read.

"This way," says Tuyet. We turn off of the main aisle into a narrower one, pushing our way between stalls selling cheap clothes, shoes and handbags. Seeing my white face, all of the vendors perk up. "Ma-dam! Ma-dam!" they yell. One lady tries to grab my arm and I brush her off, the heat and lack of light and space making me feel increasingly claustrophobic. "There it is," says Tuyet. Measuring about 20 square feet, the stall is stacked with plates, bowls and vases produced in a village on the outskirts of Hanoi. According to Tuyet, this village has been making pottery since the 1500s.

Dressed in rust-colored satin pajamas, the stall's middle-aged owner resembles a great, shiny hen in a nest of colorful crockery. When we arrive she is in the middle of getting a pedicure, requiring us to share the space that fronts her stall with her feet, a discontented-looking manicurist and a basket full of dirty rags and nail polish.

We're examining the plates on offer when Tuyet slaps my thigh with a glove. "Oh, I forgot to tell you!" she says. "I met my friend Van yesterday. Remember, I told you about her before? She is an anthropology student working with ethnic Dao people in Mai Chau?"

Hunkered down beside a stack of blue and white plates, it takes me a moment to remember who Tuyet's talking about. "Um, yes," I say. "She's the one you asked about Highlands Outreach, right?"

Sigrid turns towards us. Mention of Highlands Outreach has gotten her attention. A swinging fan is attached to one wall and when the breeze sweeps over Sigrid her hair ripples. I wait for the breeze to hit me. It is stifling in here and the reek of acetone is overpowering.

"That's right," says Tuyet. She picks up a bowl painted with pink peach blossoms and turns it over to examine the underside. "So one of Van's contacts told her that Highlands Outreach is building a community center near Sapa. The local ethnic minority women can meet there to sew, and staff will help them to design more desirable embroidery products and sell them to a wider market. The groundbreaking ceremony was held last year and the center will open next month."

I mull over this information. "Do you know anyone in Sapa?" I say. "Maybe they could stop by and check this place out?"

"I don't know anybody there," says Tuyet. "It's a long journey, you know, an overnight train ride from Hanoi." She sets down the pink bowl and reaches for a blue one. "But why are you so interested in Highlands Outreach? There are lots of NGOs in Hanoi that you could write about."

Faced with Tuyet's quizzical expression, I decide to fill her in about Lindy Tran. Tuyet listens carefully, then clucks her tongue in disgust. "This Lindy sounds like a terrible woman," she says. "You should go to Sapa and investigate."

"I can't," I say flatly. "My parents will be here in less than two weeks. I have too much to do before they get here."

"But that's perfect!" says Tuyet. "Foreign tourists love Sapa. The mountain scenery is beautiful and the weather is pleasant and cool. You can take your parents to Sapa."

"Tuyet's right," says Sigrid. "The scenery is fantastic. And your parents can't stay in Hanoi the whole time."

I consider it. Every time my dad calls he does talk about seeing the jungle. But that's only because he's seen too many Vietnam War movies… "Is there any jungle up there?" I say doubtfully.

Tuyet promises to find me some photographs. She holds up a cream plate painted with yellow goldfish. "How about this one?"

My head swimming with china patterns, I'm unsure about the goldfish motif. I'm not sure about going to Sapa either. My parents, after all, consider Canada an exotic vacation spot.

"I could come too," says Sigrid. "I have a lot of vacation days that I have to use up before my contract gets renewed at the end of September. I love the mountains. It'd be fun. What do you think, Jane?"

Faced with Sigrid's enthusiasm, I find myself agreeing. With a stranger along my parents might be on their best behavior. They may even enjoy themselves. I cross my fingers and look for some wood to touch. Since there's none around, I have to settle for knocking on my jeans, which are made of cotton.

"Hey, this is nice," says Sigrid. She hands me a pale green plate embossed with lotus leaves.

I nod. The light green is gorgeous and the design is pretty yet subtle. "They're great," I say. "How much are they?"

Tuyet volunteers to handle the bargaining. Sigrid says that she'll wait outside. I don't blame her. It's crazily hot in here.

A price having been reached, the vendor wraps my plates in old newspaper. She ties them in two stacks with

twine. I count out the money, Ho Chi Minh's face on every note, his smile as serene as the Buddha's.

The plates are heavy. Tuyet and I each carry half of them. I wonder how I'm going to hold them on the back of Sigrid's motorbike. We're about 30 feet from the parking lot when I spot Sigrid. She's talking to a *xe om* driver and another guy, both of whom are in the process of strapping a gigantic cage covered with fine-meshed chicken wire onto the back of the xe om driver's Honda Cub.

"I got some birds," says Sigrid, when we get close. Sure enough, I can see a couple of bright green birds flitting around in the square cage. Looking closer, I see that they're lovebirds, and that they're both missing some feathers.

"I thought of releasing them," says Sigrid. "But if they were born in captivity they won't be able to survive in the wild." She removes her sunglasses and wipes some sweat off the bridge of her nose. "So I got them a bigger cage. The one they were in was pathetic. They can live out on my balcony."

I set my stack of plates on the ground. The *xe om* driver is threading twine through the bars of the birdcage. I've never thought of Sigrid as sentimental but I guess that she is. "That's nice," I say, surprised to find a lump forming in my throat. I retrieve a bottle of La Vie from my bag and drink some, the water tepid. I offer it to Tuyet, who declines, and then to Sigrid.

"Thanks," she says. Looking at her new birds, Sigrid looks happy, her face pink and shiny. Getting to know Sigrid better has been the one good thing that's come out of my breakup. I want to tell Sigrid that she's a good friend, and that I owe her, but am afraid of sounding trite or overemotional.

Perhaps sensing that I'm about to say something corny, Sigrid tugs at the cage. Satisfied that it's secure she retreats to fetch her motorbike. Tuyet follows. The *xe om* driver lights a cigarette and retreats to crouch in the shade. He is wearing an olive-green army pith helmet with a little gold star in the center. I move into the shade too and watch the passersby. Across the street a blind beggar is making his rounds, armed with a microphone and trailed by an accomplice who wheels a bicycle that has an amplifier strapped behind the seat. Faced with the beggar's earsplitting wails, people pay up in the hopes of hurrying him along. I am relieved to see Tuyet and Sigrid.

I wait for Sigrid to mount her bike, then climb on behind her. Tuyet hands me the plates and I position them on the seat between us. I use one hand to hang onto the bike and the other to keep the stack steady. "Ready?" says Sigrid.

"Ready," I say. We both say goodbye to Tuyet.

Every few minutes I turn around to check that the *xe om* driver is still behind us. When we get to Sigrid's place I dismount first, carefully setting first one stack of plates and then the other onto the sidewalk beside me. Carrying both stacks at once is difficult and I'm scared that I'll drop them but I have no choice, since it takes both Sigrid and the *xe om* driver to maneuver the massive birdcage down the long tunnel into Sigrid's courtyard. I let them go first and make frequent stops. By the time I reach the fourth floor my arms are shaking. Sweat has left dark patches all over my blue cotton top. I feel sticky and disgusting.

Sigrid's front door lies open. I kick off my sandals and step inside. I can hear Sigrid and the *xe om* driver out on the balcony. I set the plates on the kitchen floor, pour myself a glass of water, and go into the bathroom. I splash cold water on my face and neck, letting it run down my back. I can hear Sigrid thanking the *xe om* driver and walking him to the door. I strip off all of my clothes and step into the shower.

Feeling cleaner and cooler, I go out to find Sigrid. She is standing on the balcony, a few feet away from her new birdcage. Set on the ground in the shade of the adjacent building, the birdcage stands about chest-high. Seeing me, Sigrid smiles. "They seem to be settling down," she says happily.

I nod. The birds are no longer flying about frantically but are perched on a thin stick in the far corner. Their little black eyes look scared and suspicious. "I'm trying to think of names for them," says Sigrid. "Any ideas? Can you think of any famous couples?"

"What have you got so far?" I say. My hair is wet and I bend over and fluff it.

"Well, Romeo and Juliet, obviously, and Adam and Eve."

"Anthony and Cleopatra?" I say. "John and Yoko? Rhett and Scarlett?"

"Bonnie and Clyde?" says Sigrid.

"God," I say, straightening up. "None of those stories ended well, did they?" A small white butterfly appears over the railing of Sigrid's balcony and flutters across her terrace. There are a few potted plants up here but no flowers; it seems like a long way for that butterfly to have come for nothing. "There must be *some* famous couples with happy endings," I say. We both try to think of some. "Santa and Mrs. Claus?" I say, finally.

Sigrid snorts. "Mrs. Claus doesn't count," she says. "She's like an afterthought. Do you even know her full name?"

I admit that I don't. We both sit down on the floor, the birds still watching us warily. I look around. The butterfly has vanished. I hope that it's found someplace more promising close by. "Cinderella and the Prince," I say, then admit that I don't know his name either. I offer to fetch Sigrid a glass of water and she thanks me. When I come back from the kitchen, she's still sitting on the floor thinking. The birds are still sitting in the far corner of their big cage. Seeing me approach, they shuffle deeper into the corner. I ask Sigrid if she's thought of anything.

"Uh uh," she says. "I was just thinking that even in fiction two independent, well-developed characters don't seem to be able to live happily ever after."

"Real people *do* stay together," I say bravely. "But nobody writes books about them."

"That's 'cause their lives are too boring," says Sigrid. We sit and watch the lovebirds.

In this heat, my hair is almost dry. "Fred and Wilma Flinstone?" I say. "Marge and Homer Simpson?"

Sigrid makes a face. "This is tragic. The only long-term couples we can come up with are cartoon characters."

"Fred and Ginger?" I say.

"Hmmm, they weren't an actual couple but that sort of suits them. Fred!" she calls out to the birds. "Ginger!"

There is no reaction.

"Which is which?" I say.

One of the birds, which has a big bald patch on its chest, hops closer to the other one, whose head is missing a bunch of feathers. For a moment I think that they're going to cuddle but then the one with the plucked chest pecks the other one on its bald spot. Sigrid shakes her head in disgust. "We should be thinking up famous adversaries," she says. "Like Moby Dick and Captain Ahab."

"Or Tom and Jerry," I say.

The bald-headed bird has retreated to the far corner, from where it's now screeching at its companion.

Sigrid stands up. "I give up," she says. "I'm going to have a shower."

"You have to call them something," I say. "Brad and Angelina? Posh and Becks?"

"How about Bash and Pecks?" says Sigrid.

I groan.

She has the grace to look contrite. "Sorry, bad pun," she says.

When Sigrid's out of the shower we both sit on her terrace drinking cold beers. The lovebirds are still squawking at each other. I wonder if they'll keep Sigrid awake at night. Sigrid must have the same thought because, out of the blue, she asks me if I think that her friend Andre would like them. "He has a big back yard," she says glumly. "They could sit out there."

Since I doubt that Andre would remember to feed them I say that I don't think so. For some minutes the two of us sit in silence. The birds, if anything, have grown even noisier. Sigrid scrambles to her feet. "I'm going to let them go," she says. "I don't know if they'll make it or not but they're obviously as miserable as hell in there." She walks round to the back of the cage and unlocks the flap, then returns to the front of the cage and tries to shoo the birds towards the opening.

I stand up and join her, the birds flapping from one end to the other but stubbornly ignoring the gaping hole in their cage. After a few minutes of flying back and forth the one with the patchy chest flutters towards the opening. Sigrid and I freeze and out it goes, hesitating for an instant at the threshold before rising and flapping over the balcony. A flash of color catches my eye and I turn to see that the second one is out too, flying fast as if to catch up to its companion.

"There they go," says Sigrid, her voice oddly stretched. Looking at her, I see that her eyes are shining.

There is something moving about seeing those birds fly up Hang Gai Street towards the lake, the street far below packed with honking commuters. It's late afternoon, the light that warm golden color that makes even ordinary things appear strangely beautiful. I take in the ornate façade of the colonial townhouse across the street, the balcony of the next house festooned with clothes hung out to dry, the sapling that's taken root in a crack of dirt on an old tiled roof. In the golden glow this seedling appears doomed yet heroic.

The lovebirds fly side-by-side, two splotches of green and yellow that grow smaller and smaller until, somewhere near the intersection of Luong Van Can, I can no longer see them. I wonder if we've done something good or bad. Lovely as it was to see them fly off, I'm afraid that they'll

end up as some housecat's dinner. I hope that they get a shot at happiness first.

"Want another beer?" says Sigrid. Her wet hair is brushed back straight and her face is free of makeup. Again, I want to thank her for being such a good friend. Again, I can't quite manage it. Instead, I say that that sounds great and offer to fetch them. "I'm hungry. Let's go inside," says Sigrid.

I nod.

We retreat indoors, leaving the big empty cage on the terrace, where I'm sure that it'll stay until Sigrid eventually moves someplace different.

· · ·

The Hanoi Professional Women's Group meets for dinner once a month at a different restaurant. Women of all nationalities are welcome. When I arrived in Hanoi, Wyatt had encouraged me to join as a way to "network". I'd come in the hope of making some friends here. Most of the group's members are in their twenties and thirties, and most don't have kids yet. I've been to two of the meetings and have met a few people I like, which is why I'm attending tonight's dinner.

Tonight's venue is a large, starkly decorated Japanese restaurant on the top floor of a new shopping mall. Going up, I'm alone in the glass elevator, the city's lights stretching further than I'd imagined. From up here, Hanoi seems utterly silent, the city's constant honking, clanking and revving replaced by the soft whoosh of the elevator. This sudden quiet makes me feel as though I've been whisked someplace else. In the dark, the city looks vast and generic. I try to imagine where I'd like to be but can't come up with anyplace. My brain feels dull and my spirits low, maybe because I'm hungry.

When the doors open I smell tempura grease and hear women's voices and laughter. A bunch of tables have been arranged in a row and about 20 women are sitting together, talking and nibbling on appetizers. I spot Jen, a textile designer who I don't know very well but really like, and am glad to see that there's an empty seat beside her. Jen is talking to two other women I've also met, a British high school teacher named Georgina and an American who works in advertising named Annalise Miller.

When Jen looks up and sees me she does a double take, her anxious expression a sure sign that she, Georgina and Annalise were talking about me. "Jane!" says Jen, her feigned enthusiasm edged with shame. Annalise and Georgina say hi too, then pretend to scan their set menus.

I put down my bag and take a seat, wishing that I hadn't come out tonight. Curiosity is radiating off of Annalise like too much perfume, while Georgina has the look of someone caught shoving office supplies into her handbag. Jen, meanwhile, just looks scared, as though she's afraid to say the wrong thing and cause me to hurl myself off of the 11th floor balcony.

"How are things?" I say.

"Good," says Jen.

"Fine," says Annalise.

"Alright," says Georgina.

Hanoi Jane 133

The conversation expires like an ant hit by a jet of bug spray. I can practically see its little legs kicking feebly on the tablecloth.

A waitress appears and sets down some small plates full of things that I don't recognize but look pretty. "Mmmm, I'm starving," says Annalise. We all pick up bits of this and that with our lacquered chopsticks and start chewing.

"Ooh, that one's delicious," says Jen, pointing at some rolls covered in orange fish eggs. She smiles at me encouragingly and I know that she's still worrying about how much I overheard when I walked in.

"Yes, that's lovely," says Georgina.

"I just love Japanese food," says Annalise.

Since I know that they know about me and Wyatt, and they know that I know they know, conversation about anything else is impossible. We can either keep this stilted dialogue going all night or I can acknowledge the cheating elephant in the corner. "I'm not getting married," I say.

Georgina blinks, Annalise brightens, and Jen frowns worriedly. There's a pause as they all figure out whether to act surprised or not.

Jen twists her napkin. "We heard that something happened between you and Wyatt."

"He cheated on me," I say.

They all shake their heads disapprovingly.

"So is it over between you guys?" says Annalise, her eyes avid behind navy D&G eyeglasses.

While she isn't the first person to have asked me this, each and every time I'm faced with this question I don't know how to answer. You'd think that I'd have worked out an articulate response by now, but my feelings seem to flip-flop every five minutes. I bite my lip and stir some wasabi into my soy sauce. "I don't know," I mutter. My soy sauce takes on a green tinge.

Annalise frowns. "Is he still seeing her?" Her voice is a low, eager whisper.

I nod. "He says he's confused."

Georgina snorts.

I dip a dynamite roll into my soy sauce, shove it in my mouth and feel some wasabi shoot up my nose. The other three pat me on the back, pass me a glass of water and wait patiently for me to stop coughing.

"Who is she?" says Annalise, when I've stopped spluttering. Jen and Georgina study their plates.

I'd bet my favorite jeans that they all know as much about this story as I do. This question was voiced partly to assure me that my business remains my own (as if) and partly to allow me to recount the tale in my own words, thereby adding to their existing knowledge. I can't actually fault them for this; in their place, I'd be curious too. At least Jen and Georgina seem genuinely sympathetic. I'm not so sure about Annalise. She has the fixated, hungry look of a serious gossip.

"Her name's Lindy Tran," I say. "Do you guys know her?"

"No," says Jen.

"Uh uh," says Annalise. "Is she Vietnamese?"

"I do," says Georgina.

Mine, Jen's and Annalise's eyes flick to Georgina, waiting for her to elaborate. But at just that moment a woman in a maroon blazer down at the far end of the table starts tapping her wineglass with a spoon and calling for attention. She stands up, smiling like a TV talk show host. "Hello Ladies!" she trills. "I'm Kerrilee Martinez and welcome to another Hanoi Professional Women's Night. We haven't done this recently but I thought that tonight we could go around the table and introduce ourselves! I see some new faces here tonight!"

One by one everyone has to stand up and say something like: "Hallo, I'm Kerstin Ekstrand from Sweden and I'm head of marketing for Oriflame cosmetics." It takes forever. I'm so scared of public speaking that even standing up to voice my name, nationality and job description causes my heart to pound. By the time we've gone all the way around the table I feel too tired to care what Georgina knows about Lindy Tran. I just want to get out of here.

"So what were we talking about?" says Annalise, the second the last woman has finished introducing herself. It's totally obvious that this question is a setup to get us back onto the topic of my and Wyatt's breakup, but Jen actually seems to be trying to remember. "Um, I'm not sure," she says. Annalise turns to Georgina in ill-concealed desperation.

"I was saying I know Lindy Tran," says Georgina.

Annalise, Jen and I are back where we were 20 minutes ago, waiting for Georgina to elaborate. "And?" I say. By right, this question has to come from me.

Georgina shakes her head. "I can't stand her."

I try not to look too gratified. Jen tops up my tiny cup of sake.

Given this intro, I now expect all of Lindy's sins to be revealed, in the manner of a Discovery channel

Egyptologist lifting the lid off a coffin to reveal a shrunken, 2,000-year-old mummy. Georgina will shed light into Lindy's depraved past and nefarious present, her cheating ways, her falsehoods and her foul thievery.

"My dog hates her," says Georgina. She dabs at her mouth with a napkin.

I swallow some sake the wrong way, which requires more back-slapping, water-sipping and waiting. "Wh-what do mean?" I finally manage to stammer.

Georgina pushes her dark hair behind her ears, which, like the rest of her visible skin, are covered in freckles. "I have a dog," she says. "His name is Alfie. He's a mutt, you know, the kind that they eat here."

We all nod. Dog meat is a delicacy in northern Vietnam, reputed, like snakes and tiger penises, to make men more virile. While all sorts of dogs are considered edible here, the ones bred for consumption are of medium size and resemble Australian dingos. They look ugly but hardy.

"Lindy used to live next door to me," says Georgina. "This was…" She stops to think about it. "Oh, about a year ago."

I wait. Maybe Georgina actually knows something after all.

"Lindy was constantly complaining about my dog. He barked too much. He was crapping in the front yard, which he wasn't. There was dog shit out there, but it wasn't Alfie's." She takes a sip of sake. "When she moved out I was thrilled." More sake. "Anyways, about a month ago I was walking Alfie around Hoan Kiem Lake and I ran into Lindy. Now Alfie loves people. He's the world's friendliest dog. But when he saw Lindy all the fur on his back stood up and he started growling at her. He's never behaved like that with anybody."

Jen looks thoughtful. "Do you think he remembered her?" she says. "Did you use to leave him outdoors back when she lived near you? Maybe she hit him or something and he remembered."

"I thought of that," says Georgina. "Once in a while I would leave Alfie in my back garden. But to get to that garden you have to go there specially. It's not on the way to where Lindy lived at all." She shrugs. "I just think that my dog sensed something off about her," she says. "And that makes me distrust her too."

I consider this. Clearly, this tale wasn't what I'd been hoping for. Alfie's disdain isn't going to hold up in court. But Georgina's story fits with my overall feeling about Lindy Tran: She's a bad piece of work. "I've never met Alfie," I say, "But he sounds like a good dog."

"Oh he is," says Georgina. She smiles. "He's more loyal than a lot of men I know."

I drain my cup in a single gulp.

Georgina signals the waitress for more sake. "And a lot of women too, for that matter," she says.

I like this addendum. Even though I'm disgusted with Wyatt, I'm not ready to turn into one of those bitter scorned women who think that all men are assholes.

"Do you think you'll stay in Hanoi?" says Georgina.

"For a while," I say. "I just got my own place."

"Good for you." She fills my cup again. "I'll drink to that."

"Me too," says Jen. We clink glasses.

When it became clear that no more gossip was forthcoming and I wasn't going to burst into tears or start cursing Wyatt, Lindy and their unborn children, Annalise dropped out of the conversation. She's now talking to the woman on her other side, an accountant who's currently explaining how hard it is to find cross-stitching supplies here in Hanoi. Annalise looks like she's about to fall asleep, which serves her right, the gossipmonger.

Jen, Georgina and I raise our tiny cups. "To fresh starts," says Georgina. By now I feel pleasantly tipsy.

The three of us ride down together in the glass elevator, none of us speaking. In the dark, Hanoi still looks massive and anonymous, lights extending in all directions to the horizon. For every one of those lights I know that there's at least one person out there, maybe reading, or watching TV or driving home from their grandmother's house. The lights twinkle white and red and orange.

As we near ground level the sounds start coming back: first the ear-splitting shriek of truck horns, then the clang of metal from some nearby construction site, then the motorbike horns and engines, the sounds of music, and people yelling, bickering and laughing. Maybe due to the sake or because I've made some new friends, stepping out of that elevator, I feel oddly at home here.

9 Letting Go

The six cardboard boxes that I'd had shipped from New York are now piled in my new living room. I guess it's a good thing that I never got around to unpacking them back at Wyatt's place after all.

I'm sorting through a box of kitchen supplies while Sigrid and her friend Andre are trying to work out how to hook up my TV and DVD player. Andre's boyfriend, Phi, is in the bedroom assembling my newly-bought lotus lamp.

Once the lamp is finished, Phi insists that we all go and look at it. "That lamp is fabulous," he says. "But you need some more throw pillows on the bed. This room needs color."

"And sparkle," says Andre. He puts his hands on his hips and scans the still-bare walls. "You want a harem vibe, jewel colors and exotic patterns. I'm thinking Turkish boudoir…"

"Ooh yes," says Phi. "A four-poster would be perfect. With organza drapes."

"And a velvet duvet!"

Sigrid and I return to the living room. Phi and Andre are busy discussing how many meters of silk would be required to hang billowing swathes of it from my bedroom ceiling. (This is not going to happen). Phi and Andre are as alike as a blond Caucasian and an Asian man in their early thirties could be, both of them having perfect bodies, boyish features and bright, naughty eyes beneath velvety crew cuts. They've been dating for a year and a half and look as if they were made for each other.

Andre and Phi's eagerness to decorate my new place stems from two factors: first, they are so obsessed with style that they can't help themselves; and second, as a friend of Sigrid's, I'm now a friend of theirs by default, and therefore, I can't be living somewhere ugly because it would reflect badly on them.

I return to my cardboard box and pull out a wooden spoon and two spatulas. Sigrid starts to unpack another box. Phi and Andre are still discussing how to sex up my bedroom.

"Where do you want this stuff?" says Sigrid. She holds up a paperweight shaped like Mount Rushmore and a pair of fluffy pink earmuffs.

I shrug. "Toss them over here. All the stuff I don't know what to do with can go to charity." I can't believe that I had these objects sent halfway around the world. In the half year since I packed these things, I haven't thought about any of them. What does this say about me? I throw both of the spatulas onto the charity pile, since I don't cook, then take one out again.

I reach back into my box and pull out a dress, a gift from Wyatt the first Christmas that we were together. The sight of it makes me wistful. Aware of my love of 1920s and 1930s fashions, Wyatt had found this 1930s gown in a vintage clothing store. A long column of sapphire-blue cut velvet decorated with an art deco circle motif,

the dress is perfect—except that it's a size six and I'm a size eight, 10 or 12, depending on how much junk food I've eaten lately and how honest I'm being. I have never been able to fit into it. (When Wyatt gave it to me, I was flattered, since it proved that he thought a size six would actually fit me.)

"Wow," says Sigrid, having noticed what I'm holding. "That's gorgeous. Can I see it?"

I hand it over and she stands up, holding my gown up against her. If the dress were shortened, it might actually fit her.

"It's from the 1930s," I say.

"Nice." She rubs the fabric against her cheek. "This silk velvet feels wonderful. It's in great condition."

Sigrid lays the dress on my sofa and delves back into her box, resurfacing with an ugly pink teddy bear that I won at a fair as a teenager. I pull out a curling iron that I haven't used in at least a decade and a string of plastic worry beads. The charity pile keeps growing.

Some minutes later, Andre and Phi say that they have to get going. I thank them for their help. They say we'll meet soon to discuss their decorating ideas. They exchange air kisses with me and Sigrid.

"They seem like a really good couple," I say, after they've left. The four of us had takeout Thai food for dinner. Sigrid is scraping bits of noodles off of our plates and putting them in the sink to soak. I am making tea, peppermint for me and Earl Grey for Sigrid.

Sigrid turns off the tap. Her thoughtful expression makes me wonder if maybe she doesn't like Phi after all. Sigrid first came to Hanoi to visit Andre, who's lived here for three years. They met in college and have been good friends for more than a decade.

"They are a good couple," she says, and I realize that she's spent the last few minutes considering it. "Phi makes Andre happy and that's a good thing. He deserves it."

The implication that Andre hasn't always been happy takes me by surprise. Phi and Andre, like my sister, exude fabulousness. They're the sort of exceptionally stylish and successful people who seem to sail through life on a stream of lesser mortals' envy.

Sigrid sighs. "Andre's partner Rupert died five years ago. The three of us went to college together." She swallows hard. "Andre and Rupert were soul mates."

I set down the kettle with a clunk. Firstly, I'm stunned to learn that Andre, who seems about as deep as a muffin tin, has lived through a bona fide tragedy. Secondly, I can't believe that Sigrid actually used the term "soul mate". I distinctly remember her scoffing at the concept and stating that sooner or later we'll all run into a few people who are compatible with us.

Sigrid has a faraway look in her eyes. "Rupert was amazing," she says. "They both were. They were together for eight years and I'm sure they'd have spent the next 50 together. They were just so…" She shakes her head, obviously frustrated by her inability to explain what had made Andre and Rupert so special together. "They adored each other." She runs a hand through her hair. There are tears in her eyes.

"How did Rupert die?" I say. Even his name is romantic, in a tragic way. I imagine a pale, fine-featured youth wasting away from consumption.

Hanoi Jane 143

"He had a heart defect that nobody knew about. There were no symptoms. He was really fit. One day he was playing tennis and had a heart attack." She stares up at my empty wall as though a film of Rupert's last tennis game were being projected there. I can see her throat working to damp down a sob.

I hand her a mug of tea. "That's awful," I say, "Poor Andre."

Sigrid manages to tear her eyes from my empty wall. "Yes, after Rupert died, Andre was a mess," she says. "He started taking pain meds to help him sleep. For a while I actually thought he'd end up dead too. He cried all the time. He barely ate."

I try to equate Sigrid's glib, charming friend with the tragic figure that she's describing. "How did he get over it?" I say.

"I don't think he has," she says flatly. "He's just learned to live with it."

"But he seems so…" I shrug. "Happy." Andre's not loud or boisterous but quietly hilarious. He can be mean but is never boring. At a party, he's the guy standing in the corner surrounded by laughing people who all feel a little bit cooler because they know him. If his insouciance is an act, Andre should move to L.A. and get an agent.

"I think he is for the most part," says Sigrid. "But he's totally different from how he was before Rupert died."

Downstairs, one of my landlord's kids is practicing the violin. Luckily, he or she is fairly good at it. "How so?" I say.

Sigrid shuts her eyes as though she's trying to identify the tune. I've heard it before too but can't place it. "Before

Rupert died Andre was doing a PhD in English Literature, about the World War I poet Wilfred Owen."

I rack my memory but draw a blank. Sigrid sighs. "Wilfred Owen was a soldier who wrote about his experiences at the front. His poetry didn't glorify war or extol patriotism but just told it like it was. His poems are amazing and totally, brutally depressing." She reaches for a spoon and stirs some honey into her tea, then licks the spoon. "Wilfred Owen was killed in action a week before the war ended. News of his death reached his family's home just as the village's bells were tolling to celebrate the end of the war."

Since I've never heard Andre talk about anything more serious than what party to attend next weekend, it's hard to imagine him devoting years of his life to studying this doomed poet. Tea in hand, I follow Sigrid into the living room. We sit on the floor because it's cooler and there's stuff all over my sofa.

"After Rupert died, Andre gave up his PhD. He was almost done but he refused to finish it. Then about a year after Rupert's death, he moved here, which is when he started working in PR. He wasn't exactly antisocial before, but he wasn't a party animal either. He's always been funny and outspoken with people he knew, but he used to be really shy around new people."

This academic, introverted version of Andre is hard to equate with the version I've seen, who'll say anything to anybody. I wonder how Phi feels about Andre's lost lover. It'd be pretty tough to compete with a dead soul mate.

When I say this to Sigrid, she shrugs. "Andre appreciates Phi," she says. "I don't think he compares them."

I wonder about this. Did true despair teach Andre to appreciate what he's got? Could I learn the same lesson without somebody I love dying?

After Sigrid has gone home I walk from room to room and close the tall wooden window shutters. I turn on a few table lamps and light some scented candles. It is my first night in my new apartment. Despite the mess, it looks good. I like the periwinkle color that I chose for one of my bedroom walls, and the cheery yellow cupboards in the small kitchen. Since I don't have a lot of furniture, there's a bit of an echo. I put on an Ella Fitzgerald CD for company. That done, I go back to unpacking my cardboard boxes. By the time the last box has been emptied, it's past 11:00.

I'm about to flick off the living room light when I see the cut-velvet dress on my couch, still lying where Sigrid had left it. I pull off my t-shirt and slip the dress over my head, then step out of my shorts and tug the dress down. Since I've lost weight, it actually fits on top. Unfortunately the hips, butt and thighs are a different story.

Since it's too tight to walk in, I hop over to a mirror. I am so close to fitting into it. I wonder how little I'd have to eat to look good in this dress. I spin around. Ella Fitzgerald is singing *Under my skin*, her voice low and plaintive.

A pause in the music is filled with the sound of tearing fabric. I freeze and curse myself.

When I manage to get the dress off, I see that one seam has ripped at hip level. Looking at the frayed fabric, I want to cry. After it's fixed, the dress will be even smaller. I look at the box full of stuff that I've set aside for charity.

I could donate this dress to some good cause or I could give it to Sigrid. She's small. There's a high chance it'd fit her.

Instead, I carry the dress into my bedroom and fit it onto a hanger. I place the hanger at the far end of the closet, right next to the wall. There's a lump in my throat, a lump that's too big to have been caused by a small tear in a dress that I've never worn once in the five-plus years that I've owned it. I shut the closet door but the lump is still there. If anything, it's growing.

It's a hot night. My air-conditioner is humming. Outside, I can hear the buzzing of cicadas. I wonder why I'm so upset. Why am I keeping that dress anyways? Am I holding onto it because it reminds me of Wyatt? Or does some small deluded part of me actually believe that one day I'll be able to wear it?

I open the closet door and pull the dress off of its hanger. The silk velvet feels cool against my arm. I raise it to my cheek. It smells of mothballs. Holding onto this dress is stupid. I'm either trying to cling to a past that is gone or dreaming of a future that won't happen. I carry the dress back out to the living room, drop it onto the sofa, blow out the candles, and walk to the bathroom to get ready for bed.

Sleeping in a new place always feels strange. There are all sorts of unfamiliar sounds: the different tone of the air-conditioner, the on-again, off-again hiss of the cicadas, the creaks of an old house, the muffled sounds of new neighbors. I toss and turn but cannot get comfortable.

After what feels like a long time I get out of bed. The floor tiles are cool beneath my bare feet. The cicadas

have stopped buzzing. The whole neighborhood is quiet. I walk into the living room and pull the dress off of the sofa. In the dark, the velvet looks black. I carry it back into my room and replace it in my closet.

I know that this is wrong. I should give the damn dress to Sigrid. But I still want it, and for all the wrong reasons.

• • •

My landlord, a mathematics professor named Dr. Trung, speaks Vietnamese, English, French, German and Russian. In the typical Vietnamese way, he and his wife and two kids live with his father (his mom passed away) and his two younger brothers and their families. All of these people share a space about one and a half times the size of my flat, located beneath and to one side of me. The entire family is obviously highly educated and cultured. One brother is a physicist and the other a biochemist. The kids, whom I rarely see, seem to spend all of their time studying or practicing the violin.

From what I can see looking down into their courtyard they all get along fine, the only fly in the familial ointment being the octogenarian grandpa. Now retired, this distinguished-looking, white-haired gentleman was once an eminent lawyer. He must have been politically important indeed to have been granted such a fine home in such a central location. Even now, in his late eighties, he has a commanding presence.

The problem, which his eldest son confesses to me when he stops by to collect the rent, is that grandpa has a dark secret. "Has my father asked you for money yet?" says Dr. Trung. Behind thick, tortoiseshell glasses, he looks mortified.

"No," I say, my curiosity piqued. I have only met Dr. Trung's dad once, on which occasion he spoke French to me. I learned French in school but could not claim to speak it. Our conversation had been limited to the basic grilling that all foreigners in Vietnam face when meeting a local for the first time: name, nationality, age, marital status.

Dr. Trung studies the floor tiles, which were undoubtedly installed when the house was first built, back in the 1920s or 1930s. Featuring an art nouveau pattern of wavy yellow and orange lines, the tiles are striking, but I doubt that Dr. Trung is actually seeing them. He clears his throat. "I have a problem with my father," he says. "It is sensitive."

In the close to five months that I've been in Vietnam, I've heard this word on a daily basis. Here, it's not being used to describe teeth or moody kids, but in reference to all of those things that are better left untouched: politics, religion, the rightful ownership of the Spratlys.

"How so?" I say. We are standing in my hallway. I'd invited Dr. Trung to come into the living room and sit but he'd declined, saying that he could only stop for a moment.

If Dr. Trung were wearing a hat he'd now take it off and start ringing it. He is the picture of misery. "He wants money." He hangs his head. No suitable response comes to mind so I keep quiet.

Dr. Trung tries again. "If he comes by to collect the rent money, please do not give it to him. Please make

some excuse, tell him that you do not have it yet…" His voice trails off. The cost of speaking these words aloud is evidently so great that he must steady himself against a wall. This done, he speaks again, his voice little more than a whisper: "This money," he says, "belongs to our family. I use it to buy family things…"

I nod encouragingly.

"My father wants to spend the money on… on something else, something that my brothers and I feel is…" He shudders, the effort of further speech beyond him.

I am so bewildered that I don't know what to say. Dr. Trung is a good man, I am sure of it. He is conscientious at work, patient with his kids, and helps his wife to set the table and take out the garbage. If you were trying to exit a building carrying twin babies and heavy shopping bags, most people in Vietnam would let the door slam in your face, but Dr. Trung would sprint across the room to hold it open for you. If he wants me to pay him instead of his dad, so be it. I did sign my rental contract with Dr. Trung, after all. "Sure," I say. "I'll give the rent money to you. It's not a problem, Dr. Trung."

"My father is not well." He shakes his head sadly.

"I'm sorry to hear that," I say. I wonder what the old dude wants to spend the money on. There are no racetracks or casinos in Hanoi but gamblers will always find some way to gamble. I imagine Dr. Trung's dad buying bushels of lottery tickets or burning cash at some local cock fight. Fast cars, drugs and hookers seem unlikely, given that the sinner in question is in his late eighties.

I figure that the conversation is over but all of a sudden Dr. Trung starts to talk. A couple of years ago I was on a plane from New York to Chicago and the lady beside me spent the entire flight telling me about her ex-husband's battle with sex addiction. As she went into increasingly graphic detail I just sat there, stunned, because she was a well-dressed, nice-looking older lady, who certainly didn't look the type to go around sharing intimate details with total strangers. Thinking about it later, I figured that the fact that she didn't know me and would probably never see me again had allowed her to unburden herself. As the plane was coming in to land she'd admitted that she'd told me stuff that she hadn't even shared with her therapist. She looked so stricken that I believed her.

Standing in my hallway, Dr. Trung has the same dazed look as that divorcee on my flight to Chicago. "My father has a girlfriend," he says. "She lives in Saigon. He sends money to her. It's been going on for years, even back when my mother was alive. We don't know what to do about it. He gives her whatever she asks for."

I am, and do my best to look, sympathetic. As he keeps talking—about the family heirlooms that his dad has pawned, the times that Pop has vanished only to resurface, following their frantic search, in Saigon—I try to imagine the woman who's responsible for this turmoil. I recall a photo of Anna Nicole Smith leaning over her decrepit billionaire husband, each of Anna's breasts appearing about twice as large as her hubby's bald, liver-spotted head. I don't know if that old guy had any kids, but if he did, I bet they looked as worried as Dr. Trung here.

"We have endured this for more than 40 years!" says Dr. Trung, and I reassess my portrait of his dad's girlfriend.

"How old is she?" I say.

"Seventy-nine!" says Dr. Trung. "And my dad's 88. Can you believe it?"

Later that evening, I recount the tale to Sigrid over the telephone.

"Hmph," she says, when I get to the part about Gramps' and his girlfriend's respective ages. "It's always the same old story, isn't it?"

"What do you mean?" I say.

"I mean that it's always some younger woman."

"She's 79," I say, wondering if Sigrid had misheard me.

"That's 11 years younger than him!" says Sigrid. "She's practically a spring chicken."

I shake my head in disbelief. "You're missing the point, Sig," I say.

"Which is?"

"That they're still at it!" I say. "This man is 88 years old and still chasing some woman."

"He's been at it for at least 40 years!" says Sigrid. "Why's he going to change now?"

It is dark outside. I stare down into Dr. Trung's unlit courtyard. "What happened to old and wise?" I say indignantly.

"The only way that people change is if they get too tired or bored to keep going," says Sigrid.

"What about Andre?" I say. "You told me that he's changed."

"Okay, you're right. Major tragedies can cause *some* people to change. But most people just keep doing the same things over and over again until they get sick of them."

I wonder if Wyatt's taking up with Lindy counts as a tragedy. "I don't get it," I say. "The old guy's wife is dead. Why don't he and his mistress just make it official so that his family will stop hassling them?"

"Maybe she's married to somebody else," says Sigrid. "Or maybe they just like it this way."

That night I dream about Dr. Trung's dad and his septuagenarian mistress. They are in an old-fashioned dance hall, dancing a tango, and Wyatt and I are dancing beside them. I am having trouble following the steps and keep apologizing. "I'm tired," says Wyatt. Then he turns and strides from the dance floor, leaving me standing there, alone and mortified.

The next thing I know Dr. Trung's dad has grabbed me and is twirling me around. "You're practically a spring chicken!" he says, as we spin faster and faster.

At that point I wake up, my heart pounding. The bed sheets have gotten wrapped around my feet. It takes me a few panicky moments to squirm free of them.

Lying in the dark I think of Dr. Trung, his dad and his dad's lady friend. I think of Dr. Trung's wife, who died two years ago, and feel sad for all four of them.

I think of all the wasted energy, people loving each other and not loving each other, everyone worrying about it. And I remember what Sigrid said about people not changing until they're too tired or bored to go on. Am I doomed to keep making the same mistakes? I feel tired of myself and my endless worrying.

10 Makeovers

As pleased as I am with my new apartment, the closer it gets to my intended wedding day, the sadder I feel. The day that Wyatt and I should have returned to North Carolina came and went, and now it's the night of my planned bachelorette party. Wallowing in solo misery seems like a good option, but Sigrid and a few other friends won't hear of it. Despite my obvious reluctance, they invite themselves over to my place for Classic Movie Night.

At just after 6:00, Sigrid, Andre and Phi show up bearing a stack of Chinese counterfeit DVDs and two bottles of merlot. Jen from the Professional Women's group and her friend Allyson arrive next, armed with microwave popcorn and more wine, followed by my assistant Tuyet, carrying a shrink-wrapped fruit basket.

As Tuyet and I unpack takeaway pizzas and Caesar salads in the kitchen, the rest of the gang debates which movie to watch. Andre and Phi want *Some Like it Hot* and Sigrid is keen to see *Bladerunner*. Allyson, who works for UNICEF, suggests *There's Something About Mary*, but that's nixed as being too recent to qualify as a classic. By the time that the food and drinks are distributed the choice has been made. We're to see *Dirty Dancing*.

I take a slice of sausage pizza and sit back to watch the movie. Phi clicks off the lights and Sigrid throws me a pillow. I am glad that they're here after all.

I was 12 years old the last time that I saw Baby and Johnny Castle dance. Just as the plot comes back to me, so does that night. There I am, dressed in hideously unflattering purple stirrup pants and a loose aqua top, sitting in the Odeon Café with my then-best-friend, Leanne Miller, and her sister Tiffany, who is almost 15. The movie has just ended and we are waiting for Leanne and Tiffany's mom to pick us up in her gold Camaro, my head still swimming with sultry dance scenes and the thrill of having seen a PG movie.

"That was so unrealistic," scoffs Tiffany, scanning the café for patrons with more to offer than me and Leanne. "I mean, as if those two would be together in real life."

I wait for Leanne to ask what she means, but she doesn't, so I have no choice but to request clarification. "Because Baby's family was rich and Johnny wasn't?" I say, dismayed that Tiffany—the epitome of teenage cool—isn't as enraptured with *Dirty Dancing* as I am.

"No," says Tiffany, her scorn now as thick as her turquoise eyeliner. "Because Patrick Swayze is, like, so much hotter than that Jennifer chick. He's like, gorgeous."

"What's wrong with her?" I ask, a wave of uneasiness causing me to set down my vanilla milkshake. I thought Jennifer Grey was amazing, especially in that dance scene in the lake, but Tiffany Miller's opinion cannot be discounted. She has all of the teenage cool boxes ticked: big hair, big boobs and a face that veers effortlessly from blinking-Bambi-innocence to sly, been-there-done that cynicism.

"She isn't pretty enough for him," says Tiffany flatly. "They so chose the wrong actress."

Hanoi Jane 155

"Jennifer Grey is pretty," I say, but it comes out more like a wish than a declaration, a wish that has nothing to do with Jennifer Grey and everything to do with me, round-faced, flat-chested Jane Moxley.

"Her nose *is* pretty big," says Leanne.

I flush with outrage. Leanne had seemed as enchanted with Baby and Johnny as I was. Betrayal causes the milkshake to curdle in my stomach.

Looking back, I see that that night marked the beginning of the end of a Friendship Era, since for the past year Leanne had already been too cool for me, and the glue of childhood-friend-loyalty was almost out of stickiness. Perhaps sitting there in the Odeon Café I already sensed this, for I was destined to become a Nerd and Leanne, like her sister, a Popular Girl, or at least until she got pregnant and dropped out of school in her senior year, which is when I lost track of her.

That night after first watching *Dirty Dancing* I didn't know Leanne's fate, or mine, for that matter. All I knew is that my looks, like Jennifer's, didn't fit the teen definition of pretty. Teenagers don't value faces with character. They don't value any deviation from the norm, which explains Miley Cyrus.

This is what I'm thinking about as the credits roll, as Sigrid turns on the lights and Phi and Andre stretch and Allyson gets up to use the bathroom. "Did you like it?" I ask Tuyet, for she is the only one of us who has never seen *Dirty Dancing* before.

"Yes," she says. "But I don't think it would work between them, Baby and Johnny, I mean."

I steel myself. "Why not?" I say.

"They come from different worlds," she says. "It would be too difficult."

I consider this, my thoughts drifting to Wyatt and me, who come from the same world and have failed anyway.

Then Andre asks whatever happened to Jennifer Grey.

"She's been in a few other things," says Jen. "But *Dirty Dancing* was her biggest hit."

I wonder if that's because the movie-going public is dominated by Tiffany Millers, or because of some other factor. Maybe Jennifer just got sick of Hollywood and went off to do other things that were even more fabulous.

That night, after everyone has left, I Google Jennifer Grey. I see that she was engaged to Matthew Broderick and Johnny Depp, which sounds vaguely familiar, and that at some point in the early 1990s she got a nose job. There's an "After" photo in which she looks pretty in a standard way, although her eyes still look smarter than those of most Hollywood starlets and her smile more sardonic. Looking at this pretty, alert woman I can't help but feel a bit sad that she no longer resembles my teen heroine. I feel like she sold out to a beauty standard that, seen from the relative wisdom of my late twenties, looks banal and boring.

But then I think that I'm just being selfish and hypocritical too, because if you offered me my sister Lauren's cheekbones or Tiffany's much-admired teenage boobs, would I turn my nose up at them? No. I can't help but think that maybe with those features Wyatt would still want me.

I am almost asleep when I recall an article that I read years ago in *The Economist*, a magazine that Wyatt subscribes to. The story, which was short, had recounted how a team of ornithologists (who presumably had nothing better to do) had placed tall red hats on the heads of some male finches, then turned the birds loose to see what would happen.

What soon became clear was that the males wearing red hats were much more popular with the lady finches, an attraction that had the scientists baffled. The females should have been drawn to inheritable traits like strength, agility and speed, but instead they were going for males in totally useless red Pope hats, which, if anything, would have added risk by attracting the attention of hawks and owls.

So why were the hat-wearing finches getting more love than normal? The conclusion, which you don't need a PhD to reach, was that the males wearing hats stood out. I guess that those female finches were all looking for someone out of the ordinary.

Stretched out in my big new bed, I wonder why I'm thinking about those finches. What lessons do those hat-loving birds hold for me, or is this train of thought, and indeed the entire finch study, totally pointless?

Then I get it: I don't have the guts to undergo plastic surgery like Jennifer Grey. For starters, I'm scared of the pain. And as much as I'd like bigger boobs, a refined little nose or Lauren-like cheek implants, I don't think that fake ones would work well on me. But the status quo isn't flying either. If I want to regain Wyatt's attention, I'm going to have to try harder. I have to make him see that I'm special.

Hugging my pillow, my mind fills with frisky finches.

What I need is a new hat.

• • •

Chic! runs makeovers in every issue and, more often than not, I think that they're total scams. First, you take a pretty girl with unwashed, unbrushed hair and no makeup and photograph her straight-on in sweat pants looking sullen. Then you turn a crew of hair and makeup professionals loose on her, dress her up in designer clothes, pose her at an angle so that she looks slimmer, and tell her to smile. Voila! She looks better.

Except that about a third of the time she doesn't look better at all, merely stunned, as though she's nodded off to sleep and woken up in someone else's clothes wearing far too much makeup and hair product. So despite my resolve to improve my appearance, I am nervous. I don't want to end up like one of those uncomfortable 'After' girls, who you know will run home and shower, then get back into her sweats and wear a hat until her absurdly trendy haircut grows out.

For help, I have turned to the most style-conscious people I know, Phi and Andre. Beautiful themselves, they have opinions about everything related to appearance, and aren't afraid to voice them. "This color is so wrong for you," says Phi, fingering a strand of my hair as if it were a limp lettuce leaf. "It washes you out. You need to go brighter."

Since I've had this color all of my life, my heart sinks. Why, in 29 years, have I failed to realize this?

We are in Phi's salon, which is full of photos of Phi and Andre posing with similarly beautiful people. Sigrid and Andre are lounging on a black sofa eyeing me thoughtfully.

Hanoi Jane 159

I am sitting in a swivel chair, my jeans and t-shirt covered by a giant plastic poncho. "Blonder?" says Andre.

"No, red," says Phi.

Sigrid and Andre nod, as though the meaning of life were suddenly clear to them. "Yeah," says Andre. "She'd be great as a redhead." The plastic poncho, like a hospital robe, seems to have rendered me invisible, since my friends are behaving like medical staff and talking about me as if I weren't present.

"*Red*?" I say. What I mean is: *I don't think so*. I can count the number of attractive redheads that I've seen in my whole life on one hand. When they do look good, they are stunning. But most of them? I don't see why I'd go there.

"It is such a hot color," says Phi. "So now."

Andre and Sigrid are still nodding like holy rollers at a revivalists' meeting. I turn to study myself in the mirror. Do they see something that I'm missing? "Um, what kind of red?" I say. "Strawberry blonde?"

"No, red red," says Phi. "Like that model, you know, what's her name?" He waves his fingers around as though he's burned them.

"The tall, thin teenage one," I say, trying to be funny, but Phi, Sigrid and Andre just stare at me blankly until Andre yells: "Lily Cole!" They all nod happily.

As Phi mixes up the dye, he, Andre and Sigrid chat about a mutual acquaintance who is pregnant with her third son. I don't really listen. Phi starts to spread the dye onto my hair and I wish that I hadn't agreed to this. I pretend to read an old copy of *In Style* but am unable to concentrate, my thoughts turning to every style blunder that I've ever made, practically all of which are recorded in my parents' oversized family photo album.

Every time I go home my dad hauls this album out of the liquor cabinet. If we're alone, it is bad enough. If we have guests, it is mortifying. I know, you probably think that I'm exaggerating; everyone has embarrassing childhood photographs, especially if they were alive in the 1970s and 1980s. What you don't understand is that my obsessively fashionable mother insisted on dressing us in the year's hottest trends, which unfailingly suited Lauren and made me look as if I'd been found wandering the streets suffering from amnesia and dressed in a circus troupe's castoffs. There I am, small and pigeon-toed in bell-bottoms, awkward in puff skirts, ridiculous in Madonna-style lace gloves and shoulder pads... What stays constant, besides my pained expression, is my hairdo: plain, shoulder-length with straight-across bangs. I've always *hated* going to the hairdresser.

The one and only time that I got anything more than a trim was in 1989, when I was 14 and desperate to look more grown up. With no breasts I had to do *something* to signal that I was no longer a little kid, and what I chose to do was to get a perm. Anyone too young to remember 1980s perms is blessed. This was the era of big, blocky crinkle perms and Pac Man bangs, so named because half of the top layer of bangs was teased straight up and the other half was sprayed stiff and left to cover the forehead, like the open jaws of a Pac Man.

When Leanne Miller, who was by then way too cool to be my friend, saw my new 'do she dubbed it "instant noodle hair", probably the most accurate and witty observation that she's come up with to date (not that I'm bitter).

The phrase stuck and I spent the next six months washing my hair several times a day in a bid to get rid of that tenacious ripple. Never again, I told myself, and yet here I am, 15 years later, having a foul-smelling paste rubbed onto my head and wishing that I hadn't succumbed, yet again, to peer pressure.

The process seems to take forever. Sigrid, Phi and Andre go out for coffee, leaving me in the care of Phi's androgynous assistant, who surfaces every five minutes to prod at my scalp as though my head is a cake that he's baking. Finally I'm deemed done and led off to the hair-wash station, where yet another young, black-clad gay man massages my head for 20 minutes. The massage is so relaxing that I forget why I'm here, and it's in this dazed, blissed-out state that I catch sight of myself in one of the salon's countless mirrors.

Back when I was a kid, my Uncle Dwayne had an Irish setter named Pluto, a dog so dumb that at the age of 10 I resolved to never, ever get a canine that was any sort of purebred. Give me a smart, ugly mutt any day! When Pluto wasn't drooling or sniffing his crotch, he was launching himself into Uncle Dwayne's swimming pool, from which he'd scrabble out and shake himself all over me. Looking into the mirror is like seeing my long-forgotten nemesis. My hair is the exact same shade as a sopping wet Pluto.

"Ooh!" says Andre.

Sigrid looks thoughtful. When I try to meet her eye, she looks away.

"Now for the cut!" says a freshly-caffeinated Phi, waving the hairdresser's poncho as if I'm a stray sheep that he's trying to herd towards his swivel chair. I eye the door as if to bolt but know that it's too late. I should have had the guts to speak up an hour and a half ago.

The moment that my buttocks touch the seat Phi swivels the chair so that the mirror is behind me. Sigrid and Andre have resumed their positions on the sofa. They have brought me back a Highlands ice latte, for which I am pathetically grateful. No matter what happens, at least I'll be high on caffeine. I toss in some sugar. "Just a trim," I say.

Phi ignores me.

I try again. "Don't take too much off." I form a narrow U with my thumb and forefinger to demonstrate.

Phi makes an impatient noise, like I'm ruining his concentration. Light flashes off of his scissors.

Upsetting someone who is wielding scissors a few millimeters from my ear seems unwise, so I keep quiet and stay as still as possible. The scissors make a humming sound. Kelis is promoting her milkshake over the stereo.

The poncho and the surrounding floor are soon coated with tiny red hairs. I clear my throat. "Not too short," I say. "That seems like a lot already."

"I'm almost done," says Phi. "Hold on a minute."

After Phi has set down his scissors, his assistant reappears, armed with gel and a blowdrier. I am subjected to an age of hot air and vigorous brushing, and then Phi takes control of the blowdrier, presumably to put the finishing touches on his oeuvre. I study Sigrid's face for clues as to just how bad it is, but she is uncharacteristically stone-faced.

This can only mean one thing: I look horrendous.

"Ta da," says Phi. He spins my chair to face the mirror.

My first impulse is to laugh, mostly with relief, since it's not as bad as it could have been. Does it suit me? Not at all. But I think it's salvageable.

The red—now like Pluto's fur when dry—seems to drain all color from my face, while the sweeping, asymmetrical bangs might look good in a magazine but would drive me crazy. After a few hours of trying to push that hair out of my left eye I'd surely end up with an eye infection.

"So what do you think?" says Phi.

I look at Sigrid. She frowns and I know that she's torn between telling the truth and trying to be diplomatic. Then she shakes her head. "I don't know," she says. "It just doesn't seem quite right for you."

Phi looks outraged. "It is so cute on her," he says. Then Andre shakes his head too and Phi stops talking.

I squint into the mirror. I feel bad that Phi went to all of this trouble to create something that I'm not cool enough to carry off. Why is it that every absurd Back to School outfit that my mom bought made Lauren a trendsetter while I simply looked like I was trying too hard? "It's too trendy for me," I say glumly. "Maybe if you straighten out the bangs?"

"And tone down that red," says Sigrid. "Strawberry blonde might be better on Jane after all."

By the time I get out of the salon it is dark. I have wasted an entire day in there. Well, maybe not wasted, because my hair has a few more face-framing layers than it did and has gone from dirty blonde to a shade somewhere between honey and chestnut. I think it looks nice but most people, I am sure, will fail to notice.

"You look good," says Sigrid, after she's dropped me off in front of my apartment. We have just gone out for beef noodle soup and reek of garlic.

"Thanks," I say. I toss my head like a girl in a shampoo commercial. Sigrid revs her motorbike's engine and waves at me, then heads off towards her place.

Climbing the stairs to my apartment, I feel lucky. My hair didn't turn green. Clumps didn't fall out. Considering that I ignored my intuition and caved to a style that is so now and so not me, I got off lightly.

I head for the shower, then change my mind and retrieve my digital camera from my closet. Figuring out the various settings is something that I've failed to do, since I always used to ask Wyatt to set it up for me. Through trial and error I finally manage to set the self timer, then position the camera on a bookcase in such a way that it's pointing at the sofa. I hit the self timer button, sprint to the sofa and pose, over and over again until finally, I get a shot that's half decent.

Although it's late, before getting ready for bed I type out an email to my dad and send the photo of me as an attachment. I imagine him going to Kerr Drug to get the photo developed, then pasting it into the family album. I doubt that he'll actually do this but it's a nice thought.

Before shutting down the computer I take one last look at the photo. While my face is sweaty following repeated sprints to the sofa, my hair looks shiny and I'm smiling.

Hanoi Jane 165

. . .

I drive down Ngo Quyen Street, an ironing board, a bulk pack of toilet paper and a bag of kitty litter strapped to the back of my Vespa. I've just come from the supermarket.

I'm almost home when I remember that my fridge contains nothing but Diet Coke and ketchup. Luckily, I'm just a few blocks from one of my favorite restaurants, a small Thai place where Wyatt and I were regulars. They serve the best pad thai, papaya salad and crab cakes in town. While going there solo feels sad, hunger wins over self-pity.

I step into the restaurant and the waitress smiles at me. "Oh hello," she says. "Table for two?" A plump, cheerful young woman, she motions towards my and Wyatt's favorite table.

"No, takeaway tonight," I say. It's still early enough for the restaurant to be mostly empty.

"The usual?"

I shake my head. "No, just for one."

She nods. "Is your husband away on business?"

Before I can answer the door swings open, causing some door chimes to jangle madly. I look up and freeze. It's Wyatt.

He looks equally surprised to see me, and not in a good way. "Uh, hi Jane," he says. Wyatt has clearly just come from work, since he's wearing his banker's uniform of grey pants, white shirt and red striped tie.

"Hi," I say, my throat too constricted to get anything else out.

No doubt noticing our discomfiture, the waitress

looks confused. "So, usual table?" she asks again, this query now directed at both of us.

"No," I say. "Just a *pad thai* and one *som tum* to go."

Wyatt casts a worried look at the door, which is when I realize that he's expecting someone. My heart sinks even lower. I bet he's waiting for Lindy. "How's Grannie Beryl?" I ask, more for something to say than because I'm genuinely concerned. Given the way that my heart is pounding I'm sure that Beryl is healthier than I am.

"She's doing well," says Wyatt. "The doctors called it a miracle." He checks his watch and clears his throat, his eyes sliding towards the exit as though his pupils are magnets and the door made of solid iron. There are two crescents of sweat under his arms.

I realize that in a strange, nasty way, I'm enjoying seeing Wyatt acting so nervous. "So, are you expecting someone?" I say innocently.

"Yes, yes, I am," says Wyatt. He licks his lips. "I'm meeting Lindy, if you must know." He sounds defensive.

"So you're still with her," I say. "She sure is popular."

"What's that supposed to mean?" he snaps, then holds up a hand. "No, forget I asked. I can't believe that you're being so…" Hand fluttering, he searches for the right word. "So juvenile."

Watching Wyatt's fluttering hand it occurs to me that my mom is right: He does have gay mannerisms. "Wyatt," I say. "Are you gay?"

He scowls at me. "Am I what?"

"Gay," I say. "Homosexual."

He shakes his head irritably. "Really, Jane, you're behaving like a spoiled 14-year-old."

"I'm serious," I say. "And it's not like there's anything *wrong* with being gay, Wyatt. Some of my best friends are gay. I was just wondering, that's all."

"I am *not* gay," says Wyatt. He peers towards the door again. "What are you talking about anyways? I mean, come on, how long have you known me?"

"I don't think I know you at all," I say. "I just thought I did."

Wyatt tugs at his ear. "Just because I don't want to be with *you* doesn't mean I'm gay."

I shrug and smile sweetly. "Sure, whatever you say, Wyatt."

From the constipated look on his face I know that I've finally gotten to him in a way that I never could with tears, admonishments, or hysterics. While I know that Wyatt isn't gay, it seems that he's insecure enough to fear looking gay. He looks ready to have a coronary.

The waitress, evidently still confused, hands me a bag of food and then passes the bill to Wyatt. I smile broadly. "Aw, thanks Wyatt," I say, then turn to go before he has time to say anything. I hear what sounds like someone choking behind me but keep walking.

As I push open the restaurant's door I feel positively buoyant. I have faced Wyatt without crying, begging or otherwise making a total fool of myself. I feel invincible. I walk towards my motorbike with a new spring in my step. If I had curls they would be bouncing.

I'm just maneuvering my Vespa off of the curb when a large, fancy new scooter pulls up. Without even having to look up, I know that it's Lindy Tran. Dressed in short shorts and a tank top she looks like an Asian Barbie doll, her long hair newly curled into perfect, inky ringlets. All of my bravado melts into a puddle of angst. I wish that I could sink into the pavement.

Instead of looking directly at me she looks at my luggage rack, taking in the ironing board, the toilet paper, the kitty litter. She looks at these items as though they reveal everything there is to know about me, as though such things have no place in her perfect world of glamour and romance. And then she sweeps past me.

That I manage to kick-start my Vespa on the first try really *is* a miracle—a much bigger one than the fact that tough old Granny Beryl is still breathing. But even though I'm grateful for this little miracle, as the bike picks up speed I start crying. Why doesn't Wyatt love me? I feel old and alone and pitiful. I cry all of the way home but at least it's dark and no one can see me.

11 The Relapse

I'm well aware that there are real tragedies in this world: pregnant women felled by drunk drivers; downed passenger jets; entire families buried by mudslides. On the scale of human hardship, my situation doesn't even warrant a One, and yet, knowing that others have it worse doesn't make me feel any better.

If anything, this awareness adds to my misery, since, as well as feeling unloved and humiliated by my recent breakup, I must face the fact that I'm a drama queen who should just buck up and get on with it. I have all of my limbs, after all, and am, so far as I know, physically healthy.

So call me a complainer, but this has been the worst month of my life, and tonight and tomorrow promise to be even tougher. It's August 14th, the night before what should have been my wedding day.

Eight days from now my parents will arrive. This means that I have one week to get my new apartment and new life into order, and to grieve my old one. My plan for this weekend was to stay home alone, eat ice cream and watch artsy European films that end badly. I intended to cry copiously in a bid purge all self-pity from my system. But for better or for worse Sigrid has nixed this idea and insisted that I go out, for tonight is the highlight of Hanoi's expat calendar.

Since Hanoi's few bars and nightclubs tend to shut at midnight, the city's *bon vivants* have been forced to make their own fun. Held once a year, the Blue Fantasy Ball is part costume party, part rave and part Moulin Rouge-style stage show, the latter performed by a bunch of elaborately dolled-up gay guys. Phi is one of the performers and Andre an organizer. All of their fabulous friends are, naturally, in attendance.

In line with tonight's theme, which is 'Diamonds', Sigrid and I are dressed as cat burglars in tight black jumpsuits and slim-fitting hoods that leave only our eyes exposed. Vodka sevens in hand, we are craning our necks to see the stage, where a young man dressed as Marilyn Monroe is singing Happy Birthday Mr. President. The song over, a dance number starts up, three strapping young fellows cavorting on stage clad in nothing but gold briefs and body paint.

Since it's hard to see the stage I turn to survey the crowd. Katy Demoines of the NGO Resource Center waves at me from her perch on top of a speaker. My friends Jen and Allyson are at the opposite end of the room, dressed in fake furs and tiaras. It seems that everyone I've ever met in Hanoi is here, many of them barely recognizable in their costumes. How some of these get-ups relate to diamonds is anyone's guess. I spy fairies, pirates, a gorilla and a banana, along with an entire troupe of Indian maharajas and three rhinestone cowboys.

"I'm going to the bathroom," I tell Sigrid. "Want me to get you another drink on the way back?"

Having arrived fairly late we're a lot more sober than most people here. Half of the crowd appears blind drunk

and the other half seems to have consumed some pill or another, likely obtained without a prescription at their local pharmacy.

"Sure, another vodka seven would be great," says Sigrid. She runs a hand through her hair. We've both removed our cat-burglar hoods since they made drinking impossible.

I down the last of my vodka and replace my hood, then wade through a throng of bodies towards the exit.

Beside the door sit three folding chairs occupied by three middle-aged Vietnamese guys. Dressed in grey pants, white shirts, shiny black shoes and white sports socks, they all have Lego-man haircuts with low side parts. Two out of the three are wearing square, thick-framed glasses.

Just by looking at them I know that they work for the Ministry of Culture and are here to keep an eye on things. All three have a glass in one hand and a cigarette in the other. They all share an expression of slack-jawed incomprehension. I wonder what Mr. Thai's doing tonight.

Turning to look back at the stage I see a row of guys who look like beautiful girls dancing the cancan in fish-net tights and tutus. Watching this spectacle the Ministry of Culture minders look neither impressed nor upset but merely baffled.

I step into a long corridor. There are less people out here but it's still fairly crowded, party-goers who've tired of the stage show standing around chatting, smoking and drinking.

The Ball is being held in the ballroom of a state-run hotel that was built in the 1970s to house a visiting Fidel Castro. Designed in a blocky Soviet style, the lobby features oversized rattan armchairs, chandeliers made of seashells, and a row of clocks that show the time in Hanoi, Moscow, Beijing, Berlin and Havana. Beneath the smell of cigarette smoke there's an underlying odor of mold and mothballs.

Since there's a long line outside the bathroom closest to the ballroom I go in search of another one. The further I walk the less people I see, until I'm wandering down hallways so dim and devoid of decoration that it's like being in a penitentiary. I wonder if any guests have actually stayed here since Mr. Castro.

By the time I do find a washroom and start to make my way back, a good 15 minutes have elapsed. I bet that Sigrid is wondering what the hell happened to me. All of the corridors look exactly the same and I start to worry that I'm walking in circles. The air-conditioning is lousy back here and my polyester jumpsuit doesn't breathe. I peel off my black hood and use it to fan myself.

I'm considering retracing my steps when I turn a corner and see a bunch of guys dressed up as women. But unlike the cross-dressers in the stage show, this bunch looks neither convincing nor beautiful. I wonder why so many seemingly ordinary straight guys are so eager to dress up like hookers.

Seeing me, a tall, gangly guy in a pink bustier and blonde wig waves: "Hey Jane!" he says. "How's it going?"

"Brian?" I say. "I didn't recognize you." A couple of weeks after arriving in Hanoi Wyatt and I had met Brian and his fiancée Julia at a house party. Their wedding is the week after ours was supposed to be, so we'd all bonded by bitching about the stress of wedding-planning.

"It's my stag," says Brian. He motions to his outfit and looks apologetic. "This get-up wasn't my idea." He tries to tug up his bustier.

"Oh right," I say. Looking at Brian and his stag mates all decked out in bras and far too much makeup I feel my throat constrict. It's not fair that a week from now Julia will be walking down the aisle looking like a princess while my nuptials are on hold, perhaps indefinitely.

The idea that Brian might be aware of my situation and feeling sorry for me causes my brain to freeze. I can't think of anything to say. Brian seems tongue-tied too. "So, uh, where's Julia?" I finally mumble.

Brian readjusts his wig. "Oh, her sister's here visiting and they went to Hoi An for the weekend."

"Right," I say. "Nice." I feel like a total loser. I don't know if it's the look on Brian's face or something else that causes me to turn but when I do, I see Wyatt.

"Um, hi Jane," he says.

Brian looks stricken. "So uh, great to see ya, Jane." He bids as hasty a retreat as his high-heels will allow. Judging by Brian's excessively hearty tone and his eagerness to teeter out of here, I guess that he does know about Wyatt and me after all. I'm so flustered that I can barely wave at him.

Wyatt, who hasn't smoked in years, is attempting to light a cigarette. Dressed in a tight red dress that I've never seen before, he is obviously and sloppily drunk. When he asks what my costume is supposed to be it comes out as: "Wash-oor-cosh-choom-Chane?"

"I'm a jewel thief," I say as haughtily as I can. "And who are you meant to be, Wyatt?"

He twirls around shakily and grins. "I'm a lay-dee."

I'm not used to seeing Wyatt dressed in drag or looking and acting so goofy. Part of me wants to smack him and part of me wants to throw myself against his spandex-covered chest and sob.

"How ya been?" he says. He looks genuinely interested.

"Okay," I say warily. I ask how he's been, aware that I should probably just walk away. Being near him is too difficult. I have too many questions swirling around in my head, starting with whose hideous dress is he wearing, anyways? I feel as though anything that he says or fails to say could push me over the edge to hysteria.

Wyatt seems to be working out how best to answer. I wait, steeling myself. Maybe he'll say that he's great, that he and Lindy are deliriously happy, or maybe he'll tell me that he was wrong and that he can't live without me.

"This makeup is making my face itch," he says. He rubs at one stubbly cheek. "It's really disgusting, ya know?"

My heart plummets. "Uh, yeah," I say. "Look Wyatt, I better get going now."

"No," he says. "No Jane, wait, please."

That forlorn 'please' causes my heart to bounce up and whack me in the chin. I'm too stunned to move away from him.

"I-I...we should talk." He looks beseeching.

I'm sober enough to know that this is a bad idea. Wyatt is far too drunk to be doing anything besides sleeping it off. What he needs is a couple of Ibuprofen, a tumbler full of water and some makeup remover—not a serious conversation with his heartbroken on-hold fiancée.

"What about?" I hear myself say.

He tugs at the hem of his stretchy dress. "About everything."

Brian and the other guys have vanished, the hallway empty. From around another corner come the sounds of drunken voices and laughter. I lean up against the wall and so does Wyatt, a few feet of naked cement between us.

"I, uh, miss you," he says.

The word 'miss' comes out as 'mish' but I don't care. I tilt my head forward and screw my eyes shut. A couple of tears squeeze out. I don't even know why I'm crying, just that I feel too much sadness, relief and fear to hold myself together.

"No, don't cry," says Wyatt. He raises a hand and strokes my hair, running his fingers through it. I raise my head and he massages my neck. And then he kisses me.

He tastes like booze and cigarettes, a fairly nasty taste, but I keep kissing him anyways. When we stop, I lean back and look at him. His eyes are unfocused but he's grinning.

I want to ask what this means. Is it over between Lindy and him? Has he decided who he wants? Can our life go back to normal?

I hold my tongue because I'm scared that he'll step away from me, scared that he'll say that he needs more time, that he doesn't know yet. It's so much nicer to just shut my eyes and allow him to pull me closer.

He asks if I want to get going and I nod. All thoughts of the Blue Fantasy Ball and Sigrid still waiting for her vodka seven have evaporated. When we start walking it's as if some miraculous force is guiding us through this maze of corridors, the universe ensuring that we'll have an easy passage back to our rightful place, together. Or at least that's how it feels to me. I am giddy with happiness.

I'm wearing higher heels than I normally wear and Wyatt is staggering from side to side, but before we know it, we have found the exit. We manage to get a taxi without having to call for one, another sign that this is meant to be. And then all of the traffic lights are green and our driver—unlike most—actually knows how to work the gearshift. Talk about miracles! We don't have to stop once. The taxi glides through the dark empty streets of Hanoi and Wyatt keeps kissing me.

Then the ride is over and I'm standing outside of Wyatt's house—our house—and Wyatt is trying to unlock the two padlocks. "You do it," he says, after he's dropped the keys a couple of times. Sure enough, both locks spring open as though they've been waiting for my touch. I step inside and Fergus bolts out. But then he stops, turns around and stares at me. I figure that he's happy to see us reunited.

Wyatt and I climb the stairs together, Wyatt pausing on the second floor landing to tug off his mini-dress and toss it over the railing. We kiss again, a bit more sloppily than I'd like but it doesn't matter because we're going upstairs to our bedroom and our bed. Wyatt's body feels totally, wonderfully familiar and yet exciting and strange to me. I am desperately happy.

The sex isn't great since he's too drunk to get very hard and falls asleep partway through. But I don't care, really.

It is lovely just to lie in his arms and to feel his breath on the top of my head, to know that when I

wake up everything will be back to normal and we'll be together again.

I fall asleep thinking of our wedding. We'll have to wait until there's a cancellation at the country club since it's booked solid for the next year straight, but sooner or later some other bride and groom will pull out and then we'll be ready to go. I see the tables with their antique pink tablecloths and myself smiling in my silk dress and tiara. I see Wyatt's hand on mine as we push the knife through the cake, slicing through the layers of cream and sponge as easily if they weren't there, then laughing and licking the icing off of our fingers. I can practically taste it.

• • •

When I wake up the bed—our bed—contains only me. I go to the bathroom and wash my face, then borrow Wyatt's toothbrush and brush my teeth. Given how drunk Wyatt was last night I'm amazed that he woke up before me. I figure he's downstairs downing cup after cup of black coffee.

Since all of my clothes are now at my new place I put on one of Wyatt's shirts. My cat burglar jumpsuit is lying like an oil spill on the floor. I pick it up and sniff it, then drop it again. It smells of sweat and cigarettes.

After turning off the air-conditioner I go downstairs to find Wyatt. I hope that he's made breakfast. I am hungry.

The more stairs I descend the unlikelier this seems since there's no smell of frying eggs or toast or pancakes. I can't even smell coffee brewing. When I peer over the railing I see Wyatt sitting at the kitchen table with his head in his hands. "Wyatt?" I say. He looks up blearily.

I ask how it's going and he shrugs. "I'm hungover," he says.

"Yeah," I say. "I figured you would be."

He says he was really drunk. I ask if he wants coffee and he nods. "Coming right up," I say.

To get to the coffee maker I have to walk past the table and when I do, I bend to kiss Wyatt. I don't expect a big kiss back since, for all I know, he hasn't even brushed his teeth yet, but I do expect a little close-mouthed kiss or a peck on the cheek or one of those affectionate, unremarkable touches that couples exchange all the time without even thinking about it.

Instead Wyatt leans back, his eyes fixed on the none-too-clean floor tiles. "About last night," he says.

I freeze, one hand outstretched towards the coffee pot.

Wyatt clears his throat. "I don't want you to get the wrong idea," he says.

I bite on my lip and wait. A minute ago my stomach had felt empty. Now, it feels hollow. "How so?" I say.

"Well, I don't want you to think that we're, you know…" Wyatt rubs his temples. "Like, back together or anything."

I wish that the coffee pot were full so that I could hurl scalding coffee at him. I'm tempted to throw the empty pot anyway but resist. My arm is shaking so badly that I'd probably miss. "So what were you doing last night?" I say. "What was the point? You said you missed me!"

"I do miss you," says Wyatt. "But I'm still confused. I mean I still have feelings for Lindy too." He rubs his

hands through his thick, dark hair. I remember how that hair had felt in my hands last night and want to pull out clumps of it. Instead I grip the black marble countertop as though letting go will result in my sliding off the edge of the earth. I feel sick and angry but mostly just disgusted with myself.

I imagine leaving without another word. I see myself stalking past the coat rack and the motor oil stains that are still visible on the cracked green tiles. I see myself sliding back the retractable gate and striding down the street with nary a backwards glance. I am resolute and dignified and Wyatt is left staring after me, his haggard face filled with regret and anguish.

Unfortunately, I am wearing nothing but Wyatt's shirt, which means that no matter how dignified my exit, I'd probably end up being arrested. The other option holds no dignity whatsoever but I have no choice but to trudge up the four flights of stairs to our—now Wyatt's—bedroom, put on my smelly, silly cat burglar jumpsuit, and then face Wyatt all over again.

The last straw comes when I'm waiting for Wyatt to unlock the retractable gate. Somehow, last night, the keys to the padlocks were mislaid, and it takes ages to find them. When he's finally unlocked the second padlock and pulled back the metal gate, he turns sheepishly towards me. "So, um, I'll, ah, call you," he says, his eyes firmly fixed on my polyester-covered ankles.

His tone of voice, body language and facial expression all scream, "One night stand who never wants to see you again!", so loudly that I'm stunned into immobility. This guy, who reeks of booze and cigarettes and is obviously desperate to hustle me out the door, this *turd* was my beloved fiancé. This is *Wyatt*.

I stop and stare at him and he meets my eyes, then glances away again. He looks furtive and embarrassed.

Luckily I make it out the door before the tears start, but when they do, there's no stopping them. For the second time in three weeks I walk past the pagoda sobbing my eyes out. This time, it's not raining and there are plenty of spectators to watch a foreign woman in a black cat-suit perform a tearful walk of shame away from Wyatt's house.

• • •

"What a prick," says Sigrid, when I've finished recounting my latest debacle. "Wyatt knows that you still have feelings for him and totally took advantage of you."

We are sitting in Sigrid's tiny living room drinking tea and eating cinnamon rolls. Although it's 1:00 in the afternoon, we're both wearing pajamas. Sigrid never took hers off this morning and I put on a pair of hers after I'd arrived at her door in tears, peeled off my catsuit, and had a shower. "He was drunk," I say.

Sigrid snorts. "Come on, why are you defending him?"

I shrug. Why am I defending him? Do I actually believe that we'll be together again? I start to unfurl my cinnamon roll and pick out the raisins, which I love, lining them up on the edge of my plate to save for later.

I can't, or rather don't want to, imagine my life without Wyatt. But given the hurt and humiliation that I feel right now, it's hard to imagine the two of us living happily ever

after. "God," I say. "I can't believe I slept with him. I am such an idiot."

I wait for Sigrid to say no, it's not that bad, but instead she says, "Yeah, tell me about it."

Noticing my hurt expression she laughs. "Oh come on, that was a really dumb thing to do," she says. "But we've all been there."

"You haven't," I say sullenly.

Sigrid shakes her head. "You'd be surprised." She swallows a big chunk of her cinnamon bun. "But this isn't about me. It's about you and Wyatt."

"I love him," I say, then hang my head, horrified, yet again, by how pathetic I sound.

Sigrid pulls a face but her eyes are kind. "I know," she says. "I really do. But you've got to ask yourself whether he's actually worth it."

She goes into the kitchen to make more tea. A bookcase covers one wall and I stand up to see if she's got any books that I might want to borrow. There's an entire row of books about World War I and II, which I bypass as too depressing, and another row full of classics, like *Wuthering Heights*, *Frankenstein* and *Great Expectations*. I'm hoping for something light and fun but can't find anything.

Sigrid calls from the kitchen to ask if I want some leftover macaroni and cheese.

"Yes, please," I say. My appetite has returned with a vengeance.

I'm about to sit down again when I spot a fat volume called *The Birthday Book*. I remember Sigrid once telling me about it. For every day of the year it gives a personality profile. While I wouldn't expect someone as logical and practical as Sigrid to be into astrology, she'd claimed that this book is freakily accurate.

I lift down the book and take a seat, then open it across my knees. I'm flipping to August 11th, which is Wyatt's birthday, when a photo falls out of someplace in November and lands, facedown, on the floor tiles. I bend to retrieve it.

The photo, in black-and-white, shows Sigrid and a tall, good-looking guy with dark hair holding each other and smiling. Sigrid is wearing a wedding dress.

Sigrid steps through the open doorway armed with a tray. When she sees what I'm looking at she freezes. I almost expect her to drop the tea things but she just sets them down. I see that she's arranged four sticks of shortbread and four chocolate digestives on a little plate. I wait for her to say something.

"He walked out after six months," she says.

I shake my head. "Why?" I say, voicing one of multiple questions vying for space in my head. *When was this? Who is he? Why have you never mentioned this?*

"We were just wrong for each other."

"You look so happy here," I say, because they do. They both look gorgeous and ecstatic.

Sigrid sits down. "I was," she says. "I thought he was too but it turned out that he wasn't."

"Why not?"

Sigrid shrugs. "He said that sometimes being in love isn't enough." She sits down and pours tea into both of our cups. When she hands one to me I see that her hand is trembling.

"I'm sorry," I say. She looks so sad that I wish that I hadn't found the photo. Even though I wasn't, I feel like I was snooping. I start to put the photo back inside *The Birthday Book*.

"November 8th," she says. "A Scorpio."

I slide the photo back into its proper place. Sigrid shakes her head. "No more Scorpios for me," she says. "We were incompatible."

"What was his name?" I say.

"Damien."

I realize that she is crying. "This is so stupid," she says. She reaches for a tissue and swats at her eyes. "I can't believe that I'm still crying about it. I haven't seen him in over a year."

I go over and hug her. My eyes are full of tears too. When I put my arms around her I'm surprised by how small she is. I have never thought of Sigrid as small. She has such a big personality. "Do you still miss him?" I say.

"Sometimes, but not really. I miss how I felt when we were first together." She blows her nose.

"Was there somebody else?" I say, thinking of Wyatt and Lindy.

"No," she says. "As far as I know he's still single." She takes a digestive and dips it into her tea. "He's a musician. I think he felt that being with me, being married, was somehow restrictive, like he couldn't focus on his music and me at the same time." She shrugs. "He said that he felt stifled with me."

Since I don't know what to say to this I ask if his music is any good.

Sigrid looks pensive. "Yeah, I actually think his music is great. I keep expecting to hear that he's made it big. He has a fantastic voice and his lyrics are smart and insightful." She lifts her half-soaked digestive carefully towards her mouth and bites off the wet part.

"Why didn't you ever tell me about him?" I say.

Sigrid pours some more milk into her teacup. "I guess I just wanted to forget about it."

"Is that why you came to Vietnam?"

Sigrid shrugs. "Maybe," she says. "I needed a change." She blows into her teacup. "This place if full of people who are running away from something, isn't it?"

I nod. From what I've seen expats are a strange bunch, all of them some extreme or another: too adventurous, too curious, too lazy, or too socially inept to fit in at home. Sigrid returns *The Birthday Book* to its shelf. I think of the photo of her and Damien on their wedding day, looking so beautiful and happy. How can people go from that to an entire year without any contact?

"Do you think that you'll be single forever?" I say, because this is what I fear even more than losing Wyatt.

Sigrid gives me the sort of smile that people give to toddlers when they've said something sweet but silly. "I felt like that for a while," she says, "but now I figure that sooner or later I'll meet someone who'll be better for me." The microwave dings and she gets up and walks into the kitchen.

A few minutes later she's back bearing two bowls of homemade macaroni and cheese. The smell of it makes my mouth water. She sets down the bowls and hands me a spoon. I say thanks and wait for my macaroni to cool.

I can't stop thinking about that picture of Sigrid in her wedding dress. "I don't want to start over again," I say. "It's like all that time that I spent with Wyatt was just wasted."

Sigrid takes a bite and chews. "If you think about it that way your whole life is a waste," she says. "I mean we all end up dead in the end."

"Geez," I say. "You're really cheering me up, Sig."

"Your problem," says Sigrid, "is that you think that life is like a romantic movie. You know, there's a big fancy wedding at the end and the happy couple drives off into the sunset as the credits roll. But in real life, if you get what you want, even if it is what you want, well, you keep wanting other stuff."

I think about this for a minute. She's right, I realize. I've always thought of the wedding as the end of the story rather than the start of a more-often-than-not unromantic life negotiating who's going to ferry the kids to school, wipe up the toast crumbs and pay the phone bill.

"Like my yoga teacher says, the journey is the destination," says Sigrid serenely. There is no sign that she'd just been crying.

I add some more salt to my macaroni and cheese. I've always found that expression annoying. The journey tends to suck, as far as I'm concerned. I mean, would you rather be sitting in an airport lounge or sipping pina coladas by the ocean? "I hate that expression," I say. "I bet it was coined by a bunch of stoners who couldn't even remember where they were going."

"At least they were happy," says Sigrid. Then she laughs with her mouth open.

12 Family Matters

My parents' flight was delayed. Since people meeting planes aren't allowed inside the airport, I have been standing outdoors, in 93-degree weather, for over an hour. A couple of guards ensure that the waiting crowd stays behind a metal bar that separates the newly arrived from those who are here to fetch them. Little girls wearing puffy, scratchy ballerina-style frocks wave bouquets of flowers swathed in layers of clear plastic. Toddlers shriek. Gold bangles tinkle on waving wrists. Old ladies fan themselves. So many bodies are pressed against the bar that it's a wonder that it doesn't give way. I stand about 20 feet back, craning my neck to look into the Arrival Hall.

When my parents finally appear my relief is short-lived. They both look hot, stressed and disheveled.

Through the tinted glass I see my dad hoisting an oversized suitcase onto an X-ray machine. Tabitha is saying something to a guard, who obviously has no clue what she's talking about. Both of my parents look haggard and older than when I saw them last.

Between my folks and the exit lies one final line, where two female airport staff in turquoise *ao dais* are checking newly-arrived passengers' luggage tags. When one of these blue-clad women reaches my parents I see Skip start to search his pockets. My mom rummages through her purse, looking increasingly frustrated. While I'm much too far away to hear what's being said, it's obvious what is happening. My folks have misplaced their luggage claim tags, tiny stickers that are checked to ensure that passengers are taking the correct bags with them. Tabitha starts to shake her head violently. She waves her arms. My dad stares towards the exit, his face beseeching.

While I doubt that I can help I have no choice but to try. I push my way through the throng of people until I reach a break in the metal barrier. "Those are my parents," I say to the guard, who waves me away with an expression of annoyance. "You don't understand," I say. "There's a problem. I have to go and see them."

The guard raises his baton in a threatening gesture. I feel an urge to punch him.

At that very moment my mom has reached the end of her tether. I see her propel her cart past the two women in blue, both of whom try to grab at her arms and start squawking. My mom shrugs them off and keeps going, Skip shuffling dazedly behind her. The sliding doors open; they have almost made it. Then someone blows a whistle.

In the commotion I manage to slip past the guy with the baton. "Mom!" I yell. "They need your luggage tags!"

A few more guards have materialized, the lot of us now blocking the exit. Recently arrived passengers start to pile up, everyone pushing and shoving, overwhelming the two ladies in turquoise who are supposed to be checking people's luggage tags.

"We never got any tags!" says my mom. "I already told them that!"

"Nobody told us that we needed them," adds my dad. "What kind of system do they have here?"

By now a supervisor has appeared and the argument is moved to one side, clear of the exit. A tall, unsmiling man in square glasses, the supervisor explains that my parents will have to fill out some forms. My mom protests all the way to his office.

Filling out the forms takes a long time. It occurs to me that the guards might be after a payout. Would slipping them 10 bucks get us out of here? I'm pondering how to go about it when I hear someone calling my name, and turn to see Mr. Thai of the Department of Foreigner Control.

"Ah Miss Jane, we meet again," he says. He looks pleased to see me, which makes me nervous.

"Hello Mr. Thai," I say. "What are you doing here?" As at our last meeting, Mr. Thai looks immaculate, while my blue t-shirt has sweat stains down my back and beneath my arms and my hair is in a messy, sweaty ponytail.

"I had some business here," says Mr. Thai. I doubt that you could ever get a straight answer out of this man. He exudes intelligence and intrigue. He looks from me to my parents and frowns. "And you? Is there some problem here?"

I explain about the missing tags, then introduce Mr. Thai to my parents. My dad shakes his hand heartily and my mom glares at him, as though it's Mr. Thai's fault that she lost her luggage claim tags. Mr. Thai, his expression as elegant and inscrutable as ever, says something to the supervisor, who shrugs and says something back. He sounds defensive.

After that we're allowed to go. Mr. Thai walks us back towards the exit. I want to ask him if he ever followed

Hanoi Jane 189

up about Lindy Tran but am afraid that if I mention that night he'll say something that will alert my parents to the fact that I got arrested. We're almost at the gate when my dad asks how Mr. Thai and I know each other. I look at Mr. Thai, my mind blank. I wait for him to say something that will undoubtedly cause my parents to stage an intervention.

"Hanoi is a small place," says Mr. Thai. "It is easy to meet people and then run into them all the time." He smiles at me. I smile weakly back at him.

My parents and I are settled in a cab when I turn back to look at Mr. Thai. He is standing by the curb watching us. I wish that I could convince him take my claims against Lindy Tran seriously. Then I realize that I don't care as much about bringing Lindy down as I used to. If she is committing fraud, I'd like her caught. But I no longer feel that deep, obsessive need to make her suffer.

I wonder if this means that I've moved on or whether I've simply grown resigned to yet another of life's injustices. My mom asks the driver to turn up the air-conditioning.

"You look thin," she tells me. "Have you been eating right?"

"I'm sure I'll gain it back soon," I say. It feels nice to be told that I've lost weight and to know that my mom is concerned about me. "Sorry about that, back at the airport," I say. "It wasn't a very good introduction to Vietnam, was it?" Even though the luggage tag fiasco wasn't my fault, I feel responsible.

My dad gives me a hug. "What matters is that we made it," he says. "It's good to see you, Janey." On either side of the road lie rice paddies. Women in pale conical hats and brightly colored shirts crouch in the green fields. The sky overhead is bright blue, the scene, seen from our air-conditioned car, beautiful.

"It's good to see you guys too." I say. And I actually mean it.

• • •

My parents are staying at the Metropole, a hotel that holds a central place in Hanoi and in my heart. This is where Wyatt brought me for dinner on my first night in Vietnam, back when the city had felt so foreign and our future together was a given. This is where I met Wyatt the day that I tried and failed to alert him to Lindy's treachery. It is also where Wyatt goes to the gym, and where I used to go to the gym, until I caught Wyatt cheating on me and stopped working out in favor of eating ice cream on the sofa.

If I were visiting Hanoi for a couple of days and had the cash, I'd stay at the Metropole. Even though the rooms are small and overpriced, unlike most hotels in the world, it has atmosphere. Opened in 1901 it has housed everyone from Charlie Chaplin to Graham Greene to Don Johnson. In a 1972 visit to protest the Vietnam War, Jane Fonda reportedly crooned folk songs in the hotel's bunker as American bombs rained down on the city. Ho Chi Minh is said to have stayed here too. I like to imagine him, neat and trim, doing his morning exercises out by the swimming pool.

It's in these historic surroundings that my parents and I are sitting in the pool, each of us holding an absurdly expensive, brightly colored cocktail. Like our drinks, our swimsuits are colorful, mine a pink-striped bikini that I only dare wear because heartbreak has rendered me relatively svelte; my dad's a pair of rainbow-colored board shorts that wouldn't have looked amiss on Jerry Garcia; and my mom's a one-piece the color of an eggplant with gold piping. Since the sun is intense, we're all wearing hats. Skip and I have on baseball caps, while my mom is wearing a floppy, wide-brimmed number that looks like it was found floating near the final resting place of the *Titanic*.

In between sips of her Singapore sling, my mom is recounting the ordeal of their flight over here. Since they flew Business Class, I'm having trouble feeling too sorry for her. She's explaining how the Starbucks in Hong Kong's airport had—gasp—refused to accept American dollars when I stand up, excuse myself and wade out in search of the washroom.

I'm on my way back to the pool when I hear a familiar voice. Clad in gym clothes with a small white towel draped over his neck is Wyatt, talking on his cell phone. Judging by his sweat-stained T-shirt he'd been in the middle of a workout when his phone rang. Since there's no mobile reception in the gym, he'd wandered out into the hotel's inner courtyard, near the swimming pool. Wyatt is so focused on his call that he's oblivious to his surroundings. My folks are about 20 feet away from him.

I dart behind a bougainvillea bush.

Peering cautiously around the greenery, I hold my breath, hoping that my parents and Wyatt won't see each other. The last time I saw Wyatt was the regrettable morning after the Blue Fantasy Ball. My humiliation feels too fresh. I simply cannot face him, especially not whilst wearing a bikini and in the company of my parents.

His conversation finished, Wyatt looks up, which is when he spots Skip and Tabitha in the swimming pool. Recognition causes him to trip over nothing. His first impulse, I know, is to make a run for it.

My dad squints. "Oh look," he says. "Isn't that Wyatt over there?"

At that point, Wyatt has no choice but to walk over to my parents and say hello. Whether due to his interrupted workout, the sun, or embarrassment, he is sweating copiously. My parents say hello back. There's so much ice in my mom's voice that it's a wonder that the pool doesn't freeze over.

Wyatt dabs at his face with his towel. "So, um, when did you arrive in Hanoi?" he says with strained heartiness. Like my dad, he is squinting against the bright sunshine.

"The day before yesterday," says my father. He and my mom are sitting on a step, half-submerged in water.

Safely hidden in the bushes, my dread has merged with curiosity. What are Wyatt and my parents going to say to each other? Will my mom chastise him? Will I be further humiliated?

My dad stands up. I have a brief vision of my father leaping out of the pool and grabbing Wyatt by the throat, demanding restitution for the dishonor heaped upon his darling daughter. But that's obviously not going to happen. My dad dislodges his shorts from his butt-crack and sits down again.

If my dad were alone, he and Wyatt would undoubtedly exchange a few banal statements about the weather and

basketball scores and part ways. I glance at my mom. Tabitha is the wild card in this pack, her face hidden by her oversized hat and dark glasses.

My mother finishes the remains of her drink and sets the glass carefully on the side of the pool. "So Wyatt," she says, and Wyatt jumps. "We were so shocked to hear about you and Jane. It was so terribly sudden." She smiles grimly and Wyatt takes a step back. He looks like an extra standing on the beach in *Jaws*. *Look out, Wyatt!* I think. *Don't go near the water!*

"What happened?" says my mom. "Have you thought this through carefully?"

Wyatt looks faint. "We, uh, I, um, had, ahem, doubts," he says, "about, ahem, uh, ahem, getting married."

Still hiding in the bushes, I have to admit that I find Wyatt's discomfiture highly gratifying. My dad, on the other hand, looks almost as uncomfortable as Wyatt. I see him peering towards the pool's bamboo-clad bar, no doubt hoping that more drinks will materialize. The waitresses all seem to have vanished.

"Doubts?" says my mother, this word gaining so many layers of meaning from her inflection that Wyatt doesn't know whether to nod or deny everything. He makes an indeterminate head movement and rubs his neck with his white towel.

"Is it over between the two of you?" says my mom. "Getting a straight answer out of Jane is impossible. One minute you two are finished and the next you're taking a break. All of this indecisiveness can't be healthy. Me and Skippy have been worried about her. She's always been…" Tabitha pauses, either to search for the right word or to give her pronouncement more weight. "She's always been sensitive."

That word again, I think. I've joined all of those other things that are better left untouched. Thoroughly humiliated, I shrink deeper into the shrubbery.

Wyatt peers up at the sky, as though help might come from on high. His squint has taken on a pleading aspect and he is sweating harder than ever.

When he fails to respond my dad shakes his head. "I don't get it," he says. "Do you love her?"

"Yes," says Wyatt. Head hanging, he looks set to burst into tears. I've never seen him looking so pathetic.

"Then what are you doing?" says my dad.

"I don't know," mumbles Wyatt. "I, I …" He gives up and stares numbly into the deep end of the swimming pool.

My mom makes a noise of impatience. I expect her to start yelling at him, probably not about the real issues—his unfaithfulness and willingness to keep stringing me along—but some related matter of more direct interest to Tabitha, such as how hard it is to get a refund on a returned ring cushion. Strangely, there is dead silence.

I peer cautiously around the bougainvillea bush. In the afternoon light, the pool glows turquoise. Way up overhead, swallows are flitting across the sky, which is slightly darker than the swimming pool. Wyatt runs a hand over his eyes. He looks like he's sleepwalking through a nightmare.

For the first time I truly believe that he *is* confused and not simply claiming to be to. It's possible that he really does love me after all.

A breeze rustles the bougainvilleas, causing some

papery pink flowers to float towards the swimming pool. Wyatt looks in my direction and freezes, his face stricken. I consider darting back into the shrubbery but know that it's too late. He has seen me.

Looking into my ex-fiancé's agonized face, his recent behavior is suddenly clear to me: He loves me but is shit-scared, terrified that we'll have less and less to talk about as the years go by, that we'll become more and more like business partners and less like lovers. He's afraid that before he knows it he'll be middle-aged, just another balding guy with a paunch racing his red sports car towards a midlife crisis. Being with Lindy feels fresh and commitment-free. She makes him feel younger, cooler and more exciting.

He loves me. I wait to feel an answering rush of love for Wyatt, or at least some compassion and understanding. Instead, I feel tired and annoyed, since he is not that young, not that cool, and not that exciting.

I think of Sigrid's claim that people don't change but just get too tired or bored to keep repeating themselves. I see Wyatt's Adam's apple bob.

"Hi Jane," he says.

I step out of the bushes. "Hello Wyatt."

At the sight of my new pink-striped bikini his eyes widen. Ten minutes ago, I was sure that meeting Wyatt would cause my heart to stop and yet here I am, facing him whilst practically naked. I should be worrying about the size of my thighs or trying to suck my stomach in and yet, oddly enough, I don't care about these things. Nor do I care to make conversation. At this moment I have nothing to say to Wyatt.

I march back over to the pool and wade in, then take a seat beside my father. I can see Wyatt trying to think of something to say. His eyes keep veering away and then sliding back over to me. He scratches his ear. "So, uh, how's Fergus?"

"Fine," I say, unsure whether to be more amazed that he remembered the cat's name or that he's asking about it.

"Good." He swallows hard. "Maybe I could stop by and, ahem, visit him."

The thought of Wyatt going anyplace to visit a cat is so ludicrous that I can't help but smile. "You want to visit Fergus?" I say, unable to keep the sarcasm from my voice.

Wyatt's cheeks are now as pink as the bougainvillea blossoms. "Yes." He clears his throat. "I really liked that cat."

"We're going to Sapa," I say. "Maybe when we're back."

"Okay," says Wyatt. "That'd be great." He nods at my parents one last time before turning to go, then stops and glances back at me. "Bye," he says, then tries to smile, his face like that of an alien which, never having actually smiled before, is following written instructions on how to do so.

"See you, Wyatt."

Head down, Wyatt sways on his feet. With that towel hung around his neck he looks like a boxer who's taken one hit too many. For a moment, I think that he'll collapse, but he just turns and trudges off. I hear the door to the gym open and shut again.

My mom takes off her hat and shakes her head. "Hmmph. He looks terrible," she says. "I think you had a lucky escape." Two French women have just walked out to the pool, both carrying Prada bags and clad in chic black swimsuits.

"You want another drink?" says my dad. Before my mom or I can answer he's already on his feet, using one hand to extract his shorts from his butt-crack and the other to wave at a reluctant waitress.

• • •

It's my parents' fourth night in town and they, Sigrid and I have gone to Hanoi's historic Opera House to see a traditional *Tuong* opera. If I didn't feel obliged to expose my folks to the local culture I wouldn't be here, since I don't care for Vietnamese opera. To my ears, the singing sounds like high-pitched wailing, while the plot is impossible to follow. Unable to keep track of who's a good guy or a bad guy, I give up and focus on the building itself, which, built by the French and opened in 1911, is my idea of beautiful. I lean back and gaze at the cloud-covered domed ceiling. The wailing up on stage grows louder.

By the intermission I have a throbbing headache. Sigrid, my folks and I wander out into the lobby, where Sigrid and my mom line up to buy drinks and my dad and I head downstairs to use the washrooms. "What do you think?" I ask my dad, before we go our separate ways to the Men's and Ladies'.

"It's interesting," he says.

I shake my head accusingly. "You fell asleep."

"Luckily," he says. We both giggle.

My bladder emptied, I reenter the lobby in search of the others. Sigrid, who actually seems to be enjoying herself, is chatting happily with my mom, who prides herself on being cultured and cosmopolitan enough to appreciate this sort of event. I take the glass of wine that my mom bought me and guzzle it. My dad volunteers to buy another round. I gaze around the lobby, admiring the columns and ornate wall sconces.

All of a sudden a familiar voice says: "Aha! You see, Hanoi really is small!" I turn to see Mr. Thai. In a dark suit and white shirt he looks even more dapper than usual, although I wouldn't have believed that to be possible.

For once I look decent too. I'm wearing a cream cotton dress that is pretty without being fussy and my hair is freshly washed and brushed. Mr. Thai smiles. "You are a fan of *Tuong* opera, Miss Jane?"

If it were anyone else I might lie, but deceiving Mr. Thai seems impossible. "Not really," I admit. "I don't understand what's happening."

"That's a pity," he says, then proceeds to explain that the characters in *Tuong* are archetypes. At a glance an educated audience can read the stylized features that reveal a character's personality and intentions. A pointy black beard, for instance, signals treachery and a square jaw is a sign of courage. I see Sigrid listening intently and realize that I've failed to introduce her.

"This is my friend, Sigrid," I say. "Sigrid, this is Mr. Thai."

What happens next takes me by surprise, for the moment their eyes meet, both Sigrid and Mr. Thai become rigid. The ensuing silence is like that period after

lightning has struck when you're waiting for the thunder to start. I find myself counting: *One Mississippi. Two Mississippi. Three Mississippi...*

"Um, Sigrid works in emergency response," I say, just to fill the void. I feel embarrassed for both of them. I've never known Sigrid to be lost for words and could not have conceived of Mr. Thai being anything but cool and collected. And yet here they are, frozen and blushing.

A little bell dings, signaling the end of intermission. Sigrid and Mr. Thai both shake themselves. "Nice to meet you," he says. He looks so shaken that I consider offering him my last sip of wine. "You too," says Sigrid. She is sweating.

My dad reappears bearing four glasses of wine on a tray. "Oh hello," he says, when he recognizes Mr. Thai. "Sorry, I didn't know you were here or I'd have gotten you a glass too." People are starting to move back towards their seats now.

"No, no," says Mr. Thai. "I'd best go back in." He nods to my parents and me, then nods at Sigrid. She manages a glassy-eyed smile. "Bye," she says. We all watch Mr. Thai cut neatly through the crowd and disappear through the open doorway.

"What does that man do?" says my mom. We are all shuffling towards our seats.

"He works for the government," I say. "Something to do with public security."

"He looks like a movie star, doesn't he?" says my mother. "Like someone from a Hong Kong movie."

I'm sitting between my dad and Sigrid. When we're all seated she leans over and whispers to me: "Is that Mr. Thai the guy who interrogated you?"

I glance at my dad, worried that he's overheard, but he and my mom are busy slathering mosquito repellent onto their ankles. While one wouldn't expect there to be a lot of mosquitoes indoors, Hanoi's Opera House seems to be infested with them. Malarial mosquitoes reportedly can't survive in urban areas (they can't stand air pollution) but it'd be just my luck if Skip and Tabby came down with it. "Yes," I say. "That was him."

"Wow," says Sigrid. She folds and unfolds her catalogue. "You didn't tell me that he was gorgeous."

I consider this. Mr. Thai is handsome, but not my type. For one thing, I don't think that I could be attracted to someone who's keeping a dossier on me. When I say this to Sigrid she shrugs. "It's not like I have anything to hide," she says.

Except for the fact that you were married, I want to say. But I manage to stop myself. Sigrid must know what I'm thinking because her chin goes up. "I'm not ashamed about the divorce," she says. "I was for a while. I felt like a total failure at first. But now I don't regret any of it."

I want to ask why not but it seems rude. Luckily, Sigrid feels the need to explain further. "I learned a lot from being with Damien," she says. "Breaking up sucked but we did have some amazing times together, plus I have a much clearer idea of what I want in a relationship."

I think of Wyatt the morning after the Blue Fantasy Ball, hung over and hustling me out the door. How could I have spent six years of my life with such a jerk? The lights dim. As the great red velvet curtain starts to rise, I question why I ever loved Wyatt. But as much as he's disappointed me, I know that there are other, better

sides to him. He is hardworking, for one thing, and has done a lot of nice things for me. He bought me an MP3 player before any of my friends had one, for instance, and actually tried to teach me how to use it. Whenever I had bad period cramps or was really stressed with deadlines he'd rub my back for ages. Most guys will just give you one of those short token massages that dies as soon as they figure out that you're not going to have sex with them, but not Wyatt. And he came to every *Chic!* office party, despite being bored senseless.

My throat feels thick. I'm not sure what's worse, thinking about the good Wyatt or the bad one. Recalling both versions makes me feel miserable. I guess that's why Sigrid moved halfway around the world, just to avoid thinking about Damien.

The performers are back on stage. I look for the guy with the pointy beard, who's bound to be sneaky, and for the square-jawed, valiant one. If only it were that straightforward in real life. Then I would never, ever have been in this situation.

The music starts up and I still hate it. My forehead starts to throb. When I look over at Sigrid, I see that she's smiling.

13 True Colors

Tonight we are heading off to Sapa. My folks have been here for six days and, so far, it hasn't been terrible. That may be because they've spent most of this time in their fancy hotel, since my mom refuses to go anywhere without air-conditioning. Luckily for her, we're in the train's first class carriage, which is so cold that I'm now wearing two pairs of socks, along with a sweater that I borrowed from my dad, over my shorts and t-shirt. Sigrid's got an extra pair of socks on her hands, like mittens.

"How about some more of this red wine?" says my dad, upending the empty bottle as if he hopes that a few more drops will fall out. Our cabin has bunk beds that sleep four. My parents have the bottom ones and Sigrid and I the top, but at the moment we've folded up the top bunks and are all sitting around chatting. I'd packed cheese and crackers and two bottles of wine. Just two hours into our trip the wine is already finished.

"Try ringing that bell for the waiter," says my mom, pointing at the emergency alarm. I manage to stop my dad before he tugs it.

"I'll go and get more," I say. "The dining carriage is a little ways up." I wait for someone to offer to come with me but nobody does. Wrapped in a big quilt, Sigrid is curled up in a corner. My parents are flipping through travel magazines. I'm sure that we're all a bit tipsy.

I teeter down the corridor towards the caboose, the train shuddering and rocking. When I open the carriage's door, a blast of hot wind hits my face, my nostrils assaulted by the smells of engine oil, smoke and urine. This carriage and the next are connected by a swaying metal platform that rattles loudly. I hold my breath and step onto it. The noise and movement make me nervous.

Moving unsteadily towards the next carriage I realize that I'm drunker than I'd realized. It's a relief to get inside again, although this carriage is a lot more crowded and smellier than ours, with bench seats instead of private cabins. As I make my way down the aisle dozens of dark eyes stare up at me. Everyone looks reproachful, as though they know that I've just come from the first class carriage.

I pass through two more carriages of this type before entering another with private cabins. A glimpse through an open doorway reveals that these compartments are much more basic than ours, with ceiling fans instead of air-conditioning, hard wooden bunks, and no bedding. The passageway is dirtier too, and I realize that I've stepped in a puddle.

Before I can question what it is, the train lurches. With a great yelp, I lose my balance. My arms windmill and I run backwards in place, like a cartoon character that has slipped on a banana peel. For what feels like a long time I hang poised in mid-air, just waiting to hit the wet linoleum.

Just as gravity claims me I feel someone grab hold of my shoulders. Staggering backwards, my butt hits a hard body. Strong hands grip my arms. "Whoa," says a male voice. "You okay there?"

Twisting around I realize that I'm leaning against Graham Hall, his green eyes revealing a mix of concern and hilarity. From the look on his face, he's obviously trying not to laugh. I can feel myself turning fuchsia.

Since I'm too embarrassed to move, let alone speak, I just hang there, Graham still clutching me in the style of lovers in an old-fashioned movie. Up close, he's even better-looking than I remembered, his aquiline nose dotted with just enough freckles to make him look cute but not infantile. I struggle to stand unaided and Graham releases me. "I…um…thanks," I stammer. "I…uh…slipped."

"No kidding," he says, the effort to keep a smile from his face evidently too much for him. "I wish I had it on video."

Seeing my humiliated expression his face falls. "I mean, I'm glad you're okay and all." He peers at me worriedly. "You are okay, aren't you?"

Faced with his concerned gaze I have an urge to say no, I've just been dumped by the love of my life, my parents are drunks, and I have less grace and coordination than a beached walrus. But instead I take a deep breath and nod. "I slipped," I say again, then curse myself. I already said that. He must think I'm a total idiot.

"So what are you doing here?" He pushes back a curl of blond hair, which the wind has thrown into his eyes. "You going to the mountains for work or for fun?"

"Fun," I say, trying to sound enthusiastic. "My parents are here visiting so I'm taking them to Sapa to see some countryside."

Dressed in faded cargo pants and a white t-shirt with a Japanese-style print of a koi fish, Graham looks

relaxed and stylish. I wish that I weren't wearing my dad's ugly brown sweater, which is about as flattering as a potato sack. "How about you?" I ask. "Where are you going?"

Graham explains that he's got his motorbike onboard and will head out on a road trip. "I'll be going through Sapa in a couple of days," he says. "Maybe I'll see you up there." Down the corridor a cabin door opens and someone tosses a bag of trash into the aisle.

All of a sudden it occurs to me that Lindy Tran might be onboard too, this thought causing my pulse to quicken. I find myself peering furtively up and down the corridor, which is mercifully empty. Outside of the windows, all is dark. We're between towns, the cool wind smelling of rice paddies. The train sways around a corner and Graham reaches for my elbow to steady me.

"I was going to the dining car," I say. "Do you think they sell wine in there?"

"I doubt it, unless you want some of the local stuff from Dalat." He grimaces. "Not that I'd recommend it. You can probably find some rice whisky though, if you're into the hard stuff."

"It's for my parents," I say, lest he think that I'm drinking alone. "They'd probably like to try something local."

"Then I should take you all out to this place I know in Sapa," he says. "They make really good *ruou*." I'm no expert but his Vietnamese pronunciation sounds perfect. I ask if he goes to the highlands a lot and he nods. "Yes, I like to get out of the city every chance I get. It's gorgeous up there and the roads are empty."

He starts telling me about his last road trip, enthusiasm making his green eyes sparkle. Listening to him, I want to ask if he's traveling alone but it seems too forward. Girls must come on to him all the time. I don't want him to think that I'm interested in him, because I'm not, really. It's just that he's cute and seems really nice and I'm emotionally fragile right now. The last thing I need is some crazy rebound relationship—not that Graham would be interested in me anyways, I remind myself. He's into Lindy.

This recollection leaves me feeling deflated. All of a sudden I don't know what's worse, the thought that Lindy is here with Graham or back in Hanoi with my intended.

I have a crazy urge to ask Graham about Lindy but manage to stop myself. What would I say anyways? *So Graham, I hear you're dating this French woman named Lindy Tran who's a total slut and possibly a thief. What exactly do you see in her?* I must smile grimly at this point because Graham stops talking, an abashed look on his face. "Sorry," he says. "I get a bit carried away talking about those road trips..."

"No," I say. "It's not that. Your trip sounds amazing. I'd love to go on one too..." I stop talking. Now Graham's the one with a weird look on his face.

Following his gaze, I look down at my feet. The puddle in which I'd slipped has expanded, dark liquid sloshing across the linoleum. Graham takes a step back. "What the hell," he says. "It's coming from that cabin."

The spill, sure enough, does seem to be seeping from beneath a cabin door. "Ugh. What *is* that?" I say. I lift one foot to examine it. The bottom of my sock is bright blue.

"Indigo," says Graham. "A pot of indigo dye must have spilled. A lot of different ethnic groups use it to dye their clothing. They cook it up from plants. It's amazing stuff." He surveys my blue socks. "Those will never be white again. You should go wash your feet as soon as possible or your skin will be dyed too."

"I'm wearing two pairs of socks," I say.

Graham cocks an eyebrow in amusement.

I'm still examining the bottom of my sock when the train lurches around another bend, causing me to go flying. While Graham makes another valiant effort to catch me, I'm on the ground so fast that it shocks both of us. For a minute, neither of us moves. The train's whistle blows and we enter a tunnel, a whoosh of hot air rushing in on us and a great, rattling noise filling the carriage. The darkness is total.

"Jane?" says Graham, when we're free of the tunnel and the noise has subsided. I am on my hands and knees in a big blue puddle.

I straighten up and he extends a hand to help me, then, seeing the state of my hands, hesitates. "I'm fine," I say, staggering to my feet. "I'm just…" I hang my head. I want to cry with embarrassment.

"Blue," says Graham. And then he starts laughing.

Peering down at my legs, I can't help but laugh too. From the knees down I'm as blue as a Smurf. When I go to wipe my eyes, Graham grabs my wrist. "Don't!" he warns. "The color won't come off for weeks." Sure enough, my palms are a bright shade of cobalt.

After I've tried—and failed—to wash off the blueness in the dining car's bathroom, Graham and I sit down for a quick drink. Like he predicted, there's no wine but we do find a bottle of pink champagne—made in Moldova.

"What shall we drink to?" I say, holding up my glass of hot pink bubbly.

"Bright colors?" suggests Graham. His eyes twinkle.

"Better balance," I say.

He smiles. "I don't think this is going to help that."

Maybe it's because of the champagne but conversation flows easily. We discuss our hometowns and Hanoi, the things we miss, the things we don't. I'm just getting up the nerve to broach the subject of Lindy Tran when his cell phone rings. "Oh sorry," he says. "I'd better get this." While I can't really hear the voice on the other end of the line, I get the feeling that it's Lindy's.

Graham doesn't say much, just a couple 'yeahs' and some 'okays' but when he hangs up, he looks apologetic. "I should get going," he says. "It's late. The train gets to Lao Cai at 5:30 a.m." I nod and he rises to his feet, then says good night to me. "Maybe I'll see you in Sapa," he says, as he's turning to go.

"Sure," I say. "Have a good road trip."

Armed with another bottle of pink champagne for my parents I make my way carefully back to my cabin. The puddle of indigo is even bigger than it was but I manage to avoid the worst of it.

When I open the cabin door I see that Sigrid is already asleep. My parents are playing cards, a bottle of rice whisky between them. "Where did you get that?" I say, and Tabitha shrugs.

"A guy came by with a drink cart," she says. "It's not terrible. Tastes a bit like tequila except stronger."

She peers up at me and squints. "What's happened to your legs?"

I sigh, suddenly too tired to get into it. Luckily, my dad saves me from answering by roaring "Full house!" and throwing his cards onto the table.

"You cheated," says my mom accusingly.

"Did not."

"Oh yes you did!" She glares at him.

I peel off my blue socks and climb into the top bunk across from Sigrid's. "Good night," I murmur.

"Sleep well, Janey" says my dad. "Sweet dreams, honey," says my mom. And then they go back to arguing.

As I drift off to sleep, I dream that I'm swimming in a bright blue ocean. Wyatt is there, and so is Graham. I'm perfectly happy until I step out of the water, which is when I realize that I'm as blue as Vishnu.

14 Mountain Scenes

Sigrid, my parents and I are sharing a long picnic table with three H'mong guys, our table located under an orange tarp on the edge of Sapa's open-air market. The tables around us are full of local men, most of whom look drunk. All of the women seem to be cooking or tending babies or selling stuff in the market. If I had to be reincarnated around here, I'd hope to be born with a penis.

Although it's a sunny day it is cool and shady beneath our tarp. The guys slurping soup and drinking rice wine at our table seem to be celebrating something. They keep laughing and yelling 'Cheers', which seems to be the only English word that they know. My dad, who's about twice their size, is trying to teach them the lyrics to *One Hundred Bottles of Beer*. They seem to find this song hilarious.

We arrived in Sapa early yesterday morning and spent the day strolling around some nearby villages. This morning we climbed to a lookout that offers a great view of the surrounding mountains and terraced paddy fields. And now we've stopped for a snack—bowls of beef noodle soup and some locally-made rice wine.

"This stuff is fantastic," says my dad, one of his large, sunburned hands clutching a long, curved stick of rattan, which, being hollow, serves as a straw. The rest of us are holding cane straws too, the ends of which are immersed in a fat ceramic pot full of rice wine.

Wearing flip-flops, board shorts and a Hawaiian-print shirt, Skip looks as though he just wandered out of a beach resort. My mom resembles the member of some exclusive cult, her skinny frame clad in long, tailored white shorts, a white St. John's tunic and a white terry-cloth sun-visor. Around her neck hangs a large necklace consisting of chunks of wood, stones and colorful glass beads held together by thick twine. It looks like it was assembled by preschoolers but probably cost a fortune.

Seeing me looking at it, my mom fingers the thing. "Statement necklaces are all the rage," she says. The mints in her pocket rattle jauntily.

"Right," I say, for lack of anything better to say.

My mom is forever issuing these fashion pronouncements. Brown, white or grey is invariably the new black. "It's all about the arms," she'll say, or, "animal prints are so in vogue this season."

With a mother like this, is it any wonder that I ended up working at *Chic!*? She still hasn't forgiven me for quitting. Even though I was the most unstylish beauty editor in the history of *Chic!*, my position there had been a huge source of pride to her.

Out of guilt for having disappointed her, I compliment her on her totally impractical metallic Jimmy Choo sandals. "Aren't they divine?" she coos, then admits that they're giving her a blister.

We all suck up more rice wine. At first, I'd thought that it tasted off, but it's starting to grow on me.

Her face almost as rosy as my father's, my mom starts to fiddle with her camera. "Everybody say 'cheese'," she coos, then takes a photo before the H'mong guys have time to figure out what she's talking about. She squints into the digital camera's small screen and shakes her head. "You really need to do something about your hair, Jane. I know you wanted it up for the wedding but it's looking stringy." She pats her own sleek bob while examining my head critically. "You might do well in one of those short pixie cuts if your face weren't so round."

I grit my teeth. So not only is my hair stringy, my face is also fat. "I like my hair," I mutter lamely. I almost add that Wyatt likes long hair too, but manage to stop myself.

"Lauren got hers bobbed recently," says Tabitha. She turns to Sigrid. "That's my other daughter. She's getting married in the spring. Her fiancé—he's a neurosurgeon—he just proposed in St. Tropez." She turns back to me. "The photos were amazing. Their room had its own private swimming pool." Whatever filler that my mom has had injected into her lips impedes her ensuing smile. "And a butler too."

I gulp down some more of the rice wine.

At the mention of Lauren's upcoming wedding, Skip rejoins our conversation. "The country club is giving us a deal on Lauren's reception," he says. "Donny, the manager there—you remember him, one of my golf buddies?—well, anyways, he felt real bad for us on account of your cancellation and all, so we're getting it for half price. We've already got the seating plan and menu worked out."

"And the flowers too," says Tabitha. "Lauren's busy designing their new 4,000-square-foot house so she's leaving the wedding planning to me."

I swallow hard. "So Lauren's wedding's going to be exactly like mine? I mean, like mine was going to be?" I grip my cane straw so hard that I snap it.

"No need to look like that," sniffs Tabitha. "It's just lucky that *someone* can make use of it all. At least Uncle Dwayne didn't order that custom-made tux for nothing. And well, it's not like *you're* going to be needing those wedding favors any time soon, is it?"

Luckily Sigrid intervenes, turning everyone's attention to a passing Flower H'mong woman who's daintily carrying a baby potbelly pig in a rattan harness with a handle on top, as if the piglet were a designer handbag. Clutching her camera, Tabitha abandons the table to pursue the H'mong woman and her piglet. Within moments, she's encircled by a throng of fabric vendors, all of them frantically waving bits of brocade at her.

The Black H'mong women wear indigo tunics, leggings and hats, while the Dao women appear to have puffy red pillows balanced on their heads. Encircled by short women in bright headgear, Tabitha resembles a tall, skinny stamen in a colorful flower.

Observing the scrum, I feel queasy. I wish that I'd never let my dad talk me into sampling the local homebrew— especially so early in the morning. Checking my watch, I groan. I look at my dad accusingly but he's deep in drunken conversation with a H'mong guy.

"Number one!" yells the H'mong guy. "Cheers!" yells Skippy. They both start drinking again.

I turn to Sigrid, whose eyes look as glazed as mine feel. "I don't believe it. It's not even 11:00 a.m. and I'm drunk," I say. "This always happens when my parents are around."

"They're something else," agrees Sigrid. "After the amount of wine they drank last night I figured they'd be in bed all day." She shakes her head in amazement. "But they sure seem to be enjoying themselves."

Looking from one parent to the other, I have to agree. Both Skip and Tabitha seem to be in their element, my mom shopping and my dad and his new H'mong buddies playing some drinking game that involves coins, a lighter and paper napkins. "Yeah, at least when they're drunk they're not complaining about my cancelled wedding," I say bitterly.

"Or trying to set you up with anyone with a Y chromosome," laughs Sigrid. "Or maybe your dad's negotiating the bride price with that H'mong guy right this minute." She nods towards Skip. The H'mong guy on his left looks set to pass out. The guy on his right stands up and staggers off to vomit quietly into some bushes.

I make a face. "I guess he didn't like the idea," I say.

We're interrupted by a pretty Red Dao girl in her early teens who thrusts an intricately embroidered tunic between us. "Shopping?" she says, her round face framed by her scarlet headgear. With her sharp cheekbones, tawny skin and whisky-colored eyes, this girl belongs on the cover of *National Geographic*.

"No thanks," I say. "Try that lady." I point towards my mom, wondering what on earth she plans to do with all the stuff that she's buying.

The girl frowns. "She buy some already," she says, her near-perfect American accent taking me by surprise. While she looks like the member of some lost tribe, this girl is clearly used to dealing with foreigners. "Why you not buy from me?" she says, pouting prettily.

Faced with her unflinching gaze, I realize that this child is an experienced saleswoman. She's got a streetwise edge too; it's easy to picture her dressed like all of the teens back home in a tight t-shirt, skinny jeans and too much eyeliner. Then she smiles and her face is transformed into that of a cute little kid again. She smells of wood smoke and bubblegum.

I ask where she learned English and the girl shrugs. "From tourists," she says. "I speak Japanese too." She starts to rattle away in what I assume is Japanese.

"Um, that's great," says Sigrid. "But we don't speak Japanese."

"*Francais?*" says the girl.

We shake our heads. "English."

Obviously unimpressed by our lack of linguistic prowess, the girl smacks her gum. I notice that beneath her hand-embroidered top lies a faded Britney Spears t-shirt. Three thick silver rings encircle her neck, which, like the rest of her, could do with a good wash. Nobody seems fond of soap around here.

Just as we study her, she examines us, taking in our baseball hats, jeans and muddy running shoes. Sigrid's diving watch warrants special attention, the girl momentarily sidetracked from her sales duty as she tests its various functions.

Having tired of this toy, she gets back to business. "I

am Mai. What your name?" she says, shaking first my hand and then Sigrid's. Her fingers, like my knees and palms, are stained blue from indigo.

We ask Mai her age and what grade she's in, this query eliciting a quick frown. "I thirteen," she says. "I stop school already, go work sewing and sell for tourists." Her brave and slightly defiant tone gives me the impression that leaving school may not have been her choice. She drops her eyes. "I need make money. My family poor," she explains.

I can't help but suspect that this is all part of a practiced sales pitch. Sure enough, she digs into her woven rattan backpack and holds up an embroidered cap. "My friend, you buy from me," she says confidently. "I sell special price."

I'm preparing to decline when Sigrid reaches for the hat. "Do you have kids' sizes?" she says. "My sister has two little boys and this would be cute on them."

The Dao girl's face falls. "No small size. That style for adult."

"I think foreigners would buy it for kids," says Sigrid. "And those tunics too. If you made baby-ones, I bet that lots of people would buy them."

The girl holds up the tunic, considering this suggestion. "You sure?" She tugs at a hoop earring. "Hard to know what foreigners like."

I had, I realize, been hoping to find a way to ask this girl about Lindy Tran. This is my lead-in. "I heard that an NGO called Highlands Outreach is building a community center to help local craftswomen," I say quickly. "Have you heard of it?"

The girl bends to adjust the strap of her plastic sandal. When she straightens up, she nods. "Yes," she says. "Open ceremony last year. But then nothing happen."

Sigrid and I exchange glances. "But I thought it was supposed to open next month," says Sigrid.

The girl shakes her head, causing her jewelry to jangle. "They not build yet. Office mostly empty."

I'm about to ask more when my mom reappears, her arms filled with embroidered garments. "Look how cute this stuff is!" she crows triumphantly. "The handiwork is amazing. I'm going to give it to my quilting circle. It's so much cuter than that stuff Betty Almatoz brought back from Bermuda!"

Mai holds up a cap. "More shopping?" she says hopefully.

Tabitha purses her lips. "Hmmm, do you have any small ones? It'd be adorable for a baby, wouldn't it?" She giggles excitedly. "Hopefully Lauren and Luke will give us grandchildren soon."

Catching sight of my face, my mom looks alarmed, as though she fears that this allusion to Lauren and Luke's future progeny might cause me to tear out my stringy locks or throw myself under a passing ox-cart. Since my mom has about as much sensitivity as she does body fat, I find myself wondering if she's hit on something. Was my biological clock behind my desperation to wed Wyatt?

I imagine myself holding a baby that looks like Wyatt, but this image evokes distaste rather than sadness. A baby that looks like me is equally unappealing, so I guess that my biological clock isn't to blame after all. So what does lie behind my hard-to-quash white wedding fantasy? Is it that all of my friends back home are engaged? Have I been a bridesmaid one time too many? (Four, for the record). Or is it just that I'm about to turn 30 and am petrified of ending up alone and unwanted?

"Are you alright?" says my mother, which suggests that I don't look it.

"Yes," I lie. I think back to the night that Wyatt had proposed—and asked me to move to Vietnam with him. We'd been at his Uncle Nick's lakeside cabin in upstate New York, and had spent a perfect day walking in the woods, swimming and fishing. After grilling dinner over a campfire, we'd crawled into a single sleeping bag and lain out on the cabin's rickety dock, the sky so full of stars that it had taken my breath away.

Wyatt had pointed out various constellations and I'd seen a shooting star, which had fallen in heart-stopping slow motion. "Look!" I'd gasped. "Did you see it?"

"Yes." He'd pulled me closer. "Did you make a wish?"

When I'd replied that I had, he'd asked me to marry him, then—before I'd even had time to respond—told me that he was being transferred to Hanoi. "It's a great job," he'd said. "And the contract's just two years. Will you come with me?"

I swallow hard, this memory having brought a sticky lump to my throat. I recall the various good times that we'd had at Uncle Nick's cabin, how Wyatt had always seemed less uptight and more affectionate in the woods than he did in the city. I remember the elation that I'd felt when he'd proposed, how moving half away around the world had seemed like a minor detail. What did it matter that I'd be giving up my decent job, my friends and my

Hanoi Jane 219

whole carefully constructed life in New York, if we were finally going to get married?

My trip down Memory Lane is interrupted by Sigrid, who asks if I've got change for a 100,000-dong. While I'd been revisiting Uncle Nick's rustic cabin, Mai had been busy talking my mom and Sigrid into buying her ratty scraps of fabric. I examine the girl with fresh respect. I bet that Sigrid has even less use for this crap than my mother does.

Turning back to where my dad's sitting, we see him slumped facedown on the dirty table. "Skippy?" screeches my mother, scuttling towards him. I am right behind her.

"Dad?" I say. I am already envisioning my dad in a helicopter, being medevaced to Singapore.

When my dad emits a contented snore, I exhale. My mom, relief clearly fighting with fury, turns to glare at me, then raps my dad sharply on the shoulder.

Skip looks up blearily. "Captain Willard?" he mumbles. "Look out, cap'n! Charlie! Charlie!"

Tabitha grabs his collar and shakes him. "Really, Skippy," she says. "Wake up! It's not even lunch time! You've had too much of that zoo-drink!" She turns to me and Sigrid. "I'm taking him back to the hotel."

I offer to come too and my mom glowers at me, as if to say: *You've done enough already*. There's a streak of dirt on her white tunic and her Jimmy Choos are muddy. Seeing her grim expression, I feel sorry for my father.

"Naw, I'm fine honey," says Skip. He rubs his eyes and signals for the bill. "I was just having a nap, that's all. It's the jet lag." He yawns. "Delayed reaction." After paying for our soup and rice wine, he sways to his feet, his three

H'mong buddies doing likewise. They all shake hands, the H'mong trio looking even wobblier than my dad does.

Sigrid, Mai and I watch as my parents stagger off towards their hotel. After refolding her wares and placing them neatly into her backpack, Mai asks if we're in need of a tour guide. "You see Cat Cat village, waterfall, indigo making, rope bridge, ancient stones?" she says, holding up a clear plastic card-holder filled with faded photos of the local tourist attractions.

"Um, what's that?" says Sigrid, pointing to a picture of a pile of rocks decorated with geometric patterns and squiggles.

"Ancient rock carving," says Mai. "Very old. Two, three thousand year."

I peer at the image. The rock carvings might, as Mai says, be prehistoric. Or they could have been made last month by some entrepreneurial local, like Mai here.

"Not today," I say. "But could you show us the way to Highlands Outreach office?"

Mai eyes me curiously. "Sure," she says. "We go now? It not far." She slips her thin arms through the handles of her backpack. I expect her to set a price, but instead she just asks why we want to go there.

Flying by the seat of my pants, I explain that I work for a magazine in Hanoi, and that I'm interested in community aid projects. "Someone mentioned Highlands Outreach and Lindy Tran," I say. "Do you know her?"

At the mention of Lindy's name, Mai's brown eyes narrow. "Lindy come here some time," she says, her cautious tone further whetting my curiosity. Why has mention of Lindy Tran caused Mai to sound so guarded?

But before I can ask, she is off, leading us deeper into the market. The stalls at the back are more makeshift than those near the street. Women in traditional garb squat beside colorful blankets spread with fresh produce. Some of the women have babies strapped to their backs, the woven baby-slings split to reveal the infants' bare bottoms. Toddlers wearing nothing below their waists careen down the aisles or sit in the dirt staring up at us, while the smells of sewage, raw meat and fish, and medicinal herbs assault our nostrils.

After exiting the market we descend some stone steps and pass a silversmith's shop and another selling rudimentary farm implements. The street slopes downhill, increasingly rutted. We walk past low, tiled-roof houses towards the edge of the village.

"What does Lindy do when she's here?" says Sigrid. I can tell that she's trying not to sound too curious.

Mai shrugs. "Well, first I think she here to build community center. She seem nice. But then I see her with some guys." She glances around when she says this, as though fearful that someone might have overheard her.

"What guys?" I say.

The girl hesitates, her pretty face troubled. "Traders." She lowers her voice to a whisper. "Bad traders, you know?"

The road turns a corner. "As in smugglers?" says Sigrid.

Mai nods, then readjusts her red headgear. "They H'mong but not from here. They sell black market." Her pretty face looks ominous. "Or maybe worse."

"Like drugs?" I say.

"Maybe. My mom say they mafia. But my ⸱. everyone not from here bad." Perhaps fearing t⸱. sounds disloyal to her mother, she reconsiders. "I th⸱. they bad too."

We are nearing the edge of the village, the road leading down a hill into a green valley that is crisscrossed by snaking red footpaths. Here and there clumps of giant bamboo stand like massive, curlicued ostrich feathers. A stream runs through the valley, the water white in places and dotted with big gray boulders. The scene is so picturesque that I stop to take a photo.

Instead of continuing down into the valley, Mai turns into a small lane spread with gravel. As we walk, our feet stir up puffs of dust. The houses are further apart here, both sides of the narrow road bordered by thick vegetation.

After a few minutes, the road starts to climb. I take off my baseball hat and fan myself. The locals are fond of saying that Sapa has four seasons in a day, and while last night was cool, in the midday sun, I'm sweating. Mai leads us around another corner, then gestures towards the end of the alley. "Highlands Outreach last one, green door." She points to a single storey, tiled-roofed shack that couldn't contain more than two rooms, if that, and looks as if it hasn't been repainted in decades.

"Is that going to be the community center?" says Sigrid doubtfully. "It doesn't look like much, does it?"

"No, they say they build new place next door," says Mai. "At open ceremony they say cost 40,000 dollar."

"American?" I say. "That's a lot of money."

Mai nods sadly. "Yes. Will have computer, with

Internet and Wifi." She says these final words as though she's speaking of something sacred.

Looking at the girl's wistful expression, I shake my head. The chance that Mai and her friends are going to get Internet connection any time soon seems unlikely. "Forty thousand dollars," I say again. I look at Sigrid. "She wouldn't just take it, would she? I mean sooner or later someone would check up and realize that nothing had been built…"

Sigrid studies the red-tiled shack and shrugs. "Things are probably just delayed," she says. "It's not like anything ever happens on schedule in Vietnam. They might start building next week, or tomorrow."

Walking closer, I see a tiny plastic sign affixed to the hut's only door, its red surface bearing the words: Highlands Outreach.

"Or maybe Lindy Tran really is crazy," says Sigrid. "Or else she's not planning to stick around long enough for people to start asking questions. You know, take the money and run."

"She wouldn't dare," I say.

We're a few steps from the shack's door when Mai freezes. She puts a hand on my arm. "Shhh," she whispers. "Someone in there."

I'm wondering if the girl is mistaken when I hear a voice too. It's a man's voice, speaking in English but with a heavy accent. Sigrid is listening too. I tiptoe towards the hut's shuttered window. Sigrid and Mai follow.

"They top grade," says the man. "Look at color!"

"Would you sit down for a minute?" says a woman. "I cannot think with you looking over my shoulder like that!"

I swallow hard, recalling the imperious tone in which Lindy had ordered me to fetch her a robe. I'd recognize that snooty French accent anywhere.

While the window shutters are drawn, the wood is old and warped. I press my eye to a crack, Sigrid and Mai doing likewise. At first I can't see anything, but when I move my head a sliver of room comes into view. I see unpainted wood-plank walls and a low table. I move my eye along the crack and Lindy Tran's head appears. She is bent low over the table examining something. Strewn across the table are some pieces of brown paper. These pages bear the same strange and beautiful script that I'd found on some of the papers in Lindy's sequined handbag.

I step back to see Sigrid and Mai with their faces pressed to the rough window shutters. "Can you guys see what she's doing?" I whisper.

"She look at something," says Mai. "A man there." Her voice quakes ever so slightly.

"Do you know him?"

The girl leans back and nods. "Yes. They call him Knife. He mafia, bad man." She steps away from the wall. "We better go now."

"Wait," hisses Sigrid. "I… oh, look!"

I press my nose to the rough wood and squint. I can now see a stocky, tough-looking man standing with his hands in his pockets. Dressed in Western-style clothes, he's got darkly tanned skin and a wide, off-centered nose that looks as if it's been broken repeatedly. He's staring down at the table with an expression of impatience on his broad face. "You finish yet?" he says gruffly.

Lindy Tran leans back and I blink. Lying before her on the rough wooden table are dozens of glittering red stones. "Rubies!" I whisper.

"Wha! Big ones!" says Mai, her eyes huge.

"There are a lot of them," whispers Sigrid. She shakes her head. "Why is she buying rubies? Is that what she's doing with all the charity cash? I don't get it."

I'm trying to figure it out too when I hear a noise behind us. Turning to look, I freeze. Graham Hall is standing in the middle of the alley, staring at us.

15 Guilty Pleasures

My first thought is that Graham is involved in whatever Lindy's up to. I imagine him yelling for help and Lindy and the tough-looking H'mong guy rushing out and attacking us. What would they do? Are we in actual physical danger?

I look at Sigrid and Mai, both of whom, like me, stand frozen. Mai's mouth is open. She looks petrified. Down the lane, a dog barks. My heart is thumping madly.

I wait for Graham to say something but he just keeps standing there squinting at us. I gape back at him. In one hand he's holding a small, brown paper parcel that is tied with pale twine. The index and middle fingers of his other hand are wrapped in a grubby gauze bandage. I take in his faded grey cargo pants and his white t-shirt and his face and arms, which are more tanned than when I'd seen him on the train the day before yesterday. In the bright noonday sun, the tiny hairs on his forearms glow gold. I have a crazy urge to walk over to him and stroke them.

I've heard that fear can cause horniness, which makes sense if you think about it. You're scared and stressed so you focus on something nice, something that makes you feel alive, and glad to be. But while part of me is fantasizing about stroking Graham Hall's muscled body, another part of me is ready to run for it. Mai seems to be considering flight too. Out of the corner of my eye I can see her shaking.

"Jane?" says Graham. He shades his eyes against the sun. "What are you doing here?"

Sigrid, Mai and I all shush him in unison, as though the sound of his voice has unlocked all of ours. Sigrid tiptoes towards him. Mai and I follow.

"What the—" says Graham. He looks so confused that I feel a rush of hope. Maybe he's not involved in Lindy's dodgy dealings after all, or maybe there's an innocent explanation to all of this.

"Shhhh," says Sigrid again. "They're in there." She glares at him.

"Who's in there?" says Graham. "And what are you guys doing here?" He looks at me when he says this, as though I'm the most reasonable of the trio. His fingertips, I note, are stained with motor oil and his cargo pants are streaked black in spots.

"Lindy's in there," I whisper. "Counting rubies."

"Lindy?" says Graham. "In Sapa?" He shakes his head. "No, she's at Ba Vi Lake on a mission for her NGO. I called her this morning." He steps towards the Highlands Outreach office but Sigrid grabs his arm. "No! Over here," she hisses, propelling him towards the rear of another hut. "They might see us."

"What?" says Graham. "This is crazy. Who might see us?"

"Lindy," I say. "She's in the office. With the H'mong smuggler."

"Smuggler?" says Graham. "What are you guys talking about?"

While I'm inclined to believe that he knows nothing about any of this, Sigrid is obviously skeptical. "The guy with the rubies," she says belligerently. "Aren't you here to meet them?"

"No," says Graham. He pushes a stray curl from his eyes. "I'm here to drop off a package." He holds up the small paper-wrapped parcel that he's holding. "Lindy asked me to pick it up in Bac Ha and drop it off at the office." He nods towards the shack, his face troubled. "I wasn't supposed to get to Sapa until the day after tomorrow but I took a spill and my gearbox started acting up so I decided to cut my road trip short and take a shortcut." He holds up his injured hand like an exhibit of proof in a courtroom.

I want to ask if his fingers are broken but Sigrid speaks first. "So what is it?" she says, eyeing the parcel suspiciously.

"I have no idea," says Graham, some irritation creeping into his voice. "Why would I open Lindy's mail? She said it was important." He shrugs, then turns to me. "How do you know Lindy?" he says. "And are you sure that she's in there? It makes no sense. I just talked to her a few hours ago."

"She's in there," I say. "She's not at Ba Vi Lake and she wasn't there this morning either."

Graham bites his lip. Ba Vi Lake is at least a day's drive away. "But, but why would she lie?" he says. "She said she was running a prenatal care workshop up there." He shakes his head. "Why wouldn't she just tell me that she was coming to Sapa?"

"Because that's just what she *does*," I say. "Lie, I mean. It's like she can't help herself."

"God, this is crazy," says Graham. He looks from me to Mai to Sigrid and back at me again, then rubs his

forehead. There's a sheen of sweat on his brow. "What were you saying about rubies?"

"She's in there counting rubies," says Sigrid. "And a lot of charity money seems to be missing. The community center was supposed to open this month and look at it..." She nods towards the shack. "Any idea what's been happening?"

"She said there were problems with the license," says Graham.

"No true," says Mai. "I know for sure. My uncle work at town planning department. He say license approve before open ceremony."

Graham studies the hut, as if by doing so some explanation will come to him. "Rubies?" he says. "Why would Lindy be buying rubies?"

Sigrid glares at him. "How should we know?"

I give Sigrid a look. Can't she give the guy a break? He's obviously as bewildered as we are, plus he's just discovered that his girlfriend is lying to him.

Graham winces. "You really think she's been misusing charitable funds?" He studies his scuffed Adidas. "It seems so..." He searches for words. "So outrageous."

Looking at Graham, I feel sorry for him. It's a lot to absorb: Not only has his girlfriend been lying about her whereabouts but she might be a con-woman. I wonder if he loves her.

I'm debating whether or not to mention Lindy's goings on with Jason McCallum and Wyatt when we hear the sound of voices. Mai flattens herself against the shed, while Sigrid herds Graham and me deeper into the shadows. My heart starts to pound again. I can hear footsteps crunching on the gravel.

"I'll have the rest the day after tomorrow," says Lindy. "So I need that paperwork now."

Knife grunts. "I told you it's coming."

"You said that last week," snaps Lindy.

He stomps through the gravel. "Why you in such a hurry? It is *coming*."

"You just don't get it," says Lindy. "I can't hang around here much longer. How long do you think it will be before people start asking questions about the community center, why it's not built yet?"

Knife shrugs. "That's not my problem."

"It is if I get caught," she says ominously. "I'm not going down alone."

"Are you threatening me?" He sounds so mean that I shiver.

When Lindy replies her voice is as menacing as Knife's. "No," she says. "I'm just *reminding* you of why we need to move quickly. My flight to L.A. is next week."

From where we're hiding we can't see Lindy and the H'mong guy until they've passed us. When Lindy's shapely back comes into view I feel Graham stiffen beside me. Her sequined purse hangs over one shoulder. I imagine all those rubies inside of it. The H'mong guy says something to her that I can't hear and Lindy tosses her hair, which sways like a silky black scarf across her shoulders. I picture all of the guys who've admired that hair toss, including Graham.

With my back pressed against the hut I want to turn towards him, to see if he looks utterly crestfallen, but it seems too intrusive. But then curiosity gets the better of me and I look, surreptitiously studying the determined tilt of his jaw and the way that his big lips are pressed tightly together. I'm relieved to see that he looks more mad than heartbroken.

Knife shoves his hands into the pocket of his tight jeans. "How do I even know you'll come back?" His voice is sullen.

Lindy stops walking and puts her hands on her hips. She sounds exasperated. "Because we have a *plan*!" she says.

They both start walking again.

When Lindy's and Knife's footsteps are no longer audible we all relax. I realize that I've been holding my breath. I feel dizzy. Mai looks dazed too. I bet that she regrets having brought us here. Maybe we can find some way to make it up to her.

After peeking back inside the Highlands Outreach office to be sure that the rubies are gone, we all trudge back towards the main market. As we walk, we fill Graham in on what had aroused our suspicions about Lindy in Hanoi: the work that hadn't been done in Mai Chau, the bank statements, the expensive training courses that seem never to have happened.

"She's guilty as sin," says Sigrid, who's never met a proverb that she doesn't like. We're back on the main road, going uphill this time, so the climb is slower. "So now what?"

"I guess we could try to follow her," I say. "See what she does next?" I recall my last dismal attempt at espionage, when I'd been apprehended trying to clamber onto Jason McCallum's porch, then push this memory away. "Any idea where she could be staying, Graham?"

"Maybe Fansipan Lodge," he says, referring to a place at the other end of the village. He looks glum. "But who knows, I obviously don't know her that well, do I?"

"Don't worry. I ask my friends find her," says Mai. "Sapa small. No problem."

We're near the back side of the market when Mai bids us farewell. "I better go sell," she says, nodding towards the wicker backpack that's still draped over her shoulder.

"Let us pay you," I say. "Or else I'll buy some of your fabric." I figure that it's the least I can do given that we've monopolized a few hours of her workday but Mai just shakes her head and grins at us. "No problem," she says again. "Just make sure we get Wifi."

And with that she is gone, scrambling off up the hill at three times our speed. The three of us stand there watching her.

"Want to get a drink?" says Graham. Sigrid and I nod. The sun is still hot and we're all thirsty. As we walk I half expect to run into Lindy Tran. Every time we turn a corner I feel furtive and nervous. The streets are narrow and lined with connected shop-houses, none of which is higher than three stories. Most of the houses' doors are open and people sit on their doorsteps or out in the street doing all sorts of everyday tasks like hucking corn, sharpening knives, braiding little girls' hair, or washing the dishes. Since they're used to tourists nobody pays us much attention.

The place where Graham takes us is up on the second floor. We follow him up a narrow, rickety staircase and into a dark room, then walk outside and sit on a long, skinny balcony. The view is amazing. We can see the

valley down below and the hills on the other side, backed by a ruff of lacy green ridges.

"They make great coffee here," says Graham, "and the best strawberry milk shakes." I order a milk coffee and Sigrid goes for a shake. Graham orders one of each, plus a plate of French fries.

When we're all eating Graham's fries the conversation turns back to Lindy Tran. Watching Graham attempt to shake out more ketchup, I realize that I'm curious about something else. Even though I'd found Wyatt in bed with another woman, if someone told me that he was embezzling funds from the bank where he works, I'd defend him. He cheated on me but I know that he's no felon. And yet when we'd accused Lindy of pilfering funds from her charity Graham had barely protested.

"Graham," I say. "Do you think she's a thief?"

He dips a fry into a puddle of ketchup and stirs thoughtfully. When he speaks, he raises his head and looks right at me. At the sight of those green eyes gazing into mine I feel my stomach buzz, or maybe it's because of this extra-strong coffee. "You know, the strange thing is that when you first said it, it's like everything just clicked." He sets down the French fry. "I don't mean that I knew or even suspected. I'm still hoping that this is all a big mistake…" He pauses and looks out over the valley. "But for a while now I've had the feeling that something wasn't right with her."

Sigrid slurps down the last of her milkshake. "Like what?" she says.

Graham stirs his coffee with his uninjured hand, clearly embarrassed. "Well, she just seemed too good to be true, you know? She's been everywhere, done everything, knows how to do anything you can think of."

"So why were you with her?" I say, the words slipping out before I have time to consider them. I blush. It's really none of my business.

Graham blushes too, the freckles on his face darkening. "Part of me thought I was imagining it. I mean, why would she make stuff like that up? It's so pointless." He takes a sip of coffee and grimaces. "But I think another part of me was waiting to catch her in a lie, to have some proof." He glances from Sigrid to me, his gaze troubled. "Does that make any sense?"

"Yeah, I guess so," I say. "Part of you couldn't believe that she could really be that crazy and another part of you wanted solid proof so that you could stop second-guessing yourself."

"Right." He smiles ruefully. "And now I have it."

"But we don't really," says Sigrid. "We have nothing solid at all. For all we know Lindy just loves rubies and is buying loads of them with her own money. Maybe she's independently wealthy or maybe she's just buying those stones for someone else. Maybe she's planning to resell them, which isn't illegal."

For a few moments none of us responds. I guess we're all trying to figure out possible explanations in our heads, or work out a plan to catch Lindy. Then I remember the package that Graham had been delivering. He'd shoved it into a pocket of his cargo pants back when we were hiding by the Highlands Outreach office.

"The parcel," I say. "Do you think we should open it?"

"Of course we should!" says Sigrid. "I can't believe I forgot about it."

Graham doesn't look so sure. "I don't know," he says. "It seems kind of dishonest."

"So does stealing funds meant for underprivileged ethnic minority women and kids," says Sigrid pointedly.

Or stealing other people's fiancés, I think, but I don't say anything.

Graham pulls the parcel out of his pocket and sets it on the table. A small box has been wrapped in rough brown paper and tied with twine. I reach for it, surprised by how light it is. I give the box a little shake. Something rattles.

I'm wondering how to cut the twine when Sigrid hands me a Swiss army knife. It's exactly the sort of thing that I'd expect Sigrid to have in her bag. I bet she's also carrying safety pins, band-aids and a flashlight.

I snip through the twine with the little fold-out scissors, then peel off the brown paper, careful not to rip it just in case we decide to wrap it up again and drop it off as if it hasn't been opened. A brown box lies inside, its lid stuck down with masking tape. As I peel up the tape I feel a trill of excitement. Are there more rubies in there?

I flip up the lid and we all peer inside. The box contains a key ring attached to a tiny gold-painted owl and three sheets of folded paper. We all exhale. Glancing up, I see that the others are as disappointed as I am. I tip the box upside down. There are no rubies.

Sigrid smoothes out the pages, which are written on the same kind of rough brown paper that we'd found in Lindy's purse. Like those pages, these ones are covered in beautiful, cursive script. There are also some columns of tiny numbers too. We each take one page and stare at it.

"We found some pages just like these in Lindy's purse," I say. "Along with those suspicious bank statements."

"It's Burmese," says Graham. "And so's the owl. People there put sets of those owls in their houses for good luck. Lindy bought a few sets when we were there. She really liked them." He dangles the key ring from his index finger, studying it.

"So Lindy's been to Burma or Myanmar or whatever it's called now?" says Sigrid. She squints at the columns of figures, studying them.

Graham nods. "Yeah, we spent a few days in Yangon at the start of the year." He fiddles with his bandage, considering.

"Burma is famous for rubies," I say. "Do you think that's related?"

"I don't know," says Graham. He stares off into the distance like he's trying to remember something. Thin plumes of smoke are rising from some of the little houses down in the valley far below. I imagine women just back from working in the fields squatting beside open fires in their kitchens trying to get a meal together. I bet they'd kill for a microwave.

"When we were in Yangon Lindy wanted to buy some rubies to make a bracelet. We went to a bunch of gem markets and talked to some guys but then she ended up deciding not to buy any stones after all since it seemed too unethical, what with the gem trade supporting the junta and all."

"How are you supporting the military regime if you're buying them on the black market?" says Sigrid. As usual, I'm amazed by how fast her mind works. I'd still been trying to remember where Yangon is.

"The black market dealers have to pay off the cops and military," says Graham. "So wherever you're getting them in Burma it's like buying blood diamonds. That's what Lindy said."

"Do you know for sure that she didn't get any stones or is this just what she told you?" says Sigrid. "She doesn't seem that concerned about ethics to me."

Graham sighs. "You're right. I don't know. She could have bought some stones and carried them out. But if you got caught taking a lot out that way you could get into big trouble. You're supposed to buy them in the official government stores and pay tax on them."

"So if she wanted rubies why didn't she just buy them in Vietnam," I say. "Vietnam has rubies too. Why go to all that trouble?"

"They're not as good as the Burmese ones," says Graham. "The ones from Burma have a richer color. They're a lot more valuable."

"Okay," I say. "Say that she's paying H'mong smugglers to bring her Burmese rubies to Vietnam. There are H'mong people in Burma, Thailand and Laos, right? So it's conceivable that she's hooked up with some sort of H'mong smuggling ring."

Graham nods. "Yes, that's possible," he says. "But who's she selling them to? Don't you think that most buyers in Vietnam would get the local ones? They're not as nice as the Burmese stones but they're a lot cheaper.

And why would the smugglers need Lindy? They can sell the stones on to local buyers just as easily as she can."

"So maybe she's not selling them in Vietnam," I say. "She can take them overseas. As a foreigner that's her advantage."

"That's it!" says Sigrid. "She said she was going to L.A!" When Graham and I fail to share her excitement she shakes her head in exasperation. "The States has imposed an embargo on Myanmar. Like Lindy said, all the money from gem-dealing supports the military junta, which is terrorizing the people and keeping that lady…" She shuts her eyes in a bid to remember. "You know, the lady who won the election and was put under house arrest?" Her eyes spring open. "Aung San Suu Kyi!" she says triumphantly. "Anyways, it's illegal to sell Burmese rubies in the U.S. Lindy must be passing them off as exceptionally high-grade Vietnamese ones. That's what she meant when she was talking about paperwork."

Graham shakes his head in disgust. "So she's stealing donated money to buy the rubies and supporting those awful Burmese generals. She's really something, isn't she?"

Sigrid and I nod. *And she stole my fiancé*, I think. But I don't say anything.

"This is all starting to make sense," says Sigrid. She reaches for another French fry. "But what should we do about it? Do you think we should tell the authorities?"

I think back to the grilling I'd received from Mr. Thai of the Department of Foreigner Control. "I already tried that," I say. "They didn't want to hear about it. And even if they do go and talk to her she's a good liar.

probably just believe her and then she'd know that we're onto her and take off."

"I don't trust the cops around here anyways," says Graham. "For all we know Knife is actually a cop himself, or else his brother or uncle or cousin is." He uses his good hand to smooth down the crinkled brown wrapping paper. "I think that Jane had the best idea earlier. We should just watch her."

"What if she's leaving tonight?" I say. "She could be on her way to Lao Cai right now and take the early train back to Hanoi tomorrow morning."

"She said she was getting more tomorrow," says Sigrid. "That means we have another day."

I nod. "Hopefully Mai will find out where she's staying."

"Hopefully Lindy won't see *us*," says Graham. "It's hard not to run into people here. And if she sees me she'll know that I know that she lied about being at Ba Vi Lake."

"I'm sure she'll have some excuse," says Sigrid. "Like she was flown here by helicopter for some top secret mission."

Graham smiles grimly. "She has been hinting about being recruited by the CIA recently."

My eyebrows shoot up. "She told you that she works for the CIA?" I say. "Wouldn't people who really work for the CIA keep quiet about it?" I down the last of my coffee. "Weren't you a little suspicious?"

Graham looks sheepish. "She didn't exactly come right out and say it but yeah…" He shakes his head. "She just had so many outrageous stories that I kind of got used to ignoring them."

Sigrid shakes her head in disgust. "It sounds to me like you were blinded by her boobs and big hair." She reaches for the last remaining French fry.

Graham looks hurt. He starts to defend himself, then shrugs. "Maybe," he concedes. "Anyways, I screwed up big time." He checks his watch. "I have to go get my motorbike before the mechanic closes." He signals for the bill.

"And I should go check on my folks," I say.

We troop down the rickety staircase together, then stand in the street, now in shadow. Before going our separate ways Sigrid asks Graham if he wants to join us for dinner. While I hope that he says yes, I also worry about him meeting my parents. Who knows what they might say to him?

"Sure." His eyes crinkle into a smile. "Have you guys eaten at Ong Gia's? It's a bit out of the way but the food is really good." When we shake our heads he gives us directions. We agree to meet around seven.

"You like him don't you?" says Sigrid when we're walking up the hill towards our hotel.

"Sure," I say, trying to keep my voice neutral. "He's a nice guy."

"Ha," she says. "I mean *like* him like him."

"I do not," I say. I'm still not sure that it's over between me and Wyatt.

"Whatever," she says. The incline is steep and she's huffing slightly but she still manages to sound smug.

"You don't know what you're talking about," I say. "I mean sure I like him. He's cool—"

"And cute."

"And cute," I admit. I have to slow down. My hamstrings are burning. I take a deep breath. "What makes you think that I like, *like* him?"

"I can just tell," says Sigrid.

"Well you're wrong," I say.

Sigrid smiles. "Sure. Whatever."

I want to ask if she thinks that he likes me too, but of course I can't do that since that would be an admission that I do like him. Which I don't. At least not in the way that Sigrid thinks. I still love Wyatt.

In the street down below us two H'mong guys drive by on an ancient Minsk motorbike. Some wooden planks lie across the bike's luggage rack and strapped to these wooden boards is a large, hog-tied pig. As they drive past I can see the pig's little eye staring up at me, its expression beseeching.

I stop walking and watch the motorbike drive away. One of the H'mong guys turns back to check on the pig, which is just lying there. Staring after that pig I try to imagine Wyatt here in Sapa with me.

I try to picture him dressed in shorts and a t-shirt, smiling and holding my hand, but all I can manage is an image of him in his suit and tie, clutching his briefcase.

16 Getting Closer

Graham wasn't exaggerating when he said that Ong Gia's is out of the way, since it's reached by a series of alleys that grow progressively smaller and steeper. The restaurant is set on a hillside and has a big low terrace that overlooks rooftops and some streets sloping down below.

There's a chill in the air but we've all brought sweaters and opt to sit outdoors. The air smells like some unknown flower, a sweet smell that for some reason makes me feel nostalgic, as though this moment were already gone and I'm looking back on it.

I'm seated between my dad, who's at the end of the table, and Graham, who's sitting across from my mom. Sigrid is sitting across from me. She's wearing a red beret that makes her look even jauntier than usual. We're all holding menus and pretending to look at them, although we're actually going to let Graham order for all of us since the menus are in Vietnamese and have no pictures.

I'm guessing that my mom must be nervous about eating here; it's not the sort of place where she'd usually go. But she's being a good sport and my dad seems to be in high spirits. He slept most of the afternoon and my mom got a massage.

"Cocktails?" says my mom.

"It's either beer or rice wine here," says Graham. He scans the menu. "Or wait, there's some plum liqueur."

Given that we'd indulged in rice wine only this morning, Sigrid, my dad and I opt for beer. Graham has beer too, while my mom orders the liqueur.

"How is it?" I ask, after we've all clinked bottles and glasses and she's taken a sip.

"Delicious," declares Tabitha. "You really must try some."

I take a dutiful sip and have to admit that it's not bad. Graham orders what sounds like way too many dishes. As we wait for our food we talk about where we're from, our jobs, my dad's golf handicap, Vietnam and what there is to do around Sapa. I keep waiting for someone to mention my cancelled wedding but nobody does. My parents seem relaxed and friendly and Graham is making my mom laugh, telling her all about his recent bike crash and how he'd ended up in a duck pond with mud all over him and been charged by an irate goose that had thought he was threatening its territory.

The food comes and it's delicious, with so many plates appearing that we keep having to rearrange our napkins and chopsticks and beer bottles to allow everything to fit. We eat beef stir-fried with green peppers and pineapple, sticky rice cooked with coconut milk, pork and tofu in a clay pot, fish steamed with cat's-ear mushrooms and vermicelli noodles, and two plates of sautéed morning glory stalks.

"This is a feast," says my mom. She's wielding her chopsticks like a pro. Back in Hanoi she'd used a fork the whole time.

I can't believe that my mom isn't complaining about the beef being too spicy and that my dad actually eats his tofu. It's like my parents have been kidnapped and replaced by this pair, who are adventurous, chatty and charming.

The dishes have just been cleared away when I hear someone calling my name. I turn around to see Mai standing on the pavement below our terrace, waving at us. We all say hi. I ask her if she's eaten yet.

"Already," she says. "I come tell you Lindy stay Gold Mountain hotel. Room nine." She explains how to get there.

"Great! Thanks," I say. "But how did you know where we were?"

Mai shrugs. "My sister see you go here."

We all say goodnight and watch Mai walking back down the lane, her wicker backpack still strapped to her narrow back. I wonder if she managed to sell anything. In the fading light her dark tunic, backpack and leggings grow less and less visible until all we can see is a slim dark shadow topped by her bright red headgear. Then she turns a corner and is lost to us.

"What was that about?" says my mom. "Who's Lindy?"

"Oh, just this girl we know," I say. I'd rather not explain the whole long, complicated saga to my parents. They'd both advise us to leave things to the cops, I am sure. I change the subject to whether or not anyone has room for dessert. There's a chorus of 'none for me's' and one 'sure, why not?' from Sigrid.

The hotel where we're staying is the most expensive one in town, managed by a French company and designed like a stylish ski lodge. Being French-run, it serves good pastries, so we decide to go there. We can sit beside the fireplace in the lobby and drink tea and brandy while Sigrid has her dessert.

Of course, by the time that we get there the rest of us are ready for dessert too. We grab a bunch of French magazines and sit on corduroy-covered sofas with our shoes off and our feet tucked up. We order three kinds of cake and share, then order another slice of the *mille feuilles* since my dad ate most of the first one.

"Do you think that you'll stay in Hanoi for much longer?" my dad asks Graham. The firelight is making the little hairs on Graham's forearms sparkle again. Again, I have an urge to reach over and stroke them.

Graham nods. "Yes, I think so. My graphics business is going pretty well and I like this." He spreads his arms towards the picture window to one side of us. Although it's dark outside we all know that he's referring to the mountains beyond, the seemingly endless ridges that run to and past the Chinese border. "I like getting out on my bike and exploring these far-off places. I like that Hanoi's still got its own vibe, that there aren't McDonald's and Starbucks on every corner and that every day I still feel like I've seen something new." His eyes crinkle into a smile. "I still don't know what'll happen next and I like that." He looks right at me when he says this.

Not much later my parents decide to call it a night. "It's been a great day but I'm beat," says my dad.

"All this fresh air," says my mom. "We're going to sleep like babies."

I kiss them goodnight and they hug Sigrid, then shake Graham's hand. "Great to meet you," says my dad.

"See you tomorrow," says my mom, who's already ascertained that Graham's planning to stay in Sapa for another couple of days. She stands up and smoothes down the back of her sweater.

Before they walk out the back door to cross the courtyard to get to their room, my dad turns back and looks at me. I smile and my dad nods towards Graham and winks, a great big conspirator's wink, as though we're in on something together and he's happy about it.

The door swings shut behind him. Staring at the still swinging door, I wonder what my dad had meant by that wink. Does he think that there's something going on between Graham and me? Was that a wink of approval?

Maybe it's the heat of the open fire or maybe it's the brandy but all of a sudden my cheeks feel hot. Graham asks if we want another drink and I can't even look at him.

"We should go check out Lindy's hotel," says Sigrid. She gives me a funny look. "Are you alright Jane?"

I say that I'm fine, it's just hot in here.

"Your parents are great," says Graham, as we're walking towards the hotel's front door.

You don't know them, I think, but manage to stop myself from saying it. "They seem to be having a good time here," I say. We leave the building and start walking down the hill. The air is a lot colder now.

"They seem really well suited to each other," he says. "How long have they been married?"

"Forever," I say, then do the math. "Thirty-one years." Graham has his hands in his pockets. Mine are pulled up inside my sweater.

"Wow. That's impressive," he says. "My parents divorced when I was six." He sounds sad when he says this.

I don't know how to respond so I don't say anything.

"Same," says Sigrid. "They split when I was nine." She kicks at a rock, sending it rolling down the hill. "Most of my friends' parents are divorced. It makes me wonder why people bother."

I am surprised. While she's spoken of the pain and shame of getting divorced, I've never heard her question the institution of marriage. I wonder if her parents' divorce or her experience with Damien is behind this reluctance to commit. "Would you rather stay single?" I say.

"No, I just don't see the point of getting married," she says. Her face is hidden to me but there's some strain in her voice. I realize that Sigrid has told me only the bare minimum about her past. I, on the other hand, have told her everything.

"Think of all the weddings you've been to," she says. "It seems that everyone's so focused on the cake and champagne that they forget that the odds that they'll actually stay together are less than one in two." She kicks at another rock. "That means that sooner or later more than half of them will be tossing out those wedding photos."

I recall various weddings that I've attended, a row of pretty, smiling brides parading through my head. My cousin Suzanne. My college roommate Molly. My friends Alex, Mila and Stephanie K. Mixed in with the real brides are ones from movies and magazines, images gleaned way back in childhood and on through the years: Princess Diana looking demure and divine despite her 25-foot-long train that could have done with a good ironing; *The Princess Bride*'s ethereal Robin Wright long before she was married to Sean Penn; Donald Trump's latest wife, her ring almost as blinding as her teeth are... At the end of the lineup I see myself, dressed in my made-to-measure silk gown. But unlike all of those other brides, I look worried.

"My older brother got married last year," says Graham. "His wife's Catholic and he's not so he had to go to classes so that they could get married in her family's church. It was a total nightmare. The golden retriever that he'd had since he was a kid had just died and he got into a yelling match with a nun about whether or not there are dogs in heaven." He runs a hand through his hair and grins. "Vegas sounds like a better idea to me. No hassle. No squabbling relatives."

From the sharp way that Sigrid looks at Graham I think that she's going to say something. I remember that she and Damien had gotten married in Vegas. But instead she just hunches her shoulders and stuffs her hands deeper into her pockets.

"I do agree with Sigrid that people get carried away focusing on the wedding details," I say cautiously, recalling all those hours I'd spent agonizing over font for the invitations and which shade of pink to pick for the napkins. "But I like the idea of a celebration, some kind of event to declare your love and make it official."

"I'm not saying that there's anything *wrong* with marriage," says Sigrid, "just that it's not for me." She readjusts her beret. "I guess I'm just not a romantic like you are."

I consider this. I am a romantic, for sure. And there's nothing more romantic than a wedding. But it's not just the wedding that I want. I want the secure feeling that comes from being with someone who you're totally comfortable with. And I want to know that the fun things that I'm doing with my partner are things that we'll look back on later, together. I want the shared fun and the joint history. I want forever.

I don't say any of these things because Graham is here and we're veering dangerously close to the topic of my broken engagement. I don't expect Graham to add to the discussion since romance and marriage aren't topics that most guys are dying to discuss but he surprises me. "But what's the alternative?" he says. "To never fall in love? To always be thinking that it's going to end badly?"

Sigrid laughs. "It seems I'm outnumbered," she says. "You're both romantics."

I glance at Graham and he smiles at me. "No, we're just optimists," he says.

I find myself grinning back at him. I've never thought of myself as an optimist before but walking down this dusty road I feel positively buoyant. I'm not going to end up like my Great Aunt Lucia after all, ditched at the altar and spending the rest of my days sewing outfits for my massive doll collection. Sooner or later I will find true love. And then I'll fight like hell to keep it.

We're some distance from the center of town on a quiet street. There are no streetlamps. It's a clear night. I lean my head back and see dozens of stars, cold and remote in the distance. Gazing up at those stars I realize that all of these thoughts about love weren't in any way linked to Wyatt. I haven't been thinking about Wyatt at all. I haven't been missing him.

The air smells of wood smoke. The only sounds are those of our footsteps on the dusty pavement. I shut my eyes and keep walking, one foot in front of the other, pretending that I can see where I'm going.

• • •

"That's it," says Graham. We follow him across the street, then stop and stare up at the place.

"Damn, that's ugly," says Sigrid.

The Gold Mountain Hotel features about a dozen little chalets arranged in rows across a hillside. Made of cement, the huts are meant to look like log cabins, complete with knots and whorls in the "wood". In front of each hut rest two cement chairs and a table shaped like tree stumps. Fake-stone cement paths link everything together.

The closest row of chalets is about 20 feet from us, the hillside steep enough so that all of the rooms overlook the road. The lights are on in five chalets.

Even though the street is dark I feel my skin crawl. Lindy Tran could be looking out of her window right now, staring down at us. Graham must have this same thought because he leads us into the shadow of a pine tree. "Room nine," he says. "That must be one of the back ones."

Huddled under a pine tree in the dark my idea to spy on Lindy doesn't seem so brilliant anymore. What are the odds that we'll actually see her do something felonious compared to the chance that we'll get caught sneaking around and be hauled off to the local penitentiary? I hear

Mr. Thai's warning ringing in my ears: "*And remember, Miss Jane. It is you who we are watching!*"

Sigrid clears her throat. "So what are we waiting for?" she says. "See those bushes to the right? We need to stay low and keep close to them."

I wait for Graham to say that this is a dumb idea after all but he just nods and starts moving towards the bushes. Like him, Sigrid moves in a crouch. Not wanting to be left behind, I follow them.

Number nine is the second-furthest hut in the last row, one of two chalets in this row with its lights on. We all crouch in the bushes and catch our breath. "We should go round back," whispers Sigrid. "It's darker back there."

Graham and I nod. Graham's hair shines in the dark. Luckily he's wearing a hooded sweatshirt so I tell him to put his hood up. "Your hair's so light," I say.

He touches his head as if to remind himself that he actually has hair, then pulls up his hood and grins at me. "Good thinking," he says. "But yours is pretty fair too." Then he reaches out and touches it.

I'm too surprised to speak or move so I just crouch there looking at him. Once, when I was a kid a hummingbird flew right up to my face and hovered there staring at me, its round black eyes gazing into mine as though it thought it recognized me. Its wings were pushing air against my cheeks and if I'd wanted to, I'm sure that I could have reached out and touched it. But I was so awed that such beauty was so close to me that I just held my breath and froze. I have never forgotten it.

"Hurry up," hisses Sigrid. Graham drops his hand. We turn towards the row of chalets.

Sigrid is already moving towards the first hut when its door swings open. We all freeze. A fat woman with her hair in pigtails that she outgrew at least three decades ago steps onto the chalet's narrow balcony. "It's stuffy in there," she says.

"Shut the door will you?" says a male voice. "You're letting the mosquitoes in."

"It needs airing out," she says. "It smells like your socks in there."

"For God's sake, Dawn, would you shut the door please? We'll end up with malaria."

Sigrid had recently informed me that malarial mosquitoes can't survive at elevations above 5,000 feet. I feel like enlightening this guy, but of course I keep quiet, as do Sigrid and Graham. We all crouch in the bushes trying to make ourselves as small as possible. My knees hurt. I hope that Dawn will go back inside soon.

When she's finally retreated indoors, still complaining about her beloved's socks, we all creep forward again. We reach number nine without further incident, although the throbbing in my knees has worsened.

The cabin has three windows, one in the front, one on the side and one in back. The back curtains are open. While the back room is dark, the door to the front room is partly open so that enough light shines in for us to see that it's a bedroom. I can make out a double bed, a wooden bureau, two bedside tables and another door, which must lead to the bathroom.

Lindy's voice is audible in the front room, although from here we can't hear what she's saying. She sounds irritated.

"Let's try the side," whispers Sigrid. Graham and I nod. With Sigrid in the lead we creep round to the side. We can't see anything because the curtains are drawn but we can hear better from here. My thighs are starting to quiver from all this crouching.

"Why are you being so difficult?" says Lindy. "After I sell the stones we use some of the cash to build that stupid community center. That way, people will continue to donate. I'll sign the construction contract with your company and we'll split the profit. We've been over this so many times so what's your problem?"

"Maybe you go to America and not come back," says a sullen male voice.

"Knife!" mouths Sigrid. Graham and I nod.

"Why would I do that?" says Lindy. "We've got a good thing going! But what we don't need is people nosing around asking questions!"

"Nobody come to check."

"How would you know?" says Lindy, her voice rising. "I *told* you to hire a couple of guys to start digging. How much does that cost? Nothing! Hire a couple of your cousins to dig a hole beside the office. That way, if people come by, at least it'll look like *something* is happening!"

Knife grunts. "Is not necessary."

"*Mon Dieu*! Was any of this your idea?" says Lindy crossly. "No? I've come up with everything! So when I tell you to do something, just do it!"

"You not my boss."

Lindy makes an exasperated noise. "I'm tired," she says. "We'll have the rest of the stones tomorrow and the paperwork will be done, right?"

Knife grunts again.

"Good, then see you tomorrow."

Some moments later the door opens. We all crawl hurriedly round back and crouch in the shadows. We hear the door shut and the sound of footsteps descending the steps. Inside the chalet the sitting room light goes off. A second later the bedroom light turns on. Hiding on one side of the window, I stand up cautiously, my hip creaking so loudly that I'm scared that Lindy must have heard it.

I peer into the window and see Lindy sitting on the bed with a small cardboard box in her hands. She's still wearing the same tight black jeans that she'd worn earlier in the day but has pulled on a fluffy pink sweater. She opens the lid of the box, inserts her hand and then stares at her palm. Against her pale skin the stones appear black. She moves her hand and the ceiling light catches the stones, which give out quick red flashes.

Graham and Sigrid have stood up too, Sigrid peering in at the opposite end of the window and Graham standing behind me. Sigrid, being short, has to stand on tiptoes while Graham, being tall, is looking in over my head. With him standing so close to me, it's hard to concentrate on Lindy.

For a few minutes she just sits there and plays with the stones, letting them run through her fingers. It occurs to me that the stones are the same color as the nail polish that she'd been wearing when I found her in my bed with Wyatt. I remember her red toenails poking out from under my duvet and Wyatt's head popping out, his hair in disarray and the smear of red lipstick on his chin. I recall Lindy's sly smile when she first caught sight of me.

All of the details are so clear that it's like I am back there, except that this time I don't feel sick with betrayal. Thinking back on it, I feel angry. I want to kill Wyatt. What a fucking moron!

I imagine going back in time and redoing the scene, maybe whacking Wyatt over the head with my purse, or throwing my engagement ring in his face, or at least telling him to go fuck himself.

Then I realize that it doesn't actually matter. The hurt and humiliation that I felt at that moment has lifted in the same way that a fever breaks. When you're healthy again you can picture yourself lying in bed and drinking nasty medicine but you can't really remember how the sickness *felt*. This is a blessing. I think our minds are just made that way.

I can feel Graham's warm breath on my left ear. All of this standing around has left me cold. I wish that I could lean back and snuggle up against him. Maybe without even realizing what I'm doing I do lean back a little or else Graham leans forward, because all of a sudden my back is up against his chest and both of his arms are around me.

Lindy stands up and carries the box of stones over to the dresser. She pulls out the bottom drawer and tucks the box down under some clothes, then walks towards the bathroom. On the way there she realizes that the curtains are still open and comes over to shut them. Sigrid, Graham and I all shrink back, deeper into the shadows. When Lindy yanks the curtains shut, I catch a whiff of her perfume, heavy and flowery.

We hear the shower turn on. A few minutes later there's the sound of a body getting into bed. Then the light turns off.

"Now what?" whispers Sigrid. "There's no point in us hanging around here all night freezing our butts off. She's going to sleep."

We creep quietly back towards the bushes.

Graham's guesthouse is in the same direction as our hotel. We walk for a couple of blocks in silence. It's been a long day and we're all tired.

While the closeness that Graham and I had shared outside Lindy's window has left me elated, I can't help but feel anxious too. Maybe it hadn't meant anything and was just a friendly hug between friends on a cold night. Graham isn't looking at me now. My hands are back in my sleeves and his are stuck in his pockets.

The town seems almost unnaturally quiet, the houses' doors and windows all boarded up. There are even more stars than there were earlier, high and tiny above us.

"Tonight wasn't a total waste," says Sigrid. "We did learn a few things."

"Like what?" I say. I feel too tired to think clearly.

"We know that she is planning to build the community center after all but that she's hired Knife's company to do it, which means that for every dollar they *claim* to spend only a fraction will actually be spent."

"Man, she's got every angle covered," says Graham. He sounds tired too.

Sigrid nods. "We also learned where she's keeping the rubies."

Behind a fence a big dog barks at us. "She doesn't trust hotel safes," says Graham.

"That figures," I say. "Dishonest people always think that they're about to be ripped off. I guess it's just in their nature to think about it."

"Well in this case, she might be right," says Sigrid.

I look over at her. Sigrid's got her beret pulled down low over her ears and the collar of her jacket turned up. She looks sexy and mysterious. I imagine her in a movie playing a secret agent. "How do you mean?" I say.

"I mean that we should take them," says Sigrid. Her eyes shine in the darkness.

"As in steal them?"

"As in reclaim them. Those stones were bought with money donated to her bogus charity. We can sell them and build that community center the way it's supposed to be built, with the right materials and good equipment."

"That sounds like a lot of work," I say.

Sigrid shrugs. "We won't do it ourselves," she says. "I'm sure some other non-profit would be happy to manage the project if we give them the funding for it."

I fight back a yawn, struggling to get a grip on all of this. Taking the stones does seem like the obvious thing to do but also the most likely to get us into major trouble. And how would we actually take them?

Having kept quiet throughout this exchange, Graham stops walking. "This is my turnoff," he says.

I want to reach out and grab his hand or better yet to kiss him but I don't because Sigrid is here. If she weren't here I wouldn't do it either, but I still wish that Graham and I were alone. I can feel my heart pounding.

Sigrid asks Graham what he thinks, should we try to take the stones?

He's still got his hood up. Against the dark fabric his skin looks very pale. A few curls poke out, the same cold bright color as the stars above us. "We can try," he says. "She said she'll get the rest of them tomorrow so we'd better get up early to keep an eye on her."

"How early?" I say. I'm not much of a morning person.

"8:00 should be fine," he says. "Lindy never gets up before 8:00."

I'd rather not either.

"Meet for breakfast at 7:00?" says Sigrid. She's one of those people who can wake up and instantly resume whatever complicated conversation she'd been having before she fell asleep. Before coffee I can't even form full sentences.

"7:30," I say. "Up at our place?" I think of the French pastries at our hotel and feel hungry already.

"7:15," says Graham. He shifts from foot to foot. "Do you think I should call her?" he says.

"Who?" I say, then realize that he means Lindy. He's right: She would expect him to call. "When did you talk to her last?" I say, trying to sound nonchalant. The fact that both Wyatt and Graham have dated this girl makes me feel hopeless. If that's what men want, I'll die single.

"Yesterday, before I met you guys," he says. "When she told me that she was over at Ba Vi Lake, remember?"

"Yeah, call and ask where she is now," says Sigrid. "Maybe she'll let something slip. Just make sure you don't sound like you suspect anything."

Graham twists at one sleeve anxiously. "Should I say that I'm in Sapa?" he says. "What if she wants to see me? I don't think I could pretend to…" He grimaces. "I couldn't, you know, act like everything was normal."

The thought of Graham meeting Lindy makes me queasy. I can't help but worry that, whatever the evidence to the contrary, Lindy would manage to convince him that *we're* the crazy ones.

"Better to say that you'll be in Sapa tomorrow and see how she reacts," says Sigrid. "That way we might get an idea of her plans for tomorrow."

Graham pulls out his mobile phone, then frowns. "The battery's dead." He shoves the phone back into his pocket.

"Use mine," I say, handing my Nokia over. "She doesn't know my number."

In the quiet, we can all hear Lindy's phone ringing. When she answers, her familiar purr causes the hairs on my neck to stiffen. "Oh *mon cheri*," she coos. "It's so late. Whereabouts are you?"

"In Bac Ha," says Graham. "I'm going up to Sapa in the morning." He clears his throat. "How about you? You still at Ba Vi?"

"I can't really talk about it," says Lindy. She lowers her voice to a whisper. "This is an unsecured line."

"What are you talking about?" says Graham. "What's happening?"

Both Sigrid and I can hear Lindy's exaggerated sigh. We exchange knowing glances.

"The CIA," she hisses. "I can't discuss it over the phone. We're supporting the Hmongs' bid for independence. I can't tell you my location… The Hmongs deserve self-rule. It's such an ancient and distinct culture. Do you know what I'm saying?"

"Um, as in a revolution?" says Graham. "Where are you?"

"Shhh," says Lindy. "I shouldn't be saying anything. *Mais oui*, all of the ethnic groups are oppressed." She lowers her voice even further. "I have to go now, *mon chou*. It's time to move...Do you miss me?"

"Uh, yeah," says Graham. "Any idea when you'll be back in Hanoi?"

"When my mission's complete," whispers Lindy. "Sorry I can't tell you more but it's classified."

"Okay, uh, be careful," says Graham. Sigrid rolls her eyes.

"Oh I will be," says Lindy. "I'm used to it."

"Wow," says Sigrid, after Graham's handed my phone back. "That girl really is crazy. Does she actually think that you'll believe that she's working for the CIA to foment an ethnic minority rebellion?"

Graham rubs his eyes and shrugs glumly. "I guess so," he says. "Sorry. We didn't learn anything."

"We learned that she's a genuine crackpot," says Sigrid. She lays a consoling hand on Graham's arm. I wish that I could touch him too but it would feel forced and awkward. Graham sighs. "Yup," he says. "Well, we'd better get to bed. We have to be up pretty early."

In a nearby house a baby starts to cry. It sounds really young and extremely angry. I imagine this tiny new person complaining about how hard it is to be out in this world, where there's always the risk that you'll be left alone and uncared for. I imagine some exhausted new mother hauling herself up out of bed, moving on auto-pilot.

"Goodnight," says Sigrid.

Graham and I say goodnight too. I try to meet Graham's eye before he turns to go but he isn't looking at

me. I wonder if maybe I'd imagined that shared intimacy outside of Lindy's window. I feel deflated.

The baby must have been picked up because its wails have ceased. Walking through the cold night I imagine it lying safe and warm in its mother's arms, sure, at least for this moment, that somebody loves it.

17 Hot On the Trail

I am not at my best first thing in the morning, either mentally or physically. Waiting for a waiter to appear with coffee I feel as though my head had been stuffed with cotton batting in the night, and that this stuffing has caused the flesh below my eyes to bulge. In stark contrast, Sigrid is as bright-eyed as the proverbial early bird. At any moment I expect her to start chirping about what a lovely morning it is.

Graham is somewhere between me and Sigrid, appearing slightly more crumpled than when we'd left him last night, but still handsome and fully conscious. I rub my eyes. It feels awfully bright out here.

We are sitting in the hotel's back garden, gazing out over the village towards Mt. Fansipan. Or rather Sigrid and Graham are gazing. I am blinking stupidly at my still-empty coffee cup, as though desire alone could cause a cappuccino to appear.

"How'd you sleep?" says Graham.

"Great!" says Sigrid. "You?"

"Okay."

Nobody re-extends this question to me, because, judging from the catatonic state that I'm in, the answer is obvious. What Sigrid and Graham don't realize is that I actually slept very well. I wake up like this every morning.

The terrace on which we are sitting is set beside a patch of lawn. About 20 feet from our table stands the hotel's mascot, a large pot-bellied pig. Its dark, hairy flank is painted with the hotel's red and white logo.

I watch as the pig snuffles across the grass, the picture of porcine contentment. Fed on scraps from the hotel kitchen, it is probably the luckiest pig in the country. I wonder if it will one day end up in a cooking pot, replaced by a pig that is younger, smaller and cuter.

The waiter arrives bearing a pot of tea, an espresso and my cappuccino. I inhale this beverage like the addict that I am. Sigrid adds milk and sugar to her tea, stirring slowly.

"About last night," says Graham, and in my dopey state I actually think that he's referring to the embrace that we'd shared outside of Lindy's hotel room. "I think Sig is right and we should try to get the stones," he says.

Feeling stupid, I drain the dregs from my cup. Graham has probably forgotten about that embrace all together.

"I've been thinking about stuff that Lindy's done and said," says Graham. "Looking back, I can't believe that I wasn't more suspicious."

The waiter returns bearing three glasses of orange juice, yogurt and a basket full of muffins and croissants. I reach for a banana muffin.

"Such as?" says Sigrid.

Graham peers into his espresso. "Little things," he says. "Like she had a bunch of designer purses, you know, really expensive ones…" He racks his brain, obviously trying to remember the names. "Like Gucci and Louis Vuitton." He shakes his head. "I asked her about it once, since it seems crazy to be working for a small charity and buying a 2,000 dollar purse."

"What'd she say?" says Sigrid.

"She said they were fake and that she'd bought them in the market in Hong Kong." Graham laughs. "But the thing is, I knew she was lying." He takes another sip of espresso. "I just figured that she'd had some rich boyfriend before who bought her that kind of crap."

I imagine Wyatt buying Lindy an ugly brown purse from Louis Vuitton. Could he actually have been that retarded?

"What else?" says Sigrid.

Graham reaches for a croissant. "She was supposedly organizing a training workshop about prenatal care in Cat Tieng." He rips the croissant in half. "So one night we were out and we met this Finnish guy I know who's an obstetrician. I mentioned Lindy's workshop and he started asking questions about it, you know, just regular questions like who was doing the training and how had the curriculum been developed and what sort of stuff were they teaching."

I can feel the caffeine starting to sink through the cotton in my head. I look out over the village towards Mt. Fansipan, its massive slopes dotted by minuscule green bushes. It really is a beautiful clear morning.

Graham swallows a bite of croissant and rips off some more. "She had no clue what she was talking about," he says. "I knew it, the doctor knew it and so did Lindy."

"But you didn't say anything," says Sigrid.

Graham shakes his head. "Nope," he says. "The doctor and I just changed the subject to the World Cup." He plays with his watch strap, his face sheepish.

"But why?" I say, enough caffeine having penetrated my brain to allow my mouth to function.

Graham rips into a new croissant. His eyes water and his freckles darken. "It sounds awful but maybe because she's so pretty we both kind of expected her to be a bit dumb." He rakes his hair from his eyes and glances worriedly my way. "Just because someone seems ditzy you don't automatically think that they're dishonest..."

"God, guys are pathetic," says Sigrid disgustedly. "It's like you want women to act like bimbos and lie to you."

Graham starts to squirm, but then indignation kicks in. "Do you think that women are any different?" he says. "Do you have any idea how many women are attracted to jerks? They always want the guy who didn't call or the guy who can't decide."

He looks at me when he says this. I blush scarlet. Does he know about me and Wyatt? I busy myself with spreading pineapple jam onto my muffin.

"Okay, okay," says Sigrid. "I admit that there's poor judgment on both sides."

For some minutes, nobody speaks. Graham and I chew glumly on our pastries.

I tilt my head to read Graham's watch: 8:10. "Shouldn't we get going?" I say.

We all scramble to collect our belongings.

I signal for the bill on our way out. The pot-bellied pig makes a beeline for our empty table.

As we stand near the cashier waiting for the bill, I turn to see that the pig has clambered up onto the chair that I'd been sitting in. How it did so, I have no idea. Its belly is so big and its legs so short that I wouldn't have believed such a maneuver possible. The pig extends its snout and delicately picks up a croissant, its little tail twitching delightedly. It is a ludicrous-looking animal, and yet it has its own elegance. Then the waiter spots it and starts running.

"Go pig!" says Graham. The pig gulps down the last of its croissant and reaches for another. The waiter, still running, waves a napkin. The pig takes no notice of him.

"Do you think that pig will end up being eaten?" says Graham, as we're crossing the hotel's lobby a few minutes later.

"I was wondering the same thing," I admit.

"Come on. Do you think there's ever been a pig that's died of old age in the entire history of Vietnam?" says Sigrid.

Graham and I both shake our heads. Sigrid has a point, given that everything that moves, including grasshoppers, grubs and rats, is on the menu in Vietnam. We all start to trudge down the hill, retracing the way that we'd come last night, back to the Golden Mountain.

When the fake-log chalets come into view I'm still thinking about that pig. I'm glad that it got that extra croissant, especially considering what lies in store for it.

• • •

In daylight, hiding out behind Lindy's chalet is clearly impossible. We decide that Sigrid, who's the least likely to be recognized, will don a hat and sunglasses and sit at a tea stall across the street from the Golden Mountain. Graham and I will hide at opposite ends of the street, prepared to follow Lindy if she passes our way. Since we all have mobile phones, at any sign of movement, Sigrid will call us.

I take a seat in a dark coffee shop, the only other customers a pair of old guys hunkered down in a back corner. Identically dressed in navy berets and brown sweaters, they could pass for twins, each holding a hand-rolled cigarette in one gnarled, yellowed hand and a tiny cup of coffee in the other. The sight of me has no effect on this pair. I wonder how far they can see and how many years they've been coming here.

The waitress, on the other hand, looks stunned to find a foreigner on her premises, shock causing her to perform a strange little dance of advance and retreat. Eventually she crosses the room but stops a safe distance away from me. She looks all of 14, with a spotty chin and puppy fat. "*Cafe sua nong*," I say, which means 'hot milk coffee'. Thanks to lessons from Andre and Phi, I've expanded my Vietnamese repertoire.

The waitress blinks, then waves her hands. I try again. More hand-waving ensues.

Now my Vietnamese is bad, but it's not so bad that I should be unable to order coffee in a coffee shop. The problem, I decide, is that the waitress can't even conceive of a foreigner being able to speak her language. It's as if my housecat were to suddenly start chatting to me. My disbelief, combined with the cat's shoddy accent, would result in my hearing nothing but meows. To this wide-eyed teenage waitress, I'm a talking cat. I fight an urge to hiss at her.

I point at the old guys' coffee cups but the waitress still doesn't get it. I mimic drinking coffee and, obviously unfamiliar with charades, she starts to back away from me. She looks petrified.

I decide to give up when a guy who looks like he might be her dad pokes his head through a door in the back of the room and scowls at us. "She wants coffee!" he yells. The waitress says something that I can't catch, then scurries away from me. I wish that my phone would ring.

My coffee arrives iced with no milk but I drink it anyways. I check my watch: 8:32. Too much caffeine causes my heart to race. If only I'd brought a book to read. Maybe we should have gone to the cops after all. What are we planning to do anyway? Place Lindy under citizen's arrest?

I've been waiting for about 20 minutes when a kid walks by selling postcards. Since I have nothing better to do, I buy a few. I may as well write to some friends and family. Following another pantomime with the waitress, I manage to borrow a pen. I write to Lauren, my grandparents, and my dad's brother, Uncle Dwayne.

I'm writing to my old college roommate and almost-bridesmaid Molly when I hear someone say my name. Looking up, I see Mai standing in the doorway. "What you doing?" she says. She's wearing the same clothes that she wore yesterday and carrying her rattan backpack.

I offer her a drink, which she declines, then fill her in on last night's stakeout of Lindy. As I talk, Mai's eyes keep flicking towards a glass cabinet that holds about two-dozen pastries, all of which look like they ought to have been thrown out days ago. While I wouldn't touch any of them, Mai is obviously tempted. I ask her if she wants one.

Tearing her eyes away from the cakes, the girl looks torn between hunger and not wanting to be beholden to me. "Oh go on," I say. "Let's get two." I have no intention whatsoever of eating those things.

Smiling shyly, Mai nods towards the teenage waitress. Although I can't understand the ensuing exchange, it'd be hard not to notice the waitress' air of superiority. While a foreign patron had engendered shyness and confusion, a Dao customer elicits disdain and suspicion. If I weren't here, I bet that Mai would be refused service.

As Mai eats her cake, I quiz her on her thoughts about Lindy. Like Graham, she advises against going to the cops. "They mafia too," she says glumly, then takes another mouthful of cream cake. I use my fork to break off a piece of my cake and hide it in a napkin when Mai's not looking.

Mai's moved on to my leftover cake when I change the subject to her family life. Does she have any brothers and sisters?

"Three brothers, six sisters," says Mai, using a finger to wipe some icing off of her lip. "Four my sisters older. They marry already. Have baby."

When I ask their ages, she shrugs. "19, 18, 16, 15," she says. "They marry when 14."

I try not to look too shocked but obviously don't succeed. Seeing my face, Mai shrugs. She looks down at the remaining square of cake and pushes her plate away.

"Will you get married next year?" I say.

Mai pulls a face. "I hope not. I want wait, maybe 16, 17. But my parents not agree." She toys with her fork. "I not know yet." I want to ask more but she's already stood up. "I go sell now. Thanks for cake," she says, collecting her backpack from the other chair. She gives me a crooked smile and wishes me luck in catching Lindy.

"See you later," I say. I picture myself at 14, back when my definition of tragedy was a zit or a deflated hairdo. Too much coffee, sugar and the thought of Mai being married off next year have lefty a nasty film in my mouth. I rummage through my bag in search of a bottle of water.

About five minutes after Mai's left, my phone rings. It's Sigrid. "Lindy's on the move," she hisses. "She's just walked past Graham. Come on! Hurry!"

I pay my bill and walk out of the coffee shop, the matched set of old guys still chain-smoking in the corner. I walk past the Golden Mountain. Dawn's out on her porch eating Pringles. Today she's sporting two stubby braids, bleached the same color as the potato chips. Up ahead, I can see Sigrid. Like me, she's wearing a baseball cap and dark glasses.

By the time I've caught up with Sigrid I can see Graham up ahead of us. He's got on a camo-printed bucket hat that makes him look like a tourist. I gaze up the street. "Where's Lindy?" I say.

"Up ahead," says Sigrid. "We don't want to get too close in case she spots us."

"What about the stones in her room?" I say. "Now would be a good time to take them."

"She said she'd get more today," Sigrid reminds me. "It's better to wait and get all of them."

That's the difference between Sigrid and me. I think that getting some of the stones is better than nothing. We might not get another chance, after all. When I say this, Sigrid shakes her head. "We're going to bust Lindy and get the money back," she says breezily. "She's not going to get away with this Jane, believe me." She seems so sure of herself.

While I'd like to believe Sigrid, I don't. But since the thought of breaking into Lindy's room scares the crap out of me, I drop the subject. Maybe some other, less prosecutable course of action will become clear to us. I'd rather not experience another interrogation by Mr. Thai or one of his even scarier colleagues.

Close to 10:00 a.m., it's already hot. Even though we are walking downhill, we're both sweating. I'd assumed that Lindy was heading back to the Highlands Outreach' office, but the turnoff comes and goes and Graham keeps walking. I can't help but admire his bum. His jeans look old and soft, unlike the hard flesh beneath them.

"You're staring at his butt!" says Sigrid.

I look away. "I am not!" I say, blushing.

"You were too!"

I decide not to dignify this with an answer and make an effort to keep my eyes elsewhere. Graham's Adidas stir up tiny puffs of dust. Once in a while he glances back at us. Lindy is too far ahead for us to see her.

The ground levels out as we return to the center of Sapa. To our right lies the town's sports stadium, which is just an open field, and to our left lies an old stone church, now in ruins. Despite the bright sun, the crumbling gray church appears creepy. Partially destroyed during Vietnam's fight for independence from the French, it's lain abandoned for decades. On the shady steps of this derelict building sits a group of Red Dao women, all embroidering pieces of fabric and laughing and chatting.

At the sight of us, a bunch of them surge forward. "Madam! Madam!" they yell. "You buy from me!" Several of them have gold-capped front teeth, which flash cheerily in the bright sunshine. Sigrid and I shake our heads and keep walking.

About half a block later an elderly Dao woman pops out of an alleyway to offer us a Ziploc bag full of cannabis. Since pot plants grow wild along the roadsides, I'm not surprised that someone is selling it. Sigrid and I decline and the old lady shakes her baggie to entice us. She's of the same vintage as the old guys in the coffee shop, her face as scrunched as a ball of newspaper. Despite her advanced age, she's quick and persistent. It takes us another block to outrun her.

I remove my hat and wipe my forehead, then ask Sigrid if she has any clue where Lindy is headed.

"This road leads out of town," she says. "She can't be going too far or else she'd have taken a *xe om*." Graham turns around and nods at us. Even in that goofy hat, he looks handsome.

When the road starts to slope downhill and bend, we catch a glimpse of Lindy down below. She is wearing tight jeans and a bright pink t-shirt. Like us, she's got on dark glasses. Her long hair is pulled into a ponytail. She is talking on a cell phone.

She leads us out of town, the downhill slope growing increasingly steep, houses giving way to stands of giant bamboo, the dirt road shaded. We pass two little boys herding six cows uphill, and three more Dao grandmas who try to flag us down and sell us embroidered fabric. The wind sets the bamboo to rustling, a lovely but unsettling noise. I feel increasingly nervous.

Without the cover of buildings, we are forced to hang further and further back. The distance between Graham and us shrinks until Sigrid and I have caught up with him. "Hey," he says quietly. "I'm scared that we'll lose her." The road twists and turns. Once in a while, the foliage parts to reveal a view of the green valley below us. We creep cautiously around each bend in the road, caught between the fear that Lindy will look back and see us and the fear that she'll have vanished entirely.

For some minutes, we don't talk. A glimpse of pink rounds the next bend. "There she is!" I say. We quicken our pace, relieved that Lindy is still ahead of us.

A Minsk rattles past us, the driver having switched off the engine to save gasoline. Behind the middle-aged driver squeeze four young H'mong men. At the sight of us they smile and nod shyly. I expect the one on the back to slip off at any moment.

The road starts to level. Turning a corner, we see that the road below us has straightened out. All three of us stop walking. There is no sign of Lindy. "Shit. Where did she go?" says Sigrid. "There weren't any turnoffs."

Graham takes his hat off and shades his eyes. "Do you think that Minsk picked her up?" he says. Sweat has darkened the curls on his forehead.

"It was too full," I say. "And there it is, up ahead." I point. The Minsk and its five passengers remain visible, a cloud of red dust trailing behind them. I look around. "Where could she have gotten to?"

"She must have turned off somewhere," says Sigrid. "Damn it. Maybe she saw us following her and hid." She looks back the way we've come, frowning.

Graham walks over to the side of the road closest to the valley and pushes his way through the bamboo. A moment later, he is back. "I found her!" he says excitedly. "About a hundred feet back there's a small trail going down into the valley. She's about half way down. We'd better hurry."

We all speed-walk uphill, keeping an eye out for the trailhead. "There it is!" says Sigrid. Sure enough, a green tunnel cuts through the bamboo. Up ahead, I see a circle of sky. After passing through the thicket, we find ourselves on the edge of a steep hill. Fresh footprints are visible on the muddy trail that snakes downwards. Near the bottom of the slope, I can see Lindy.

Sigrid leads the way, Graham is next and I follow. I wish that I had more bottled water. The day is increasingly hot and the sun blinding. As we pick our way down the slope I pray that Lindy won't look back, or that if she does, she won't recognize us. The path is slippery, forcing us to move slowly.

Some ways off I can see four women irrigating a field with buckets of water. When their buckets are empty they turn and head back towards a stream that lies further down the valley. Two of the women have babies strapped to their backs. A couple of little kids are playing nearby, throwing stones at a tethered water buffalo. The beast has its back to them. I hope that it kicks them.

At the bottom of the hill, Lindy turns right, in the direction of a small settlement. To call this place a village seems inappropriate, since there are just a handful of ramshackle dwellings, all of which seem to have been built out of small bits of firewood. I don't know what's

holding the houses together but it looks as though one strong gust of wind would flatten them. In the winter, it can get cold enough to snow up here. I can't believe that people survive in those places. Even from way up here I can see the cracks in the woodwork.

"It's a H'mong village," says Graham. "You can tell by the houses. The Dao houses are better made."

Lindy stops walking. The three of us shrink back against the hillside, but she doesn't turn and see us. Instead, she bends to tie her shoelaces, first one shoe and then the other. A man steps out from behind a clump of bushes. Lindy straightens up and greets him. Although we're too far away to see his face clearly, the guy looks like Knife. He and Lindy walk side by side towards the H'mong settlement.

The three of us follow at a safe distance. "Now what?" says Graham, when we've reached the valley floor. With few large trees, we are very exposed. If Lindy or Knife were to look back, they would see us.

"Lots of tourists hike around here," says Sigrid. "Walk behind me, Graham. Hopefully Lindy won't recognize you." In single file we pick our way through a field planted with rose bushes, the scent of roses mixed with the reek of the night-soil that is used as fertilizer. We pass through a cloud of small white butterflies. In the distance, I can hear the gentle clanking of a wooden cowbell.

Lindy and Knife are walking faster now. Knife starts to wave his arms. Lindy jabs a finger at him. Even from back here, it is clear that they're arguing.

"Some partners!" says Sigrid. "Those two seem to hate each other."

"Yeah, they don't trust each other," I say.

"Nor should they!" says Sigrid.

"They're going into that house," says Graham. Sure enough, Lindy and Knife have turned towards the closest of the shacks. Another man with the same short, stocky build as Knife's steps out of its darkened doorway. At the sight of us, this man says something to the others. I hold my breath. Knife looks our way and shrugs. He has clearly dismissed us as hikers. Luckily, Lindy's attention is elsewhere. Another man has stepped out of the shack. Lindy shakes his hand. Then the four of them retreat indoors and shut the door behind them.

We creep closer. A bird calls out, its shrill cry startling me. "This way," whispers Sigrid, gesturing towards a stand of small banana trees that lies to one side of the cabin. We push our way through the trees' waxy green leaves, doing our best to move quietly. Flies buzz lazily through the foliage. Up close, the shack looks even rougher than I'd first thought. I'm reminded of the *Three Little Pigs*. It wouldn't take much huffing and puffing to demolish this place.

The wall that faces us contains a glassless window, its wooden flap shut and latched from the inside. Sigrid lays her ear to a crack between the planks. Graham and I do likewise. Inside, I can hear Lindy and a man speaking softly. The sun feels hot on the back of my neck. An oversized bumblebee buzzes around me. I am terribly thirsty.

All of a sudden, the soft voices give way to shouts. The whole hut seems to shake. I take a step back in alarm, afraid that this shed really will collapse on us. I can hear

Lindy screaming in French, and what sound like a dozen male voices, all yelling in Vietnamese and some language that I don't recognize. Sigrid, Graham and I all turn to look at each other. What the hell is going on? And how can there be that many people inside this small hovel?

The next thing I know, the window shutter flies open. I blink. Perhaps dehydration has caused me to hallucinate. I shake my head but the vision stays unchanged. Staring out at me is Mr. Thai, his customary suit and tie replaced by dark pants and a tight black shirt, both of which are muddy. There's a shiny black revolver in his right hand. At the sight of me his eyes narrow. Then he sees Sigrid and his eyes widen. "Don't move," he says. "The area is surrounded."

I raise my hands. So do Graham and Sigrid. None of us says anything.

Behind Mr. Thai, I can discern movement in the hut's dark interior. The back door of the shack lies open, light filtering in through this opening and the window in which Mr. Thai is standing. Thanks to this illumination, I can make out Lindy Tran standing with her arms pinned behind her back. She looks furious. Knife and two other guys stand facing the far wall, their hands manacled behind them. Other figures, all clad in black, are visible too, a half dozen eyes staring suspiciously out at us.

I swallow hard. "Um, what are you doing here?" I say.

"I wish to ask you the same thing," snaps Mr. Thai, his voice so icy cold that I shiver. Sunlight glints off of his revolver.

Squinting, I struggle to make sense of the scene before me. Does Mr. Thai suspect us of being Lindy's accomplices or is he part of some rival gang? Are we in danger? I have trouble swallowing.

"Well?" barks Mr. Thai. "What's going on here?"

My heart pounds madly and sweat runs down the back of my shirt. All that I can see is Mr. Thai's gun pointing right at me. I shake my head, still gaping at him. I'm too scared and confused to say anything. I recall the night that Mr. Thai had interrogated me after I'd been caught scaling Jason McCallum's front porch. Dressed like a ninja and pointing a gun at me, he looks even more menacing now. If only I'd listened when he'd told me to mind my own business!

Behind Mr. Thai, Lindy Tran starts to shout obscenities in a mix of French and English. Mr. Thai spins around. "Silence!" he says, in French. He waves his gun at her and Lindy shrinks back in shock. I am thrilled to see her looking so apprehensive, then recall that I'm in the same boat. Off in the distance a cow lows. I want to explain everything but no words will come out.

"Could you please put the gun down?" says Sigrid. "You're making me nervous."

Mr. Thai's eyes slide from me to her, only to veer away from her and slide back to me again. It's like watching a man trying to look into the sun. He settles on squinting over Sigrid's left shoulder. "What are you doing here?" he says again. His gun is still pointing at me.

"We were following Lindy Tran," says Sigrid. She nods in the direction of Lindy. "She's a thief and a con-artist. She's been raising money for a phony charity and using the cash to import smuggled rubies…"

"You don't know what you're talking about!" shrieks

Lindy. "These people are crazy! They're trying to set me up! I'm here working for UNIAP to investigate human trafficking! If you don't release me at once this is going to be a major diplomatic incident! France will not stand for this! My Papa is a Senator…"

"Silence!" yells Mr. Thai. "You'll be interrogated later!"

Sigrid resumes her story. She's talked for some minutes when Mr. Thai holsters his gun. I breathe a sigh of relief. Sigrid has gotten to the part about overhearing Lindy and Knife talking about Lindy's plans to leave the country. Mr. Thai nods every now and then. Once in a while, he asks a question. He seems to believe Sigrid.

"Do you two have anything to add?" says Mr. Thai, when Sigrid has stopped talking.

"We think that the rubies are from Myanmar," I stammer. "They were bought with money that was raised to build a community center for minority women and kids in Sapa."

"We have already searched and sealed off Mademoiselle Tran's hotel room and found a box of stones," says Mr. Thai. "And we found more rubies on that man." He nods towards one of the guys with his arms behind his back. "Your story fits with what we suspected."

"But how did you know to come here?" I say. "When I tried to tell you about Lindy you didn't want to hear about it."

Mr. Thai's nostrils flare. I wish that I'd kept my mouth shut. Criticizing a guy with a gun was a lousy idea. I expect Mr. Thai to ignore my question but, following a moment's hesitation, he decides to enlighten me. "After that incident in Hanoi we bugged your cell phone," he says bluntly. He nods towards Graham. "Last night, Mr. Hall here used your phone to call Mademoiselle Tran. Their conversation proved most alarming. The Department of Foreigner Control takes claims to be working for foreign espionage agencies very seriously, and as for efforts to incite unrest and encourage partition among our ethnic minority populations, well, that is treason, and a matter of grave concern to the Socialist Republic of Vietnam." He casts a grim look at Lindy. "My team traveled up from Hanoi last night by helicopter."

"I don't think she's actually a spy," I say. I lower my voice a little. "I think she's a little crazy."

Inside the hut, Lindy starts to protest again. This time, it's Graham who tells her to shut up.

Her lips quiver. "*Cheri*, you don't understand," she says. "I'll explain everything later. Can't you see that I'm being framed by these…"

"Give it a rest," says Graham. "Nobody's buying it."

A single tear runs down Lindy's cheek, her face the picture of injured innocence. She really is a great actress. I glance at Graham. He looks disgusted.

"Crazy or not, she's a thief," says Mr. Thai briskly. "As for the other matters, our investigations are ongoing." He nods towards the back of the room. "Whatever the outcome, these suspects face several serious charges. We have found a number of smuggled and illegal items on these premises. Not just your Burmese rubies but liquor and electronics and a quantity of counterfeit pharmaceuticals, all manufactured in China and without proper stamps for import to our country. And

Mademoiselle Tran's reference to human trafficking may not have been entirely a product of her imagination. It seems that at least two of her conspirators have ties to a gang that sends young girls from this region to brothels across the Chinese border."

I turn towards Lindy in outrage. Is there no limit to how low she'll sink? Graham looks as appalled as I do.

"I have nothing to do with that!" squeaks Lindy. "I'm innocent! I swear! This isn't fair! You have no idea who I am." She starts to cry, great gulping sobs that cause her thin shoulders to shake.

While taking pleasure in another person's misery isn't admirable, I must admit that I'm glad to see her suffer. She really does deserve it. She's an ugly crier too, which makes me feel even better. Her normally pretty face is all twisted and blotchy.

"Quiet! I shall interrogate you shortly!" snaps Mr. Thai. I imagine him sitting in an English class practicing this line. He speaks with a charming precision not found among native speakers. Mr. Thai turns to the policemen and issues a sharp string of commands in Vietnamese. Lindy and her male companions are pushed towards the hut's rear exit. Lindy continues to blubber.

"We must take you back to the station also," says Mr. Thai, nodding towards me, Graham and Sigrid. He looks almost apologetic. "Paperwork," he says. "We shall need full statements."

A convoy of jeeps pulls up. Lindy and her cronies are loaded into one vehicle. The three of us climb into the back of another and Mr. Thai takes the front seat. He's now able to look directly at Sigrid, but only briefly. Sigrid, on the other hand, can't seem to stop staring at him. Even Graham notices because, once we're all settled, he asks them if they know each other.

"We, ah, met," says Sigrid.

"At the, um, Opera House," says Mr. Thai.

Sigrid smiles. "We were watching, uh, *Tuong* opera."

"Jane was, ahem, there too," says Mr. Thai. "With her, er, parents."

This reminds me that I have not yet spoken with my parents today. I'd left them a note saying that I'd be back for lunch. I check my watch. 12:40. I'd better call them.

I call the hotel but am told that they're out. I leave a message. Some time later, after I've already made my official statement to Mr. Thai, my mobile phone rings. It's my mom, calling from the hotel. "Sorry," I say. "I got delayed. I'll explain everything later. Have you guys eaten yet?"

"Oh don't worry about us," says my mom. For once, this statement sounds sincere, rather than intended to inspire guilt. "We went back to that place where we had dinner last night. It was fantastic. And so cheap! We met that lovely little Dao girl, Mai. She showed us the way back there." She rattles on like this for some minutes, describing the lovely meal and the lovely plum liqueur. It's been a long time since I've heard my mom sounding so youthful and excited about things. I guess that traveling agrees with her.

Sigrid and Graham are still finishing up their statements. I imagine Mai's face when we tell her that Lindy Tran and her gangster buddies have been arrested. Mr. Thai had said that it would take some time

Hanoi Jane 283

to work out the details but, sooner or later, the rubies would be sold and the proceeds used to build the Sapa Community Center.

18 Tropical Rain

We are back on the terrace at Ong Gia's, two onion-shaped oil lanterns resting on our table. Dusk is falling, the sky to the west a deep and pretty pink. Despite the dark clouds that are piling up against Mount Fansipan's upper slopes, we have opted to sit outdoors. Since tonight's dinner is a celebration, we've used some of Mai's embroidered fabric as a tablecloth. On the walk over here, Sigrid and I collected a fat bunch of wild flowers, now arranged in a beer stein on the table.

"So what's the occasion?" asks my dad, after taking a seat. My parents and Graham are seated across from Mai, Sigrid and me. Mr. Thai is at the head of the table. He is dressed in casual clothes instead of his city suit, tan-colored cargo pants and a long-sleeved white T-shirt, but still manages to look immaculate. I glance at Sigrid, unsure how much detail to get into.

But it's Mr. Thai who answers, his handsome face serious. "Your daughter helped to apprehend a criminal today," he says. "If not for Jane's efforts to ensure that justice was done, this individual may very well have gotten away with her crimes." He winks at me when he says this, or else he just got something caught in his eye. I recall the night that I'd blubbered to him all about Lindy Tran having stolen my fiancé and blush scarlet.

In response to my parents' queries, Sigrid and

Mr. Thai take turns explaining about Lindy Tran's fraudulent charity. Then the question that I've been dreading comes my way.

"But what made you suspicious in the first place, honey?" says my mom. Tonight, she is wearing an orange tunic encrusted with sequins, like she's about to take the stage in Las Vegas. The last rays of the setting sun set the sequins ablaze, requiring me to squint when I look at her.

I squirm in my seat and fiddle with my chopsticks, considering. I could lie and say that I'd looked into Lindy's charity for a potential story, or I could 'fess up and admit that this happy ending is the result of my having been jealous, insecure and heartbroken. I glance up to see Graham watching me. In the light of the setting sun, his skin has a warm toffee glow. I would like to lick him. I swallow hard. "She was with Wyatt," I say. I look back at Graham, who looks confused. "My fiancé," I explain. "I caught him and Lindy in bed together."

Graham looks stunned, then hurt. "When was this?" he says, then, "You have a fiancé?"

I shake my head. "No," I say. "I mean, not anymore. I did, back before Lindy came along…" The words scrape against my throat. I twist my napkin, wishing that I'd lied after all.

Nobody says anything.

My mom breaks the ensuing silence. "So let me get this straight," she says. "Wyatt has taken up with this… this charlatan? Was he in on this crime?" Her sequins quiver with indignation. I remember how she'd given Wyatt the evil eye back in the Metropole's swimming pool. I'm amazed that she'd actually think that Wyatt could be in on this.

"No," I say firmly. "I'm sure he knew nothing about it."

Mr. Thai looks grim. "We shall have to speak with this Mr. Wyatt," he says. "And to the rest of Mademoiselle Tran's men friends too." He extracts a pen and a notebook from a pocket in his pants and starts jotting something.

I glance back at Graham, who's clutching a can of 333 beer so tightly that he's denting it. Looking at his face, I see a mixture of shock and hurt. I realize that Sigrid and I never told him that Lindy was three-timing him. I try to catch his eye but he won't look at me. "Sorry," I say. "I should have told you."

Graham's face darkens. "Yeah," he says. He looks from me to Sigrid and then back at me again. He releases his now crumpled beer can.

I bite my lip. Firstly, I feel awful that I hadn't told him about Lindy's other boyfriends in private instead of out here, in front of all these people. Secondly, I am gutted that he still cares that much about Lindy's unfaithfulness. Graham glowers. I feel an overpowering need to fill the ensuing silence.

I take a deep breath and start to talk, the words gushing out of me like air out of a deflating balloon that's flying in wonky circles. "I found out that Lindy was dating you and living with this American lawyer named Jason McCallum at the same time that she was dating Wyatt so I tried to tell him that but he wouldn't believe me. He said I was just jealous and making it up and then when I met you, I figured that you wouldn't believe me either, and then later, like the past few days, I didn't even

want to think about Wyatt at all because it all seemed so stupid and pointless..." My failure to breathe is making my voice squeak. "Because, well, the whole reason I started following Lindy Tran in the first place was to find enough evidence to convince Wyatt that she was an awful person so that he would take me back and, see, I didn't want you to know that I was that pathetic so I didn't say anything about Lindy or Wyatt and that was..." I take a deep breath. "What I'm trying to say is that I'm sorry."

Even with my eyes fixed on my empty plate, I know that everybody's staring at me. I dig my nails into my palms and force myself to look up at Graham. Now he'll either hate me or pity me. I've fucked this up before it's even started.

When I meet Graham's eyes, he bursts out laughing. "What's so funny?" I say.

Graham shakes his head. "You are."

"Why?" I say, feeling somewhat offended. I just poured my heart out and admitted how tragic I am in front of everybody. Graham could at least pretend to appreciate my effort at being truthful.

"That speech!" He raises his hands in a gesture of incredulity. Still grinning, he turns to my mom. "Has she always been able to talk that fast?"

"Uh huh," says Tabitha. "In second grade she passed out during show and tell because she forgot to breathe."

"I was nervous," I say indignantly. "I hate public speaking."

"Jane was a really good kid," says my dad, "but she sure did spend a lot of time in the infirmary."

I grit my teeth. Sure enough, this is my dad's entrée into one of his favorite party pastimes: recounting my various childhood mishaps in great detail to near-strangers. There's the time a gob of rubber cement glue went flying in art class and landed in my eye; the time I fell off the stage in the school Christmas play; the time I sat on a cactus at summer camp... I just thank God that he hasn't brought the family photo album.

My dad's just finished a tale about my having got a Cheerio stuck up my nose when—not a moment too soon—the waitress appears with two bottles of plum liqueur. Mr. Thai pours a half-glass for Mai and full glasses for the rest of us. "What shall we drink to?" I say. At this point, I'd drink to just about anything.

"To justice!" says Sigrid.

"To our new community center!" says Mai. She beams. We all clink glasses and down our plum liqueur.

After that, the evening improves. The food is good and the plum liqueur plentiful. Following a few more drinks, Mr. Thai can actually gaze directly at Sigrid, who merely looks dazed rather than catatonic. While they're both perfectly articulate when speaking to the rest of us, their dialogue to each other contains more *ums*, *ahs* and *ers* than intelligible words. This isn't stopping them from conversing happily about the merits of various forms of traditional Vietnamese music.

Graham, meanwhile, seems to have recovered from his shock and is telling my parents about a motorbike trip that he took to Laos. While his reaction to the news of Lindy's cheating has left a bad taste in my mouth, I can't help but be fascinated by his descriptions of lonely mountain passes, rusted bomb casings and rope bridges across fast-rushing rivers. I picture the two of us riding along perilous mountain roads, then remind myself that I have no place in Graham's stories. My mom seems equally charmed.

"Laos," she says dreamily. "We've always wanted to go, haven't we, Skippy?"

I look at my dad. This is news to me. Since when did my parents want to go anywhere beyond the reach of a domestic US postal stamp? And of all places, why Laos? But my dad is nodding and smiling. "Next year, Tabby," he says. My mom leans over and kisses him. I take another swig of liqueur. Not for the first time during my folks' visit, it occurs to me that I barely know these people.

We've just finished a dessert of sticky rice with mangoes when Mai announces that she'd better get going. It's late and her mom will be getting worried about her. Following hugs and thanks all around, we promise to return for the opening of the community center. We all watch her scamper down the lane, some tiny bells on her bracelets tinkling merrily.

I check my watch. It's only 9:30 p.m. but feels much later. A lot has happened today. I feel tired and hazy from the plum liqueur. I'm about to call it a night when a burst of lightning fills the sky. One moment, the terrace is dim. The next it's as brilliantly lit as a movie set.

In the sudden glare, we all freeze. The light has not yet faded when the thunder starts, its roar deafening. Shock gives way to a mad dash as the thunder is followed by a flood of rain. Bags and glasses in hand, we sprint for cover, our feet splashing in already-formed puddles and our hair and clothes already dripping.

Since the restaurant's cramped interior features fluorescent lights and bad Vietnamese pop tunes, we opt to remain outdoors, huddled beneath a narrow awning. "Look at that rain!" yells my dad, and we all do, since it's impossible not to stare at it. The rain falls so fast and so furiously that the town beyond our balcony seems to have vanished. The noise is deafening. Graham is standing right beside me. I try to think of something to say to him.

The first time Graham asks I can't hear him, his voice drowned out by the rain. He leans closer and my heart quickens. "How are you doing?" he says. Wetness has darkened his hair and eyebrows.

"Okay," I say, doing my best to sound nonchalant. In truth, I feel a bit glum. Our earlier exchange keeps running through my head. Why hadn't I told him about Lindy and Wyatt? I twist my damp shirt. "You?"

"Okay too." His shirt is stuck to his chest. He tugs at it. His injured fingers are freshly bandaged.

"I meant what I said about being sorry," I yell. "I should have told you about Lindy and Wyatt and Jason."

"It's alright," he says gruffly. "That wasn't what I was upset about."

"Oh," I say. The rain seems to be growing louder. I wish that I'd had less of that plum liqueur. I clear my throat. "So, um, what were you, ah, upset about?" I realize that I sound as flustered as Mr. Thai and Sigrid.

Graham stares out at the rain, his face solemn. "I didn't know that you were engaged," he says. "That's a pretty big thing not to know about someone."

I swallow hard. "Yes," I say. "But I'm not anymore. It's crazy but…" I push my wet hair out of my eyes, trying to find the right words. The strange thing is that I can't even imagine being married to Wyatt. Our relationship feels like an episode from a past life, not something that ended a few weeks ago.

Rain pours off the awning in a shiny sheet. "What were you going to say?" says Graham.

"I was going to say that so much has changed since I caught Wyatt cheating on me that it feels like it happened years ago," I say. "It's like I've changed so much that I can't believe I was desperate to marry him... I mean, what was I thinking?" I shake my head. As usual around Graham I'm the opposite of eloquent.

Graham smiles. "I feel the same way about Lindy."

I try to restrain my own smile but am unable to do so. It takes over not just my mouth but my whole face. I recall Lauren's warning that my squinty smile will lead to crow's feet. But what the hell. This grin is unstoppable.

Graham leans closer and places his uninjured hand on my arm. The resulting tingle spreads from my arm to my chest and then, no doubt transported by my heart, through my whole body. "I can't believe I fell for Lindy," says Graham. "I was such an idiot."

My first impulse is to say *Oh no you weren't* to make him feel better, except that part of me agrees with him. If Lindy Tran weren't so pretty would Graham, Jason and Wyatt have been so willing to believe her? I don't think so. "She's pretty," I say.

He nods. "Yeah, but it wasn't just that, you know..." I wait for him to continue, half of me not wanting to hear it and the other half needing to. "She seemed interested in me, interested in the same things I'm interested in. Like vintage motorbikes and art nouveau graphics and ethnic minority culture."

"She's a compulsive liar," I say evenly. "If you were interested in reptiles she'd probably claim to have a Masters in Herpetology."

Graham smiles ruefully. "I know," he says. "But I just didn't see it. It was nice to be with someone who got excited about the same things as me…" He studies his sneakers, which are muddy. "I sound so lame, don't I?"

"No," I say, meaning it this time. "No you don't. Everyone wants that."

"The thing is that I *knew* something was off and I still stuck with her." He shakes his head as if in awe at his own folly. "Her stories just didn't add up. It was all too extraordinary."

"You didn't question her about stuff?"

"Yeah, I did, but she always had some answer. Her answers got more and more complicated and I got more and more suspicious but part of me just didn't want to know." He pushes a curl from his eyes. "God, isn't that awful?"

"No," I say. "That's how I was with Wyatt. I refused to even *consider* that we might not be right for each other or that he wasn't the guy who I wanted him to be."

For some minutes, we are silent. The rain shows no sign of stopping. I can feel warmth radiating off of Graham's body. I rest my head on his shoulder.

"Do you want to get out of here?" he says.

I smile, then turn to the others. "We're going for a walk," I yell.

"What?" shrieks my mom. "In this weather?"

Sigrid, on the other hand, nods. "Good idea," she yells. "We're going to get going too." She reaches for Mr. Thai's hand. For once he looks neither smug nor impassive but thrilled and somewhat terrified.

"Yeah, you kids run along," yells my dad. "Tabby and I are going to stay here for a while." He leans closer to my mom and puts his arm around her waist. My mom giggles. Humidity has caused tendrils of the hair around her face to curl, the effect pleasantly soft and girlish. I wish that I had a camera right now. I'd like a photo of my parents like this, head-to-head, with rain streaming down all around them.

"Let's go," says Graham. He reaches for my hand. We step into the deluge.

If you've never taken a walk in tropical rain, you're missing one of life's greater pleasures. It ranks right up there with eating a mango without cutlery, diving into the ocean when you're hungover, or stretching out on cool white sheets after an overnight flight in Economy.

At first we run, the rain inspiring a giddy, childish elation. I'm laughing so hard that water gets into my mouth and nose. My eyes are so full of raindrops and happy tears that I can barely see anything. We run along winding, rain-slicked alleyways, our feet splashing in puddles. We don't see another soul. Even the rats have taken cover.

Near the ruined church I have to stop: laughter, a big dinner and exertion having conspired to give me a stomach cramp. I tug on Graham's hand. "Slow down," I beg. I stand doubled over.

He pulls me towards him. The church is a dark shadow. The only sounds are those of our breathing and the rain, thudding against the stone and asphalt. The night smells of wet earth and wood smoke. There are no streetlamps and no stars. Graham's arms close around me.

My heart pounds like the rain. I stare up at Graham. Rain cascades down his forehead and cheeks. Drops glisten on his eyelashes. His clothes, like mine, are glued to his skin. I feel a storm of emotions: surprise that he's here in my arms, lust and trepidation.

He brushes some soggy hair from my face. I wipe the wetness off of his jaw. His strong hands stroke the back of my neck. I shut my eyes. And then we are kissing.

Maybe it's the setting or the rain or maybe there's some special chemistry between me and Graham. Whatever it is, this kiss deserves a capital K. It's a Kiss to remember, a Kiss that evokes a feeling that's both strange and familiar. When have I felt this way before?

And then I know: Every once in a while, I dream that I can fly. They are good dreams, but scary too, as I'm always flying fast and low, swooping over fields and fences and treetops. Invariably I wake up feeling elated yet relieved, since in those dreams I am never in control. I am always on the verge of crashing.

We're still kissing when the rain stops, almost as suddenly as it had started. For a few moments the town lies quiet. Then the regular noises start up—revving motorbikes, the screeching of a metal gate being opened, a radio being tuned to catch a love song.

Graham and I pull apart. He smiles. I smile. I feel ridiculously proud and happy. Hand-in-hand we start to walk, the street rising in the direction of both of our hotels. We don't speak. In a few blocks we must make a choice: my room or his room or each of us to our own rooms. My hand rests in his. I don't know if I'm ready for this.

A doorway opens and the sick sweet smell of liquor leaks out, along with the sounds of drunken voices. Four young Vietnamese men, obviously tourists like us, stumble out, their arms around each other's shoulders, staggering and weaving. Seeing us they yell hello, their tones more provoking than salutary, as though we're animals in the zoo and they want to get some reaction. Graham tightens his grip on my hand. We offer subdued hellos to the drunk guys and keep walking. Behind us, we can hear one of them retching into the gutter.

Maybe this encounter sets me on edge, or maybe it's the knowledge that we're fast approaching my turnoff. Our footsteps slow. I feel increasingly nervous. I don't want to relinquish Graham's hand. I don't want this night to end. But am I ready to sleep with him? Graham and I haven't even had a real date. And it's been close to seven years since I've been naked with anyone besides Wyatt. I recall our first time. We'd been dating for a couple of months and had gone away to a B&B. There'd been champagne in the fridge and a scalding hot tub. All of a sudden there's a knot in my throat. My wet clothes feel cold and uncomfortable.

An owl hoots. I stop in amazement and look up. I thought that every bird in Vietnam bigger than a sparrow had been caged or eaten.

"There it is!" says Graham. "In that pine tree!" Sure enough, the owl is looking down at us, dark eyes peering out of a weird white face that is unsettlingly human. I shiver. Having ascertained that we're nothing special, the owl spreads its wings and lifts off. "I'll walk you to your hotel," says Graham.

I nod. This gives me a few more blocks to decide. I sneak a look at Graham but his face is expressionless. I wonder what he wants.

We don't talk. The easy togetherness that we'd shared seems to have blown away with the rain. My whole body feels stiff and cold. Outside of my hotel, we stop walking. "This was a great day," I say. My voice sounds tight and nervous.

Graham nods. "Yes," he says. We're still holding hands. "Good night Jane. I'll see you in the morning."

Before I can respond he leans over and kisses me. This kiss is nice, but it's nothing like our first Kiss. I hear myself say good night. I feel him release my hand and see him give a little wave. Then he starts walking.

I want to tell him to stop, to hell with our barely knowing each other, but no words come out. I just stand there stupidly. Watching Graham walk down the hill, I wonder what's wrong with me. If I want to sleep with the guy, why don't I just sleep with him? If I want to wait, well, that's fine too. But why do I always have to second-guess every decision and make everything so difficult and complicated?

"Graham!" I yell. I start to run down the hill.

Down at the bottom of the slope, Graham turns in surprise. He looks worried, like he thinks that something has happened to me.

I'm running fast and the hill is muddy. Momentum and mud make it so hard to stop that I end up sprawling into his arms. It's like a repeat of the scene in the train.

For a moment, I think that we'll both collapse into a heap, but we manage to regain our balance.

"Whoa," says Graham. He grips my shoulders. "Are you all right, Jane?"

"Yes," I say. "But I want you to come with me, to my room, now, I mean...." I push a clump of sodden hair from my eyes and smile up at him. I know that I must look ridiculous but feel strangely seductive.

Graham grins. "Okay," he says. And then he Kisses me.

19 Getting Real

We are back in the Metropole's pool, the sun as searing and the sky as blue as it was the last time. My dad's got on his neon tie-dyed board shorts and I'm in my pink-striped bikini. My mom, however, is wearing a new suit, this one a turquoise creation with bronze studs up the front and an aqua fringe at the chest. It looks like something that Cowgirl Barbie would have worn in the 1970s. I find myself wondering if the studs will rust. The waiters are still M.I.A and the other guests are all French matrons in slimming black. Everything is so familiar that I'm hardly surprised to see Wyatt.

Once again, he is dressed for the gym, and once again, he is yapping on his cell phone. I wait for my stomach to sink and my throat to constrict. I wait to feel hot and cold and sickly. I wait for my heart to pound and my palms to sweat. I wait to feel fat, clumsy and disheveled.

"Hey, isn't that Wyatt?" says my dad.

My mom squints. "Hmph," she says. The fringe on her swimsuit shimmies ominously.

Wyatt's phone call ends and he spots us, or rather he spots me and freezes. He has the stricken yet hopeful look of a lost hiker who thinks that he recognizes something. He raises a hand to shield his eyes, then starts to shuffle towards me.

I wade across the pool. Wyatt moves closer to the

edge. While he manages a desultory nod in my parents' direction, his eyes never leave me.

"Hey Wyatt," I say. "How's it going?" It's not so much politeness that motivates this query as genuine concern, because Wyatt looks awful. His skin appears waxy and he seems to have lost weight, along with a fair bit of hair at the temples. Over the past few days I missed a few calls from Wyatt, which, somehow, I never got around to returning. Seeing him in this state I can't help but feel guilty. I wonder if he's been ill recently. Or has Lindy's arrest left him heartbroken?

"I, um… tried to call you," he says. He swallows hard, then crouches beside the pool. I'm about five feet away from him now, in water up to my waist. Up close, he looks even worse, his eyes feverish with dark rings beneath them. One of his gym socks is on inside out. The Wyatt I knew would never make such a mistake.

"Yeah, sorry I never got back to you," I say. "With my folks here and getting back from Sapa and everything I've been pretty busy." This is—and sounds like—a lame excuse. I'd figured that after being grilled by Mr. Thai, Wyatt was calling to learn what I knew about the charges against Lindy Tran. I didn't want to hear him making excuses for her.

"So, uh, the cops came to see me," he says. He studies his Nikes. "You were right about Lindy after all. I was so blind."

I nod. This victory should taste sweet. Instead, my tongue feels slimy. Faced with Wyatt's pallor all desire to gloat has deserted me.

"What I wanted to tell you," says Wyatt. "Is that I'm so sorry. I ruined everything." He rubs his eyes. "Can you forgive me?"

"I do forgive you," I say. And it's true. While I still think that he acted like a jerk, I'm no longer crushed by it.

Wyatt clutches his gym towel. His face is the picture of hope mixed with desperation. "I … I miss you." He takes a deep breath. "A lot. I love you. I was hoping we could, you know…" Sunlight glints off of the pool and up at Wyatt. He shades his eyes, his lower lip trembling.

I feel my stomach lurch. It's not often that dreams come true, and yet here I am, on a beautiful sunny day, with Wyatt crouched down before me, begging for reconciliation. How many times had I imagined him uttering those words? How many times had I prayed that he'd realize that he was wrong? How often had I imagined him declaring that he really, truly loved me?

The door to the gym opens and two French women emerge, obviously hotel guests and, by the look of them, a mother and daughter. The latter is about my age and her mom could pass for her sister, both of them small, blonde and chic. I bet that neither of them has ever been dumped, nor worn a bronze and turquoise tasseled swimsuit. I watch their thin brown legs walking past. There's a fat lump in my throat.

Is it life that's perverse or is it me, for here I am, getting what I'd wished for only to find that I no longer want it?

Wyatt is still staring at me. Looking up at him, I feel a great rush of sadness. Where is the sharp-dressed, smooth-talking Wyatt I loved? He looks so wan and lost and untidy. I study his face, at once familiar and strange to me. Once upon a time, we had been happy together. Not perfect, of course, and probably not good enough to have lasted as long as we did, but still, we'd had some good times. Could we make it work? I'd spent so long waiting to marry him.

"I can't," I say. There are tears in my eyes. For six years, Wyatt was the center of my world. Even when the familiar isn't good, it's hard to step away from it.

Wyatt's Adam's apple bobs. "I made a terrible mistake," he says. "I'll never do that to you again. Just give me a chance. Please, Jane. I love you."

I shake my head. I feel sorry for Wyatt and for myself, and this makes me angry. I'm mad at the waste, and mad that it's only now, when it's too late, that he should want me. Part of me (a fairly large part, if I'm being honest) is gratified to see Wyatt hurting. All of this is his fault, after all. I sink down into the water. I feel sad and reproachful and petty.

A ponytailed photographer and his two assistants enter the hotel's courtyard from the Ly Thai To entrance, trailed by a couple in bridal wear. Most Vietnamese people wed in the fall and winter, when it's cooler, and this bride, in her huge-skirted, strapless gown, looks hot and harried. I watch as the photographer positions her on the edge of a lawn chair, an assistant rushing to arrange her crinolines, while another positions a giant silver disk to reflect sunlight onto her. As the bride's wearing a lot of makeup, her features are clear to me. The groom's face, on the other hand, is indistinct. He stands awkwardly behind her.

Gazing at this couple, my righteous anger starts to fade. Maybe the collapse of our relationship wasn't all Wyatt's fault. If I hadn't been so obsessed with our wedding, I might have seen that we lacked some fundamental connection. Instead of focusing on centerpieces and party favors I might have worked harder to make myself happy. With more passions of my own, I'd have had more to share with Wyatt.

I think of Graham, who speaks Vietnamese and is always out in the countryside exploring. I think of Mai, who is so eager to learn and to get an Internet connection. And I think of Lindy's Tran's bogus charity, Highlands Outreach. Writing about bar openings and product launches isn't fulfilling. Coming to Vietnam was an amazing opportunity, but after five months here, I know next to nothing about this place. If Lindy Tran could get people to donate cash for worthwhile causes, why can't I? I'm smart, creative and resourceful. Why can't I help to make Sapa's Community Center into a reality?

Wyatt shuffles his feet. I push up my sunglasses and meet his grey eyes, which are bloodshot. I take a deep breath. "I can't," I say. "I'm sorry, Wyatt, but some things aren't fixable."

Wyatt's lips tremble. "Will we at least stay friends?"

I lean my elbows on the edge of the pool. I don't think we will but it seems harsh to say so. "We can try," I say.

Wyatt clutches his gym towel. "I... Okay," he says. He bends down to kiss my cheek. "Take care, Jane."

I breathe in the familiar smell of Wyatt, soap and Allure aftershave. It's a wonderful smell and I'm already a little bit nostalgic for it. "You too," I say sadly.

I'm still staring at the spot where Wyatt had stopped to turn and look back at me when my mom appears. "What did Wyatt want?" she says. She's holding two gin and tonics and hands one to me.

I take the drink and thank her. "He apologized," I say.

"About time," says my mom. She cocks her head, then eyes me suspiciously. "You're not thinking of taking him back, are you Jane?"

The sky is as bright as it was ten minutes ago and yet, to my eyes, that blue contains a hint of sadness. I shake my head. "No, Mom," I say.

She sips her drink. "I thought for a minute there that you were going to tell me that you'd forgiven him."

"I think I have," I say. "I just don't want to be with him again."

My mom nods. She swishes her free hand through the water. "I'm glad to hear that."

"Mom," I say. "I'm sorry for all of the trouble I caused, all of that time and money you wasted on my wedding. I know that I made you and Dad worry…" I hang my head. "I'm sorry I've disappointed you guys."

"Disappointed us?" says my mom. She's had too much Botox to frown, but if she could, I know she'd be frowning at me. "You've never disappointed us."

"But Lauren's always been so good at everything," I say woefully. "And I—"

My mom cuts me off. "Listen honey," she says. "The truth of it is, I've never had to worry about you. Lauren on the other hand, well, I do worry about that girl."

"But why?" I say, genuinely mystified. Lauren's life seems perfect. What's there to worry about?

My mom sets her gin and tonic on the edge of the pool. There's a faraway look in her eyes. "Remember how back when you and Lauren were kids you loved to watch the figure skating on TV?" she says.

"Yes," I say. "And you could never bear to watch in case somebody fell."

"Right," my mom says. She retrieves her glass and takes a swig, then sets it back on the side again. Her fingernails are painted coral. "That's how I've always felt about Lauren. Your sister is like a figure skater, so perfectly poised, her every move planned out in advance."

"And you're scared that she'll fall?" I say.

"She *will* fall," says my mom. "We all do, you know."

"But what about me?" I say. Some petulance has crept back into my voice; I fall (both figuratively and literally) all the time. Why isn't my mom worried about me? I don't get it.

"You were always falling," says my mom. She readjusts the strap of her swimsuit to check on her tan lines. "And then you'd get right back up again. I never had to worry about you. Not as a kid and not now. You're resilient."

I've never liked gin or tonic, either separately or together. Gin has a weird, metallic flavor and tonic a horrible bittersweet aftertaste. But I finish my drink anyways. I consider what my mom is saying: *I mess up a lot, therefore I'm used to it.*

A bubble of resentment starts to form, full of the familiar, self-pitying refrains of my privileged childhood: *My parents love Lauren more than me. I deserve attention too, you know...*

"Jane?" says my mom.

I nod.

"Now I don't want you to take this the wrong way, but..." says my mom. I grit my teeth. What flaws will she point out now? My hair? My complexion? My low-paid, lowly job as a sub-editor?

"You've gotten much too thin."

I look into my mom's eyes, blue, like mine, but much more shrewd. She smiles sweetly.

Now my mom is much, much thinner than I am. She monitors calorie intake and searches out fat grams the way U.N. weapons inspectors look for weapons of mass destruction. No diet is too restrictive and no weight-loss fad too weird. Cabbage soup. Atkins. Cayenne pepper. You name it. You can never be too thin or too trendy, according to Tabitha.

"I'm not *that* thin," I say.

My mom smiles. "Well, you could use a few more pounds."

I smile back at her. This, I know, is my mom's way of saying that she loves me.

• • •

The first person to visit my almost-finished apartment is Graham, who's now sitting in my living room, waiting for me to serve him some homemade fettuccini with scallops in cream sauce. Since this is way beyond my usual culinary repertoire of toast, cereal and coffee, I'm pretty nervous. I'm nervous about Graham being here at all, nervous and excited.

"Can I help?" yells Graham.

"No! I'm fine," I say, unwilling for Graham to see just how messy my kitchen is, the stove splattered with boiled-over cream sauce and the countertops littered with jars, bottles, produce, dirty cutting boards and implements. When I rinsed the fettuccini I managed to spill some of it; noodles now hang off the stone counter like melting icicles.

Maneuvering my tray out of the kitchen I shut the door firmly behind me. Pasta seems pretty hard to mess up and yet the noodles look oddly solid. I shake the tray and the mounds jiggle. I blow my bangs off of my now sweaty forehead. New place, new boyfriend, new job but I still can't cook. What am I trying to prove here? I wish that I'd ordered takeout.

"That smells great," says Graham, when I set the tray on the coffee table before him. Since I don't have a dining table Graham is sitting on the floor with his back against my sofa. I retreat to the kitchen to fetch the salad. He starts to unload bowls and cutlery onto the coffee table.

"I hope it tastes all right," I say, as I reposition our bowls to fit the salad onto the table. "I'm not much of a cook. I mean the last thing I actually cooked was tea cakes back in Grade Nine Home Economics and I got a C-minus in that and third-degree burns…"

Graham holds up a hand to silence me, his face cracking into a grin. "Stop apologizing," he says. "I'm sure it's awesome. Anyways, I'm not expecting you to be a Cordon Bleu-trained chef with eight Michelin stars. I've had enough of *that* kind of perfection." He hands me a wine glass, then fills it. I take a seat on the floor beside him.

This last statement was obviously a reference to Lindy Tran. I'm not quite sure how to take it. I remember how perfect her body is and feel a flicker of regret that I let Graham see me naked.

He must realize that I'm upset because he looks embarrassed. "I don't mean that you're not perfect," he says. "Just that you're real." He lays a hand on my arm when he says this.

"A really bad cook," I quip, because I'm nervous.

He shakes his head. "You know, even before I knew that Lindy was full of shit, her perfection was exhausting. Who could live up to that? It made me feel…" He shrugs. "Incompetent."

I consider this. I'd felt the same way with Wyatt a lot of the time, as though I wasn't quite good enough. But looking back, I ended up being too good for *him*. I may not be as skinny or as successful as some of the girls he's dated, but I do know right from wrong. I've never cheated on anyone or stolen anything except the odd old-but-interesting magazine from a doctor's office.

Graham raises his glass. "What shall we drink to?"

"Underachievement?"

He grins. "How about honesty?" The look in his eyes makes me feel dizzy and tingly all over.

I clink my glass against his, my smile matching Graham's. "I'll drink to that," I say. And then I kiss him.

By the time we get to our pasta it's cold and even gluier than it was to start with. I try to pry a scallop loose and give up. It's like a boulder embedded in a creamy lava flow.

"Want to order in?" I say, after Graham's taken a few dutiful bites. "We could get Thai food."

"Um, sure," says Graham. He sets his bowl back onto the coffee table and reaches for a napkin. "Did you really get a C-minus in Home Ec?"

"Yes," I say. "I'd have flunked except that the teacher, Mrs. Dorchester, felt sorry for me."

"Maybe she liked you," says Graham.

I consider this. "Yeah, I guess she did." I set my bowl next to Graham's. "I tried hard."

Graham looks thoughtful. "Can we make a deal?"

"What kind of deal?" I say warily.

He eyes the pasta. "A deal not to try *quite* so hard. I'm already impressed by you, remember?"

"No more home-cooking?" I say.

He grins. "Not unless you really enjoy it."

I admit that I don't, then ask if he cooks.

"Some," he says. "My parents are both small-town doctors and they were on call a lot. I have two younger sisters and it was often up to me feed everyone. I learned to improvise." He stands up and carries our uneaten pasta back towards the kitchen. I shudder at the thought of him seeing the mess but it's too late. He's already pushed the door open.

"It's a bit of a mess," I call out, which is like saying that my scallops were a bit overcooked. When I follow him into the kitchen, my cheeks are burning.

Graham is crouched down in the corner, extracting scallops from the pasta and throwing them into Fergus' bowl. Fergus is sitting a few feet away, watching him. I pray that Fergus won't sniff and reject these offerings. It's bad enough that we couldn't eat my pasta. How sad will it be if my cooking is rejected by a former alley cat?

Maybe Fergus is really hungry, or maybe he senses my desperation, because the second that Graham stands up, the cat practically pounces on the bowl. I have never felt as fond of Fergus as I do watching him chew those rubbery scallops.

After scraping the rest of the pasta into the garbage, Graham surveys the boxes, jars, bags of produce and cans that lie scattered around my kitchen. He opens the fridge and peers inside, then suggests that we don't need to get takeout after all. There's enough here for him to whip up some decent pasta with tomato sauce. How does that sound?

"Great!" I say.

Before Graham's arrival, my attempt at cooking had felt frenzied and desperate. But now, following his calm directions, I find myself enjoying the acts of chopping, mixing, stirring and draining. As we work, he tells me about his childhood in a small town in Saskatchewan. I imagine him barrel-racing in the local rodeo and snow-mobiling across the snow-covered prairies.

I watch as Graham divides the pasta into two bowls. He adds a pinch of seasoning to the sauce, stirs and tastes it. My kitchen is tiny and, like usual, I feel an overwhelming urge to touch him. He turns around and sees me staring at him. "Here," he says, offering me a taste. "Does it need anything else?"

"No," I say. "It's delicious."

Graham pulls me close and kisses me. "You're delicious," he says. I kiss him again. Graham turns off the stove, picks me up, and carries me into the bedroom.

By the time we get around to dinner, the pasta is cold again. After heating up a single bowl in the microwave we carry it and some cutlery back into the bedroom and eat in bed, wearing only our t-shirts. "How is it?" says Graham, after I've taken a mouthful.

I snuggle closer to him. Lit only by candles, my

bedroom looks old-fashioned and romantic. "This," I say, "is the best spaghetti I have ever tasted." Graham's hair glows gold in the candlelight.

"I aced Home-Ec," he says smugly.

A weird, rasping sound causes both of us to turn. "What's that noise?" says Graham.

I peer under the bed. Fergus has just puked up all of his scallops.

• • •

"Oh go on," says Skip. "I'd like to see it."

"Same here," says Sigrid. "Go put it on, Jane."

My parents are seated on my couch and Sigrid is in an armchair. Sinead O'Connor is singing about heartbreak on the stereo. Even though the air-conditioner is on full-blast, it's an old unit, and my apartment is nowhere near as cold as the hotel rooms that my folks are used to.

Probably against my better judgment I find myself agreeing to put on my wedding dress. I never did get to see it with the shoes and tiara. "Give me five minutes," I say. I walk into my bedroom. There's still a faint odor of new paint. The room contains only a tall wooden wardrobe, a full-length mirror and a bed. I turn up the overhead fan and light a scented candle.

I unzip the pink plastic garment bag and pull the dress out, amazed again by how soft it is. The silk feels cool and smooth against my skin when I step into it. I struggle to zip it up, then step into my heels and put on the tiara. Only then do I turn to face the mirror, my breath catching in my throat at the sight of myself. The strapless bodice fits perfectly, while the skirt is sweeping but not puffy. When I move, the beads on the bodice twinkle and the silk rustles.

"Are you done yet?" yells my dad. Sinead O'Connor has moved on to a faster song, also about heartbreak.

"Almost," I say, but I stay where I am, hesitating. Looking at myself in this dress I can't help but feel wistful. Will I ever get the chance to wear it?

"Honey?" yells my mom. "Do you need any help in there?"

"No," I say. I step into the living room.

Both of my parents gasp. Sigrid's eyes go wide. "Wow," she says.

"Oh Janey," says my dad. "You look stunning."

I turn to my mom, waiting for some criticism, only to see that there are tears in her eyes. "You look so beautiful," she sniffs. "Oh my little baby. You're just perfect."

I'm not sure whether it's her words, her expression or the fact that I won't actually get to wear this dress in public, but I find myself tearing up too.

"No, don't cry, honey," says Tabitha. "The silk will stain."

"Well it hardly matters, does it?" I sniffle. "It's not like I'm going to be wearing it anyways."

"Sure you will," says my dad. "Just not right away." He reaches over to hug me.

"Or if that never happens you could always dye it," says my mom. "It'd be perfect for formal wear." She eyes me thoughtfully. "Maybe blue. You look pretty in blue, Jane."

Part of me wants to get mad at her for implying that I might never marry, but part of me wants to laugh. It *would* make a great formal dress and I *do* look good in blue. "Thanks Mom," I say. "That's not a bad idea."

"Or maybe Lauren would let you wear it as a bridesmaid's dress if…" I give her a stern look and she stops talking. "No need to get huffy," she says huffily. "I was only trying to be helpful."

"She's not in any rush to wear that dress," says my dad. He turns and winks at me. "Are you Janey? You're young, smart, beautiful." He spreads his arms wide, like an opera singer. "The world's your oyster."

There's a mirror over the mantelpiece and I turn to look at myself. While not exactly beautiful, the woman looking back at me does look bright and pretty. I stare at myself. Am I really happy?

I feel myself nodding. The tiara twinkles. My smile grows bigger and I'm still nodding. I am happy. And then the tiara slides off and rolls under the sofa.

• • •

After my parents have returned to their hotel to pack, I change back into my regular clothes, shorts and a faded black tank top. I zip my wedding dress into its garment bag and hang it in my closet, right next to the cut velvet gown that Wyatt gave me going on six years ago. I can't resist slipping this dress off of its hanger and holding it up against myself. The deep blue color brings out my eyes. If only I fit into it.

I'm about to replace it in the closet when Sigrid calls out to me. "Do you want a cold beer? I'm having one."

"Yes please," I yell. The 1930s dress feels cool and

silky. Before I can change my mind I carry it out into the living room. "Here," I say, handing it to Sigrid. "I'd like you to have this."

Sigrid smiles. "Wow," she says. "Are you sure? This dress is amazing!"

"I'm sure," I say. I point out the torn seam that will need re-stitching.

Clutching the dress to her chest she stands up and twirls around. "I absolutely love it," she says. "Thank you so much."

Seeing her looking so happy I feel proud of myself. My closet is too small to be cluttered up with stuff that I'll never wear. I wonder what other clothes I can give away.

When we're both back on the couch, sipping our cold beers, Sigrid tells me that I looked great in my wedding dress.

"Thanks," I say. I pick at my beer bottle's label. "That reminds me," I say. "I met Wyatt yesterday."

"Oh yeah?" says Sigrid. "How was it?"

"Okay," I say. "Well, sort of sad, actually. He said he was sorry and asked if we could, you know, start over again."

Sigrid takes a sip of beer. She's wearing a yellow sundress and her hair is getting long. She looks relaxed and pretty. "So what did you say?"

I shake my head. "I…Too much has changed."

Sigrid nods. "Yes," she says. A painting that I'd bought, depicting a street scene in Hanoi, is leaning against the far wall. I need to borrow an electric drill to hang it. Sigrid studies this painting, her face thoughtful. "What's happening with Graham?"

I swallow some more beer. "I don't know," I say, which is the truth. I like Graham. A lot. And he seems to like me. But who knows where it will go? I feel a tingle of anticipation.

Seeing my smile, Sigrid grins. "But it's good?"

"Yes," I say. "How about you and Mr. Thai?"

"Stop calling him Mr. Thai," she says. "You make him sound like a senior citizen."

"Fine," I say. "What's happening with you and Thai?"

"We'll see," she says sweetly. But her smile is naughty.

It turns out that she and Thai are meeting for dinner. As she stands up to go, I find myself asking if she's still opposed to getting married.

"I'm not opposed to being in a relationship," says Sigrid. She carefully folds the cut velvet gown. "I'm just not sure that I'll feel the need to ever make it official again." She shrugs. "Anyways, why are you asking about this now?"

"I don't know," I admit. "I guess I just thought that now that you're seeing Mr., I mean, Thai…"

Sigrid snorts. "God, Jane," she says. "Aren't you rushing things just a bit?" We walk into my front hallway.

"Maybe," I concede. "I was just wondering, that's all."

Sigrid's eyes narrow. "If you and Graham weren't…" She waves a hand. "Together. Would you still have said no to Wyatt?"

"Yes!" I say, somewhat offended that she'd felt the need to even ask this. "Of course I would have. I've changed." I stick out my jaw. "Not that you believe that people can change," I say.

"I never said that," says Sigrid. We're both standing in my tiny front hall. Sigrid places the folded gown in her

Hanoi Jane 315

bag. She retrieves her sandals from the shoe rack, then slips her feet into them.

"Yes you did," I say.

She bends to close the heel straps. "I said that people don't change until they're sick of repeating themselves." She stands up.

With no fan, the hallway is hot. I push my bangs off of my forehead. "Do you think I'm rushing into things with Graham?" I say. "I mean, is it too soon?"

Sigrid laughs. "I don't know," she says. "Nobody but you can know that. You just do what feels right and…" She shrugs. "Well, try to have fun, right?" She pats her tote bag. "Thanks again for the dress, Jane."

"Thank you," I say.

"What for?"

"For everything," I say. I follow Sigrid onto the porch, the air cooler out here than it was in my hallway. Dusk has set in, the breeze heavy with the smell of milk flowers.

"Sapa was a lot of fun," says Sigrid. She shakes back her hair and puts on her bike helmet. "I'm so glad that Lindy Tran got what she deserved."

"Me too," I say. "I wonder what'll happen to her. And what happened to all the money she stole?"

"Well, Thai told me that she'll be in jail here for a while and then she'll be deported," says Sigrid. "Some of the money's gone but they found a bunch more at her place." She shrugs. "Enough to build the community center, anyway." She descends a couple steps and stops, then turns back and looks up at me. "Oh, I forgot to tell you," she says. "I asked my Uncle Don—you remember, he's an FBI agent? —to contact Interpol and run a background check on Lindy Tran."

"And?" I say. I can't believe that Sigrid forgot to mention this. We've spent hours speculating about what's behind Lindy's treachery.

"Well, there wasn't much," says Sigrid. "It was the standard Vietnamese refugee story: Her parents were boat people, settled by some Catholic group in Nice."

"She's Catholic?" I say.

"Yup," says Sigrid. "Mom works in a bakery. Dad's a welder. She has an older sister who's a pharmacist and an older brother in IT. No criminal records. Mom and Dad are involved in their local church group. The kids went to Sunday School. Lindy played the clarinet in the school band. Nothing unusual at all. She has a B.A. in Psychology from a public school—not that fancy academy she claimed that she went to."

"It makes no sense," I say, feeling cheated. I'd been convinced that the source of Lindy's deviancy would be as easy to pick out as black roots on a peroxide blonde. Like maybe her mom was a junkie. Or her dad had gambled away their social security checks, forcing Lindy to feed an army of younger siblings by shoplifting instant noodles. What would make a seemingly normal girl want to mislead people and rip them off? "So what went wrong with her?" I say. "I don't get it."

Sigrid shrugs. "God knows," she says. "She was interviewed in connection with an investigation into a mail-order scam a couple years back but nothing came of it. Apart from that, there was nothing on her."

I follow Sigrid down the steps. A breeze lifts my hair. As Sigrid secures her bike helmet, I tell her about my plans to quit working at the *Hanoi Scope*. "I was thinking that I could take over Highlands Outreach," I say. "I mean I could start a *real* Highlands Outreach. Like I could help set up the Sapa Community Center and help find new markets for those women's embroidery products."

Sigrid looks thoughtful. "You should talk to Thai," she says. "There's a lot of bureaucracy involved in getting that funding released and choosing a local non-profit group to oversee the center's set-up but they'll need a foreign consultant. And why don't you call Katy at the NGO resource center too? She'd know lots of great contacts."

"My assistant Tuyet's friend who's an anthropologist already agreed to introduce me to some of her friends who work for non-profits," I say.

"That's great," says Sigrid. "You'd be good at that. Have you told *Scope* that you're leaving yet?"

"Tomorrow," I say.

Sigrid nods. "Congratulations." Her motorbike is parked in the small courtyard at the bottom of my stairs. I watch as she lowers it off of the kickstand and maneuvers it to fit out of the gate. On the pavement, a woman is frying tofu on a charcoal burner. Sigrid manages to push her bike around this woman, her shoulder pole and flat baskets, then gets onto her motorbike. Before starting the engine, she waves at me.

"Have fun tonight!" I yell.

"You too," yells Sigrid. "Take it easy!"

I go back upstairs and lock my front door. Sinead O'Connor is still singing. I walk over to the stereo and turn her off, then flip through my box of CDs in search of something more cheerful. *Take it easy*, I say to myself. And then I put Sinead back on and crank up the volume, her sad, beautiful voice echoing through my nearly-empty apartment. I lie on the cool floor with my eyes shut and smile. Since when have I ever taken anything easy?

About the Author

Born in England and raised in Canada, Elka Ray has spent the past 15 years living in Vietnam, where she works as a writer and editor. Elka's articles on Southeast Asia have appeared in a wide range of magazines and guidebooks. *Hanoi Jane* is her first novel.

Married with two small children, Elka lives on the outskirts of Ho Chi Minh City, surrounded by coconut palms and encroaching chaos. For more information, please visit Elka's website at www.elkaray.com